The Double

The Double

A St Petersburg Poem

Fyodor Dostoevsky

Translated by Hugh Aplin

ET REMOTISSIMA PROPE

Hesperus Classics

Hesperus Classics
Published by Hesperus Press Limited
4 Rickett Street, London sw6 1ru
www.hesperuspress.com

The Double first published in Russian in 1846
This translation first published by Hesperus Press Limited, 2004
Reprinted 2004

Introduction and English language translation © Hugh Aplin, 2004
Foreword © Jeremy Dyson, 2004

Designed and typeset by Fraser Muggeridge
Printed in Jordan by Jordan National Press

isbn: 1-84391-087-x

CONTENTS

FOREWORD

In *Danse Macabre*, his wide-ranging analysis of supernatural fiction, Stephen King imagines a metaphorical hand of four playing cards, one each for the four archetypal tropes he suggests underpin all supernatural fiction. His assertion is that every tale of the uncanny, from the cheapest 1940s B-movie to the most esteemed Gothic novel is, in essence, built around one or more of the archetypes depicted on these cards. They are – and I'm paraphrasing – *The Ghoul / Monster*, *The Undead*, *The Werewolf* and *The Double*. As far as King is concerned, at least one of these figures can be identified stalking, arms outstretched, through the pages of every tale of terror you will ever come across. When I first read this in 1983 (or devoured it more like – I was seventeen years old and entranced by anything connected to the ghostly, particularly something that could be thrown back at English teachers who suggested that my passion was somehow juvenile and tawdry), I was a little confused by Mr King's selection. The first three figures contained something that was in essence truly terrifying – some element that had frightened me since *The Armada Book of Ghost Stories*, *Shiver and Shake* and *Appointment with Fear* had first introduced me to the delights of the horrific. There was a Platonic quality inherent in the notion of a pitiless, corrupting vampire, snarling, unbound Wolfman, or relentless, unstoppable mummy that chilled (and still chills) on a primal level. But a double? What's a double? It seemed twee – charming even. Not an object of fear. In fact, when I was eleven I'd found a photograph in the *Guardian* of a boy of my age meeting Harold Wilson. The boy bore a remarkable likeness to myself and for days I carried the torn-out picture around, showing it to everyone I could. There was some notion of reflected pride in the discovery and possession of this photograph, as if in some way it had been me meeting the then prime minister. There was certainly nothing troubling about the idea that there was somebody out there who looked like me. Quite the reverse. It wasn't until, a few months later, when I saw a repeat of an episode of *Hammer House of Horror* called 'The Two Faces of Evil', that I realised how frightening the notion of a double could be. In this story, which exhibits a palpable atmosphere of nightmarish dread, a family holidaying in a suitably bleak and rain-sodden English countryside stop to pick up a hitch-hiker. Our first glimpse is of a bright yellow sou'wester and wellington boots, not unlike Paddington Bear's – but once in the car the hitcher reveals a monstrous and feral side. All we see of him is one black fingernail, elongated and filed to a point. He attacks Dad, who is driving. The rest of the story is told from Mum's point of view. She wakes up in hospital, the car having crashed after the attack. There was no sign of the attacker in the wreckage and her husband is in a coma. When he awakens he cannot speak, his throat having been injured in the accident. She takes him to their holiday cottage in order to nurse him but he becomes increasingly violent. And then she notices that one of his fingernails is black, elongated and filed to a point...

This story opened up to me the complexity, power and richness of the double as a metaphor for so many unspeakable things that I began to realise, far from being the weakest of Stephen King's cards, it may well have been the trump.

Quite why the twenty-five-year-old Dostoevsky should have decided to play this card in his second published work of fiction is not clear. He may have been drawing on traditions of the folk tale rather than any literary antecedents (E.T.A. Hoffmann, Poe, etc.). More likely the psychological acuteness that Freud so came to admire was already burning in Dostoevsky's imagination and making him write from a place of instinct rather than analysis.

It's the very complexity of ideas that the notion of a double throws up that makes this short novel so engaging and ultimately still so pertinent.

'Our hero', as Dostoevsky consistently describes his protagonist Golyadkin, is not a hero at all. He's ratty, mean-spirited, paranoid and neurotic. In short, he is like us. Whether we want to or not, we identify with him from the start, which makes his descent into the abyss all the more disturbing.

Inexplicably, Golyadkin is suddenly joined in St Petersburg by a man who not only looks exactly like him, but shares his name and his job. Others do not even notice the strangeness of this occurrence.

When it is pointed out to them they react as if it is no more than a mild coincidence.

It's no coincidence, however, that the double's first appearance is proximate to Golyadkin's having been humiliatingly ejected from a society party which he has gatecrashed. Not surprisingly, he finds the experience devastating. He 'not only wished to escape from himself, but even completely to annihilate himself, not to be, to turn to dust'.

At first the double seems more a curio than a threat. He befriends Golyadkin and is grateful for the kindness 'our hero' shows him by inviting him into his home. But soon the double's behaviour turns, and insidiously it appears that he sets out to ruin and ultimately usurp the 'real' Golyadkin's place in St Petersburg society.

I say 'it appears' because Dostoevsky makes Golyadkin's point of view feel most unreliable and the reader is left with the job of trying to ascertain exactly what is going on. There is considerable ambivalence as to who is good and who is bad. Golyadkin himself muses that, though the other is 'a scoundrel', only by being 'honest, virtuous, meek, mild', will he prove himself the true Golyadkin.

It is as if Golydakin is being punished for having been 'found out'. 'Found out' for what? For not being a good bourgeois – for harbouring dark and self-destructive thoughts, for being less than competent, less then he wants to or needs to appear to be. Above all it is a *social* anxiety that Dostoevsky seems to be articulating – the profound tension created by the split between who one actually is and how one has to represent oneself in society. The double himself has no difficulty with this dual role – he relates to others both professionally and socially with a freedom that Golyadkin can only look on and covet.

Ultimately the most impressive thing about *The Double* is how pertinent it feels today. There is an ease with which Golyadkin's place in society is usurped, a lack of substance in the 'reality' of his identity that allows this to happen, which seems entirely contemporary. Recently our newspapers have been full of genuine tales of 'identity theft', of people who are defined by their credit cards, their passport numbers and their bank accounts and whose lives collapse when this information is stolen and abused. 'It wasn't just the money,' one victim was reported as saying, 'it was the feeling that my life had been taken from me. I wasn't sure exactly who I was any more.' The women involved ended up undergoing therapy to help them recover from the trauma. The nature of our madhouses may have changed but the route there obviously remains the same. Like all the best fiction, *The Double* reinvents and rewrites itself for the current age.

– Jeremy Dyson, 2004

The Double was Fyodor Dostoevsky's second published work, appearing in the journal *Notes of the Fatherland* in February 1846, hot on the heels of the rapturously received *Poor People*. The overnight success of his debut story had already made the young man a celebrity, but he was convinced that the follow-up would seal his literary fame for good, writing to his brother Mikhail on the day of publication that 'Golyadkin is ten times superior to *Poor People*. Our friends are saying that after *Dead Souls* there's been nothing like it in Russia, that it's a work of genius, and what else aren't they saying!... I really have made an incredibly good job of Golyadkin.' The reference to *The Double* alongside Gogol's *chef d'œuvre* at a time regarded even then as 'the Gogol period' in Russian literature is indicative of the impact the story made during the pre-publication period, when Dostoevsky was reading extracts to the most influential literary circle of the day grouped around the critic Vissarion Belinsky. Dostoevsky would later recall in his *Diary of a Writer* that almost from the time he began work in earnest on *The Double* in the early autumn of 1845, Belinsky expressed great interest in the new story, and Dostoevsky's own enthusiasm kept him busy revising *The Adventures of Mr Golyadkin* – its subtitle in the journal publication – until just four days before it made its appearance.

Yet by October 1846 Dostoevsky was already planning to publish a reworked version of the story, and since that time the original text for which such high hopes were held by its author has long been consigned in collected editions of Dostoevsky to the small print of pages headed 'Other Versions'. Nowadays only literary scholars are familiar with the text of that first publication, and the translation offered here is of the version eventually reworked and published by Dostoevsky after his Siberian exile in 1866. It is perhaps ironically fitting that real literary life has reflected the content of Dostoevsky's story, with a new, more robust Mr Golyadkin completely eclipsing the character's original incarnation.

The cause of the author's immediate desire to revise his work was the storm of criticism that *The Double* provoked upon publication. Dostoevsky was particularly upset that Belinsky's circle, his former champions, had, together with other critics and the reading public, so rapidly turned against him, labelling the story dull, limp and long-winded. For a sensitive and mistrustful young writer the sudden demotion from latest sensation to overrated disappointment was very hard to bear and was an important factor in his break with Belinsky and his allies.

And an even more significant break was not long in coming, for the publication of a series of ill-received short works in the late 1840s was followed by the discovery of Dostoevsky's involvement with the revolutionary Petrashevsky circle, his infamous near-execution and then exile to Siberia. Upon his return to literary life more than a decade later he toyed with ideas of expanding *The Double* and rewriting it in the light of the new circumstances, both personal and historical, of the 1860s. Ultimately, however, he decided to restrict himself to less drastic changes: the ending was rewritten, certain scenes and elements of the intrigue were cut and, most obviously, a considerable degree of abbreviation took place, involving the exclusion of much of the repetition deemed so superfluous by the critics of the 1840s. Also to disappear were the headings summarising the content of each of the chapters. These varied in length and complexity, but the heading for Chapter one gives some flavour of their character:

Of how Titular Councillor Golyadkin awoke. Of how he fitted himself out and set off where his path lay. Of how Mr Golyadkin tried to justify himself in his own eyes, and how he then deduced the rule that it is best of all to act on a bold footing and with a candour not lacking in nobility. Of where, finally, Mr Golyadkin dropped by with a visit.

As well as being amusing in themselves, these mock-epic features served to emphasise the work's link with the literary traditions of which Dostoevsky was highly aware in his early writings – readers of Cervantes, for example, another author renowned for his treatment of self-delusion and madness, would instantly recognise a possible reference. Their excision might have seemed to signal an intention in the 1860s to break with the past, and yet at the same time, with his alteration of the work's subtitle, the author arguably actually underscored some of *The Double*'s key literary links.

The new subtitle, *A St Petersburg Poem*, immediately recalls Alexander Pushkin's supreme contribution to the gallery of depictions of Russia's imperial capital, *The Bronze Horseman*. Although it was a work of narrative verse, the freedoms sanctioned by Romanticism in relation to genre had permitted its author to define it as *A St Petersburg Story*, using a word normally associated with prose, and to intertwine its epic themes with the story of a poor civil servant's decline into madness, set against the background of the foul weather of a St Petersburg autumn. And although the new subtitle did away with his original echoing of *The Adventures of Chichikov*, Dostoevsky retained arguably no less strong a link with Nikolai Gogol's *Dead Souls* by his paradoxical use of the word 'poem' for a work of prose; for the latter's aspiration to transpose Dante's *Divine Comedy* to Russian soil in *Dead Souls* had led him too to affix the heroic genre definition *poema* to a prose narrative of the most prosaic materialism.

Indeed, just as Gogol's influence was vital for the very concept of *Poor People*, so can it be seen in numerous features, both stylistic and thematic, of *The Double*. A number of the characters – the servant, Petrushka, for example – come straight from the pages of Dostoevsky's predecessor; the wonderful description of Klara Olsufyevna's party echoes the rhetoric of the reception scene in *The Squabble*; there is something of *The Greatcoat* in the idea of a Titular Councillor being robbed of all he holds most dear; and, still more clearly, there are unmistakable echoes of two other key Gogolian tales of St Petersburg, *The Nose* and *The Notes of a Madman*. The theme of the doppelgänger was very popular in Russian literature in the second quarter of the nineteenth century, when the tales of E.T.A. Hoffmann were widely read and admired, but its oddest manifestation was surely *The Nose*, in which an ambitious and libidinous civil servant finds himself outdone both at work and at play by his own newly independent olfactory organ. Here all finally ends satisfactorily, but in Gogol's other story a Titular Councillor is thwarted in his desire for his superior's daughter, is stripped of the remnants of his self-esteem, begins to live in a world of fantasy and, having adopted for himself the more prestigious persona of the King of Spain, is finally locked away.

Yet just as Dostoevsky did something new with Gogolian material in *Poor People*, here too he gives themes of Romantic literature of the fantastic a very modern twist, thereby prompting a good deal of subsequent interest from the world of psychiatry. His double is a manifestation of Mr Golyadkin's troubled psyche, which seems initially to incarnate all his more pitiable, self-effacing features. But once Mr Golyadkin has revealed his intimate secrets to his double (or admitted them to himself), so the double adopts all the negative, despicable characteristics that make up the other side of Golyadkin's nature. Thereafter he is able to rid himself of feelings of guilt by transferring blame for anything untoward onto his double, whom he endows with all the vices he cannot accept in himself. Golyadkin's creation of a double is carefully anticipated in the narrative: as early as the first chapter he is seen to be prepared to go so far as to deny his own existence in order to pin his sins on someone who merely looks like him. The allusive manner in which Dostoevsky reveals aspects of Golyadkin's past and present circumstances to the reader intentionally obscures the whole truth in order to reflect the character's own need for obfuscation. And the reader is further introduced into Golyadkin's world by the tendency of the narrator to view things from the character's point of view and at times even to slip into his brilliantly evoked mode of speech. The way that the narrator also treats his hero with undisguised irony and the fact that some of the story's incidents do seem to suggest the actual physical presence of another clerk sharing Golyadkin's name and characteristics make the whole narrative even more disturbing.

It is perhaps not surprising that many of the elements Dostoevsky found so exciting during his work on *The Double* contributed to its initial critical failure. His delighted borrowing of Golyadkin's speech patterns in his own correspondence attests to his awareness of their originality, yet the convoluted repetition they demanded was neither understood nor appreciated in the 1840s. The revision of the 1860s did much to improve the readability of the text without detracting from the original concept, and in any event this remains an essential work for an understanding of Dostoevsky's consistent technique of doubling. He initiated it at the very beginning of his literary career in *Poor People* with

Makar Devushkin's nature and fate reflected in the elder Pokrovsky and Gorshkov, and it would be employed right through to the major novels of his last two decades. It is surely no mere chance that the revision of *The Double* in the 1860s coincided with work on the most famous of all his divided and doubled characters, the hero of *Crime and Punishment* Raskolnikov, whose very name is based on a Russian verb meaning 'to split apart'. Had he survived to read the works of the 1860s, Belinsky would doubtless have felt fully justified in his words in defence of their flawed precursors of the 1840s: '*The Double* bears the stamp of a huge and powerful talent, but one that is still young and inexperienced: from this stem all its shortcomings, but also from this stem all its qualities too.'

– Hugh Aplin, 2004

The Double

It was a little before eight o'clock in the morning when Titular Councillor[1] Yakov Petrovich Golyadkin came to after a long sleep, yawned, stretched and finally opened his eyes fully. Yet he lay motionless on his bed for a couple of minutes like a man not yet entirely sure if he has woken up or is still asleep – if everything that is now happening around him is in the waking world and in reality or is a continuation of the disordered dreams of his sleep. Soon, however, Mr Golyadkin's senses began more clearly and distinctly to take in their customary, everyday impressions. The rather dingily greenish, smoke-darkened, dusty walls of his little room threw a familiar glance at him – his mahogany chest of drawers, imitation mahogany chairs, table painted with red paint, reddish-coloured oilskin Turkish couch with little green flowers and, finally, the clothing removed in a hurry the day before and thrown in a heap on the couch. Finally, the grey autumnal day, dull and dirty, peeped into his room through the grimy window so angrily and with such a sour grimace that Mr Golyadkin could no longer be in any doubt whatsoever that he was not in some fairy-tale kingdom or other, but in the city of St Petersburg, in the capital, on Shestilavochnaya Street, on the third floor of a very large tenement block, in his own apartment. Having made such an important discovery, Mr Golyadkin closed his eyes spasmodically as if in regret over his recent sleep and wanting to bring it back for a moment. But a minute later he jumped out of bed in a single bound, probably having finally hit upon the idea around which his hitherto scattered thoughts had been circling before being brought into appropriate order. Having jumped out of bed, he immediately ran up to the little round mirror standing on the chest of drawers. Although the figure reflected in the mirror, sleepy, weak-sighted and quite bald, was of just such an insignificant nature that at first glance it would not have held the especial attention of anybody at all, still its owner was evidently perfectly satisfied with everything he saw in the mirror. 'What a thing it would have been,' said Mr Golyadkin in a low voice, 'what a thing it would have been if I'd had something missing today, if something for example had gone wrong, some unwanted spot or other had appeared, or some other unpleasant thing had happened. But so far it's not bad – so far everything's going well.' Very pleased that everything was going well, Mr Golyadkin put the mirror down in its previous place and, despite the fact that he was barefooted and still had on the costume in which he was accustomed to go to bed, he ran to the window and with great concern began searching for something in the courtyard of the building onto which the windows of his apartment looked out. What he found in the yard evidently satisfied him perfectly too; his face lit up with a self-satisfied smile. Then – but after first glancing behind the partition into the cubbyhole of Petrushka, his valet, and assuring himself that Petrushka was not there – he tiptoed up to the table, unlocked one of its drawers, rummaged around in the corner at the very back of this drawer, finally took out from under some old, yellowed papers and rubbish of some sort a worn, green wallet, opened it cautiously, and glanced carefully and with enjoyment into its furthest, secret pocket. A wad of green, grey, blue, red and various multicoloured notes probably also looked very amicably and approvingly at Mr Golyadkin: with a beaming face he put the open wallet on the table in front of him and rubbed his hands hard as a sign of the greatest pleasure. Finally he took it out, his comforting wad of state banknotes and, actually for the hundredth time since the day before, began recounting them, giving each note a thorough rub between his thumb and index finger. 'Seven hundred and fifty roubles in notes!' he finally concluded in a half-whisper. 'Seven hundred and fifty roubles... a splendid sum! It's a nice sum,' he continued in a quavering voice, somewhat weak with pleasure, squeezing the wad in his hands and smiling significantly, 'it's a very nice sum! A nice sum for anyone at all! Would I like to see a man now for whom that sum would be a trifling sum! Such a sum can take a man a long way...'

'But what's this, then?' thought Mr Golyadkin, 'where on earth is Petrushka?' Still retaining the same costume, he glanced for a second time behind the partition. Petrushka was again not to be found behind the partition, and only a single samovar, set there on the floor, fumed, raged, lost its temper, continually threatening to run away, and gabbled something heatedly and rapidly in its queer language, burring and lisping to Mr Golyadkin – probably that, so to speak, you should take me, good people, I'm absolutely done and ready, you know.

'The devil take him!' thought Mr Golyadkin. 'That idle beast could end up driving a man beyond his final limits; where's he wandered off to?' In just indignation he went into the entrance hall, consisting of a small corridor, at the end of which was a door into the lobby; he opened this door a tiny bit and saw his servant surrounded by quite a little knot of serving, domestic and chance riff-raff. Petrushka was recounting something, the others were listening. Mr Golyadkin evidently liked neither the topic of conversation nor the conversation itself. He immediately called Petrushka and returned to his room totally dissatisfied, even upset. 'That beast is prepared to sell a man, and especially his master, for no money at all,' he thought to himself, 'and he has done, he has done for sure, I'm ready to bet that he has, for less than a kopek. Well, what is it?...'

'The livery's arrived, sir.'

'Put it on and come here.'

After putting on the livery, Petrushka entered his master's room with a stupid grin. His costume was inconceivably strange. He had on the green, very second-hand livery of a footman with moulting gold galloons, evidently made for a man a good two feet taller than Petrushka. In his hands he held a hat, also with galloons and with green feathers, and at his hip he had a footman's sword in a leather sheath.

Finally, to complete the picture, Petrushka, following his favourite custom of always going around half-dressed as if at home, was even now barefooted. Mr Golyadkin inspected Petrushka all over and was evidently satisfied. The livery had clearly been hired for some grand occasion. It was also noticeable that during the inspection Petrushka looked at his master with some strange expectation and followed his every move with unusual curiosity, which Mr Golyadkin found extremely embarrassing.

'Well, and the carriage?'

'The carriage has arrived too.'

'For the whole day?'

'For the whole day. Twenty-five, in notes.'

'And the boots have come?'

'And the boots have come.'

'Twit! Can't you say "have come, *sir*"? Give them here.'

Having expressed his pleasure about the boots fitting well, Mr Golyadkin asked for some tea and things for washing and shaving. He shaved very thoroughly and washed in just the same way, gulped his tea down hastily and set about his most important final robing: he put on trousers that were almost absolutely new; then a shirt front with brass buttons, a waistcoat with nice, very bright little flowers; he tied a multicoloured silk tie round his neck, and, finally, pulled on a uniform coat, also nice and new and thoroughly cleaned. He glanced lovingly at his boots several times while dressing, every minute raised now one leg, now the other, admired the style and kept on whispering something under his breath, occasionally winking with an expressive grimace at what he was thinking. But this morning Mr Golyadkin was extremely absent-minded, because he barely noticed Petrushka's little smiles and grimaces on his account as he helped him to dress. Finally, having got everything that was needed, and fully dressed, Mr Golyadkin put his wallet in his pocket, had a final look at Petrushka, who had put on his boots and was thus also in complete readiness, and noting that everything was already done and there was no longer anything to wait for, hurriedly, fussily, with a slight palpitation in his heart, he ran down his staircase. A cabman's carriage, blue and with coats of arms of some sort, rolled with a clatter up to the porch. Petrushka, exchanging winks with the cabman and with some idlers, settled his master into the carriage; in an unaccustomed voice and scarcely containing idiotic laughter he called: 'Drive on!', jumped up onto the footboard, and the whole lot, with a noise and a clatter, a ringing and a cracking, rolled off to Nevsky Avenue. No sooner had the blue carriage managed to drive out of the gates than Mr Golyadkin rubbed his hands spasmodically and broke into quiet, inaudible laughter, like a man with a merry character who has succeeded in playing a splendid trick, a trick with which he is himself as pleased as Punch. But immediately after the fit of merriment the laughter was replaced on Mr Golyadkin's face by some strange, anxious expression. Despite the fact that the weather was damp and overcast, he lowered both of the carriage windows and began carefully scrutinising passers-by to the right and to the left, immediately adopting a decorous and respectable air as soon as he noticed that anybody was looking at him. At the turning from Liteinaya onto Nevsky Avenue a most unpleasant sensation made him shudder, and, frowning like some poor thing who has had a corn accidentally trodden on, hurriedly, even fearfully, he huddled into the darkest corner of his carriage. The thing was that he had met two of his fellow workers, two young clerks from the same Ministry in which he himself worked. And the clerks, as it seemed to Mr Golyadkin, were also for their part extremely bewildered at meeting their colleague like this; one of them even pointed his finger at Mr Golyadkin. It even seemed to Mr Golyadkin that the other called to him loudly by name, which was, of course, most improper in the street. Our hero concealed himself and did not respond. 'What young pups!' he began reasoning with himself. 'Well, what's so strange about it? A man in a carriage; a man needs to be in a carriage, so he's taken a carriage. Just rubbish! I know them – just young pups, pups who need to be flogged too! They'd enjoy just wasting their salaries on games of pitch-and-toss and hanging around somewhere or other, that's their business. I'd tell them all something, but only...' Mr Golyadkin did not finish and his heart stood still. A lively pair of Kazan horses, very familiar to Mr Golyadkin and harnessed to a smart droshky, quickly overtook his carriage on the right-hand side. The gentleman sitting on the droshky, when by chance he caught sight of the face of Mr Golyadkin – who had rather incautiously poked his head out of the window of the carriage – was evidently also extremely astonished at such an unexpected meeting and, bending down as far as he could, he began to gaze with the utmost curiosity and concern into that corner of the carriage where our hero made haste to try and hide. The gentleman on the droshky was Andrei Filippovich, the head of department in that place of work where Mr Golyadkin was also employed in the capacity of assistant to his head of section. Mr Golyadkin, seeing that Andrei Filippovich had fully recognised him, that he was gazing at him wide-eyed and that it was quite impossible to hide, blushed to the roots of his hair. 'Bow or not? Respond or not? Acknowledge or not?' thought our hero in indescribable anguish, 'or pretend that it's not me, but someone else with a striking resemblance to me, and look as if there were nothing wrong? Simply not me, not me, and that's that!' said Mr Golyadkin, doffing his hat to Andrei Filippovich and not taking his eyes off him. 'I, I'm all right,' he forced himself to whisper, 'I'm completely all right, it's not me at all, Andrei Filippovich, it's not me at all, not me, and that's that.' Soon, however, the droshky overtook the carriage, and the magnetic power of his superior's gaze passed. However, he still blushed, smiled, mumbled something to himself… 'I was a fool not to respond,' he finally thought, 'I should simply on a bold footing and with a candour not lacking in nobility have said, "It's like this, Andrei Filippovich, I've been invited to the meal as well, and that's that!"' Then suddenly remembering that he had come a cropper, our hero reddened like fire, knitted his brows and threw a terrible, defiant look at the front corner of the carriage, a look just designed to reduce all his enemies to dust in an instant. Finally, all of a sudden, moved by some sort of inspiration, he pulled on the cord tied to the elbow of the cabman-cum-coachman, stopped the carriage and ordered him to turn back to Liteinaya. The thing is that, probably for his own peace of mind, Mr Golyadkin needed to tell something most interesting to his doctor, Krestyan Ivanovich, straight away. And although he had been acquainted with Krestyan Ivanovich for a very short time – had visited him only once the previous week, to be precise, as a result of certain needs – still, after all, a doctor, as they say, is like a confessor – it would be stupid to conceal things, and knowing a patient is his very duty. 'Will it all be right, though?,' continued our hero, getting out of the carriage at the entrance to a five-storey building on Liteinaya, beside which he had ordered his vehicle to be stopped, 'will it all be right? Will it be proper? Will it be appropriate? But then, after all, what of it?' he continued, going up the stairs, catching his breath and suppressing the beating of his heart, which was in the habit of beating hard on all staircases other than his own, 'what of it? After all, it's about me, and there's nothing reprehensible here… It would be stupid to conceal things. So this way I'll pretend that I'm all right and for no reason, in passing… And he'll see that that's how it should be.'

Reasoning thus, Mr Golyadkin went up to the first floor and stopped in front of apartment number five, on the door of which had been set a beautiful brass plate with the inscription:

Krestyan Ivanovich Rutenspitz,
Doctor of Medicine and Surgery.

Having stopped, our hero hastened to give his physiognomy a respectable, free-and-easy air, not without a degree of amiability, and prepared to pull on the bell cord. Having prepared to pull on the bell cord, he immediately and quite appropriately reasoned that it might be better tomorrow and that now for the time being there was no great need. But since Mr Golyadkin suddenly heard somebody's footsteps on the staircase, he immediately altered his new decision and at the same time, moreover with the most decisive air, he now rang at Krestyan Ivanovich's door.

2

Doctor of Medicine and Surgery Krestyan Ivanovich Rutenspitz – a very healthy, albeit already elderly man, endowed with thick, greying eyebrows and whiskers, an expressive, flashing gaze, which was evidently all he needed to drive off every illness, and, finally, with a significant decoration – was sitting that morning in his comfortable armchair in his study, drinking the coffee his wife had personally brought him, smoking a cigar and from time to time writing out prescriptions for his patients. After prescribing the last phial for an old man suffering from haemorrhoids and seeing the suffering old man out through the side doors, Krestyan Ivanovich settled down to await the next visit. In came Mr Golyadkin.

Krestyan Ivanovich had evidently not at all expected, nor indeed wished to see Mr Golyadkin before him, because he suddenly became troubled for a moment and his face involuntarily expressed a certain strange – even, it could be said, discontented – look. Since Mr Golyadkin for his part almost always became somehow inappropriately deflated and bewildered at those moments when he happened to assail somebody for the sake of his own little affairs, now too, not having prepared the first phrase, which in such instances was a real stumbling block for him, he became very considerably embarrassed, mumbled something – an apology, actually, it seemed – and, not knowing what to do next, took a chair and sat down. But, remembering that he had taken a seat without invitation, he immediately sensed his impropriety and hastened to correct a mistake that displayed ignorance of society and good manners, by immediately rising from the place he had occupied without invitation. Then, coming to his senses and noting vaguely that he had done two stupid things at once, he resolved without the least hesitation on a third, that is, he tried to make some justification, mumbled something with a smile, blushed, became embarrassed, fell expressively silent and finally sat down conclusively and got up no more – but for no particular reason, just in case, he armed himself with that same defiant gaze which had the unusual power of reducing and pounding all Mr Golyadkin's enemies to dust in his mind. Moreover this gaze fully expressed Mr Golyadkin's independence, that is, said clearly that Mr Golyadkin was perfectly all right, that he was his own man, like everyone else, and in any event kept himself to himself. Krestyan Ivanovich coughed and wheezed, evidently to mark his approval and consent to all this, and directed an inspectorial, enquiring gaze at Mr Golyadkin.

'Krestyan Ivanovich,' began Mr Golyadkin with a smile, 'I've come to trouble you for a second time and now for a second time take the liberty of begging your indulgence…' Mr Golyadkin was clearly having difficulty with his words.

'Hm… yes!' said Krestyan Ivanovich, releasing a stream of smoke from his mouth and placing his cigar on the desk, 'but you need to adhere to instructions; I did explain to you, you know, that your treatment should consist in the alteration of your habits… Well, amusements; well, I mean you should call on friends and acquaintances, and at the same time not be afraid of having a drink; keep cheerful company at a consistent level.'

Mr Golyadkin, still smiling, hastened to remark that it seemed to him that he was like everyone else, that he was his own man, that his amusements were like everyone else's… that, of course, he could go to the theatre, since he too, like everyone else, had the means, that he was at work during the day and at home in the evening, that he was quite all right; he even remarked in passing at this point that, as far as he could tell, he was no worse than other people, that he lived at home, in his own apartment, and that, finally, he had Petrushka. Here Mr Golyadkin hesitated.

'Hm, no, a regime like that isn't the thing, and that's not at all what I wanted to ask you. All in all, what I'm interested in is to know what you are – if you are a great lover of cheerful company, if you use your time cheerfully... Well, you know, if you are now pursuing a melancholy or a cheerful way of life...'

'Krestyan Ivanovich, I...'

'Hm... what I'm saying is,' the doctor interrupted, 'that you need to make a radical transformation of your whole life and in a certain sense to master your own character.' (Krestyan Ivanovich put a strong emphasis on the word 'master' and paused for a moment with a very meaningful air.) 'Not to shun a cheerful life; to go to shows and a club and in any event not to be afraid of having a drink. Staying at home won't do... you can't possibly stay at home.'

'I like it quiet, Krestyan Ivanovich,' said Mr Golyadkin, casting a meaningful glance at Krestyan Ivanovich and clearly seeking the words for the most appropriate expression of his thoughts, 'it's just me and Petrushka in the apartment... I mean, my man, Krestyan Ivanovich. I mean, Krestyan Ivanovich, that I'm going my own way, my own particular way, Krestyan Ivanovich. I'm a man apart and, so far as I can tell, depend on nobody. I also go out for walks, Krestyan Ivanovich.'

'What?... Yes! There's nothing pleasant about going for walks these days; the climate's very bad.'

'Yes, sir, Krestyan Ivanovich. Although I am indeed a quiet man, Krestyan Ivanovich, as I think I've already had the honour to explain to you, still my way takes a separate course, Krestyan Ivanovich. The path of life is wide... I mean... by that I mean to say, Krestyan Ivanovich... Excuse me, Krestyan Ivanovich, I'm not skilled in speaking fine words.'

'Hm... you're saying...'

'I'm saying you must excuse me, Krestyan Ivanovich, for the fact that, as far as I can tell, I'm not skilled in speaking fine words,' said Mr Golyadkin in a somewhat offended tone, getting a little lost and muddled. 'In this respect, Krestyan Ivanovich, I'm not like others,' he added with a particular sort of smile, 'and I don't know how to talk a lot; I never learnt to lend beauty to my manner of speech. But on the other hand, Krestyan Ivanovich, I act; on the other hand, I act, Krestyan Ivanovich!'

'Hm... How do you mean... you act?' responded Krestyan Ivanovich. There then followed, for a minute, a silence. The doctor glanced at Mr Golyadkin strangely somehow and distrustfully. Mr Golyadkin in his turn also cast a sidelong and rather distrustful glance at the doctor.

'Krestyan Ivanovich,' Mr Golyadkin resumed, still in his former tone, a little irritated and perplexed by Krestyan Ivanovich's extreme persistence, 'Krestyan Ivanovich, I like peace and quiet and not the noise of society. There in that high society of theirs, I tell you, Krestyan Ivanovich, you need to know how to polish parquet floors with your boots...' (here Mr Golyadkin scraped his foot a little on the floor) 'it's demanded there, sir, and wordplay is demanded too... you need to know how to put together a sweetly scented compliment, sir... that's what's demanded there. And I've not learnt that, Krestyan Ivanovich – I've not learnt all those little tricks, there's been no time. I'm a simple, plain man, and I haven't any superficial brilliance. In this, Krestyan Ivanovich, I lay down my weaponry; I put it down, speaking in this sense.' Mr Golyadkin said all this, of course, with the sort of air that made it clearly known that our hero did not at all regret putting down his weaponry in this sense and not having learnt tricks, but even quite the opposite. Krestyan Ivanovich, listening to this, looked down with a very unpleasant grimace on his face and seemed to have a presentiment of something in advance. Mr Golyadkin's tirade was followed by a rather long and meaningful silence.

'You seem to have digressed a little from the subject,' said Krestyan Ivanovich finally in a low voice. 'I must confess to you, I couldn't understand you fully.'

'I'm not skilled in speaking fine words, Krestyan Ivanovich; I've already had the honour of informing you, Krestyan Ivanovich, that I'm not skilled in speaking fine words,' said Mr Golyadkin, this time in a sharp and decisive tone.

'Hm...'

'Krestyan Ivanovich!' Mr Golyadkin began again in a quiet, but meaningful voice, in a somewhat solemn vein and pausing at every point. 'Krestyan Ivanovich! When I came in here, I began with apologies. Now I repeat what went before and again beg your indulgence for a time. I have nothing to hide from you, Krestyan Ivanovich. I'm a little man, you know it yourself; but, to my good fortune, I don't regret the fact that I'm a little man. On the contrary even, Krestyan Ivanovich; and, so that everything's said, I'm even proud of the fact that I'm not a big man, but a little one. I'm not a schemer – and I'm proud of that too. I act not on the sly, but openly, without tricks, and although I could do harm in my turn, and could do a great deal of it, and even know to whom and how to do it, Krestyan Ivanovich, still I don't want to sully myself, and in this sense I wash my hands. In this sense, I say, I wash them, Krestyan Ivanovich!' Mr Golyadkin fell expressively silent for a moment; he was speaking with mild animation.

'I go, Krestyan Ivanovich,' our hero resumed, 'directly, openly and without devious ways, because I despise them and leave that to others. I don't try to denigrate those who are perhaps a little cleaner than you and me... that is, I mean, them and me, Krestyan Ivanovich, I didn't mean you. I don't like words cut short; I don't favour wretched duplicities; I abhor slander and gossip. I put on a mask only for a masquerade, and don't go around in front of people every day with it on. I'll only ask you, Krestyan Ivanovich, how would you begin to take revenge on your enemy, your most bitter enemy, the one you'd consider to be him?' concluded Mr Golyadkin, casting a defiant glance at Krestyan Ivanovich.

Although Mr Golyadkin pronounced all this exceedingly distinctly, clearly, with confidence, weighing his words and reckoning on the most certain effect, nonetheless he now looked with disquiet, with great disquiet, with extreme disquiet at Krestyan Ivanovich. Now he was all eyes, and shyly, with vexing, anguished impatience he awaited Krestyan Ivanovich's reply. But, to Mr Golyadkin's perplexity and complete astonishment, Krestyan Ivanovich mumbled something under his breath; then moved his armchair up to the desk and quite drily, but still courteously, announced to him something to the effect that his time was precious, that he did not quite understand somehow; that still he was ready to be of service in any way he could, within his powers, but that anything further and not concerning him he must leave. At this point he picked up his pen, moved his paper towards him, cut from it the sort of strip used by doctors and announced that he would prescribe what was required straight away.

'No, sir, it's not required, Krestyan Ivanovich! No, sir, it's not required at all!' said Mr Golyadkin, half-rising from his seat and seizing Krestyan Ivanovich's right hand, 'that's not necessary here at all, Krestyan Ivanovich…'

But in the meantime, while Mr Golyadkin had been saying all this, some strange change had taken place in him. His grey eyes flashed strangely somehow, his lips began to tremble, all the muscles, all the features of his face began to stir, began to move. He himself was shaking all over. Having followed his first impulse and stopped Krestyan Ivanovich's hand, Mr Golyadkin now stood motionless as if he did not trust himself and was awaiting inspiration for his further actions.

There then took place a rather strange scene.

Somewhat perplexed, Krestyan Ivanovich for a moment seemed to be rooted to his armchair and, at a loss, stared wide-eyed at Mr Golyadkin, who looked at him in the same manner. Finally Krestyan Ivanovich stood up, holding on a little to the lapel of Mr Golyadkin's uniform coat. For several seconds they both stood like this, motionless and not taking their eyes off one another. Then, and moreover in an extraordinarily strange way, Mr Golyadkin's second impulse was resolved too. His lips began to shake, his chin began to jerk, and our hero quite unexpectedly burst into tears. Sobbing, nodding his head and striking himself on the chest with his right hand, while with the left, having also grabbed the lapel of Krestyan Ivanovich's indoor clothing, he tried to speak and explain something straight away, but he could not say so much as a word. Finally Krestyan Ivanovich recovered from his astonishment.

'Come, come, calm yourself, sit down!' he said finally, trying to sit Mr Golyadkin down in an armchair.

'I have enemies, Krestyan Ivanovich, I have enemies; I have bitter enemies who have sworn to destroy me…' replied Mr Golyadkin fearfully and in a whisper.

'Come, come now; what of enemies! There's no need to think about enemies! There's no need at all. Sit down, sit down,' continued Krestyan Ivanovich, finally settling Mr Golyadkin down in the armchair.

Mr Golyadkin settled down at last without taking his eyes off Krestyan Ivanovich. With an extremely discontented air Krestyan Ivanovich began pacing from one corner of his study to another. A long silence followed.

'I'm grateful to you, Krestyan Ivanovich, very grateful, and I feel very deeply everything you've done for me now. To the grave I shall not forget your kindness, Krestyan Ivanovich,' said Mr Golyadkin finally, rising from the chair with an offended air.

'Come, come now, I tell you, come, come!' Krestyan Ivanovich replied quite sternly to Mr Golyadkin's outburst, sitting him down in his place once more. 'Well, what's going on? Tell me, what unpleasant things are going on now,' continued Krestyan Ivanovich, 'and what enemies are you talking about? What kind of thing's going on?'

'No, Krestyan Ivanovich, we'd better leave that now,' replied Mr Golyadkin, lowering his eyes to the ground, 'we'd better set that aside, until the time... until another time; until a more convenient time, Krestyan Ivanovich, when everything will be revealed, and the masks will fall from certain faces, and a certain something will be laid bare. But now, for the time being, it stands to reason after what's happened to us... you must agree yourself, Krestyan Ivanovich... Allow me to wish you a good morning, Krestyan Ivanovich,' said Mr Golyadkin, rising from his place this time decisively and seriously and grabbing his hat.

'Ah well... as you wish... hm...' (There followed a minute's silence.) 'I, for my part, you know, what I can... and I sincerely wish you well.'

'I understand you, Krestyan Ivanovich, I understand; I understand you completely now... In any event, forgive me for troubling you, Krestyan Ivanovich.'

'Hm... No, that's not what I wanted to say to you. Still, as you like. Continue the medication as before...'

'I shall continue the medication as you say, Krestyan Ivanovich, I shall continue, and I'll get it from the same chemist's... These days,

Krestyan Ivanovich, even being a chemist is an important matter…'

'What? In what sense do you mean?'

'In a very ordinary sense, Krestyan Ivanovich. I mean that nowadays, the way the world has gone…'

'Hm…'

'And it's not only the chemist's boy, but every young pup that turns his nose up at a respectable man now.'

'Hm… And what's your understanding of that?'

'I'm talking, Krestyan Ivanovich, about a particular man… about our mutual acquaintance, Krestyan Ivanovich, about Vladimir Semyonovich, for example, if you want…'

'Ah!…'

'Yes, Krestyan Ivanovich; and I know certain people, Krestyan Ivanovich, who don't particularly hold to the general opinion, if truth be told sometimes.'

'Ah!… How's that, then?'

'Well, it's like this, sir; it's a side issue, anyway; there are times when they know how to serve up a real dog's dinner.'

'What? Serve what?'

'A dog's dinner, Krestyan Ivanovich; that's a Russian saying. There are times when they know how to offer a man appropriate congratulations, for example; there are such people, Krestyan Ivanovich.'

'Congratulations?'

'Yes, sir, Krestyan Ivanovich, congratulations, as one of my close acquaintances did the other day…'

'One of your close acquaintances… ah! How's that, then?' said Krestyan Ivanovich, glancing attentively at Mr Golyadkin.

'Yes, sir, one of my intimate acquaintances congratulated another also very intimate acquaintance and, in addition, a friend, as they say, of my sweetest friend, on a promotion, on being given the rank of Assessor. It was like this, by the way. "I'm," so to speak, "deeply glad," he says, "of the opportunity to offer you, Vladimir Semyonovich, my congratulations, my *sincere* congratulations, on being promoted. And I'm all the more glad, since nowadays, as all the world knows, fairy godmothers have died out."' At this point Mr Golyadkin nodded roguishly and, screwing up his eyes, looked at Krestyan Ivanovich.

'Hm… So he said that…'

'He did, Krestyan Ivanovich, he did, and at that very moment he glanced at Andrei Filippovich, who's the uncle of our little treasure, Vladimir Semyonovich. What's it to me, Krestyan Ivanovich, that he's been made an Assessor? What's it to do with me? And he wants to get married, while the milk, with your permission, isn't yet dry on his lips. He really did say it, Vladimir Semyonovich, so to speak, I tell you! I've said everything now; do allow me to withdraw.'

'Hm…'

'Yes, Krestyan Ivanovich, do allow me now, I say, to withdraw. Well, at this point, so as to kill two birds with one stone – I cut that young buck down to size about fairy godmothers when I turned to Klara Olsufyevna (it all happened two days ago at Olsufy Ivanovich's) – and she'd just sung a sentimental romance – and I say, so to speak, "you were good enough to sing sentimental romances, but it's not with pure hearts that people are listening to you." And by this I'm clearly hinting, you understand, Krestyan Ivanovich, by this I'm clearly hinting that it's not her they're after now, but a little something extra…'

'Ah! Well what did he do?…'

'Ate a lemon, Krestyan Ivanovich, as the saying goes.'

'Hm…'

'Yes, sir, Krestyan Ivanovich. And I say to the old man himself too – so to speak, "Olsufy Ivanovich," I say, "I know how indebted I am to you, I fully appreciate the bounty you've showered on me almost ever since I was a child. But open your eyes, Olsufy Ivanovich," I say. "Look. I myself am conducting things frankly and openly, Olsufy Ivanovich."'

'So that's the way of it!'

'Yes, Krestyan Ivanovich. That's the way it is…'

'And what did he say?'

'What was he going to say, Krestyan Ivanovich! He mumbles this and that, and I know you, and His Excellency is a benefactor – and off he went, laying it on… But what of it, after all? He's got pretty doddery, as they say, in his old age.'

'Ah! So that's the way of it now!'

'Yes, Krestyan Ivanovich. And that's how we all are, well, he's an old boy! He's at death's door, got one foot in the grave, as they say, but if

17

some old women's tales get spun, then he's there listening; it can't be done without him…'

'Tales, you say?'

'Yes, Krestyan Ivanovich, they've spun some tales. That Bear of ours has had his hand in it and his nephew too, our little treasure; it goes without saying that they got in touch with the old women and cooked the whole thing up. What would you think? What did they think up to murder a man?…'

'To murder a man?'

'Yes, Krestyan Ivanovich, to murder a man, to murder a man morally. They spread it around… I'm still talking about my intimate acquaintance…'

Krestyan Ivanovich nodded.

'They spread a rumour about him… I confess to you, Krestyan Ivanovich, I'm even ashamed to say it, Krestyan Ivanovich…'

'Hm…'

'They spread a rumour around that he'd already given a written undertaking to marry, that he was already engaged in another direction… And what would you think, Krestyan Ivanovich, to whom?'

'Indeed?'

'To the mistress of an eating-house, to an unseemly German he gets his meals from; instead of paying his debts, he offers her his hand.'

'That's what they're saying?'

'Can you believe it, Krestyan Ivanovich? A German, a vile, disgusting, shameless German, Karolina Ivanovna, maybe you know…'

'I confess, for my part…'

'I understand you, Krestyan Ivanovich, I understand, and for my part I feel it…'

'Tell me, please, where are you living now?'

'Where am I living now, Krestyan Ivanovich?'

'Yes… I want… previously, I think, you were living…'

'I was, Krestyan Ivanovich, I was, I was previously too. How could I not have been living!' replied Mr Golyadkin, accompanying his words with a little laugh and rather confusing Krestyan Ivanovich with his reply.

'No, you've taken it the wrong way; for my part, I wanted…'

'I did too, Krestyan Ivanovich, for my part, I did too,' Mr Golyadkin continued, laughing. 'However, Krestyan Ivanovich, I've sat here with you far too long. I hope you'll allow me now… to wish you a good morning…'

'Hm…'

'Yes, Krestyan Ivanovich, I understand you; I fully understand you now,' said our hero, rather showing off before Krestyan Ivanovich. 'And so allow me to wish you a good morning…'

At this point our hero clicked his heels and went out of the room, leaving Krestyan Ivanovich in extreme astonishment. Descending the doctor's staircase, he smiled and rubbed his hands joyfully. On the porch, taking a breath of fresh air and feeling himself at liberty, he really was even prepared to count himself the happiest of mortals and then to set off directly to the Ministry, when suddenly his carriage set up a clatter by the entrance; he took a glance and remembered everything. Petrushka was already opening the doors. Some strange and extremely unpleasant sensation gripped the whole of Mr Golyadkin. It was as if he blushed for a moment. Something pricked him. He was already on the point of beginning to set his foot on the footboard of the carriage, when suddenly he turned around and looked at Krestyan Ivanovich's windows. So it was! Krestyan Ivanovich was standing at the window, stroking his whiskers with his right hand and looking at our hero quite curiously.

'That doctor's stupid,' thought Mr Golyadkin, taking refuge in the carriage, 'extremely stupid. It may be that he treats his patients well, but nevertheless… thick as a brick.' Mr Golyadkin sat himself down, Petrushka cried, 'Drive on!' and the carriage rolled off once more to Nevsky Avenue.

3

That entire morning was terribly busy for Mr Golyadkin. Arriving on Nevsky Avenue, our hero ordered a stop to be made at Gostiny Dvor[2]. He jumped out of his vehicle and, accompanied by Petrushka, ran into the arcade and went straight to the shop selling gold and silver goods. It was noticeable from Mr Golyadkin's air alone that he had masses to do and an awful lot of business. Having haggled a complete dinner and tea service down to a little over 1,500 roubles in notes and having struck himself a bargain over an intricately designed cigar holder and a complete silver set for shaving his beard at the same price, and after finally asking the prices of some other little things, nice and useful in their way, Mr Golyadkin concluded by promising to drop by without fail the next day or even to send that same day for the things he had negotiated over, took the number of the shop and, after attentively hearing out the merchant, who was making a fuss about a small deposit, he promised a small deposit too at the right time. After which he hurriedly took his final leave of the bewildered merchant and, pursued by a whole flock of salesmen, set off along the line of shops, looking back every minute at Petrushka and carefully searching for some new shop. In passing he dropped in at the *bureau de change* and exchanged all his notes of large denomination for small ones, and although he lost out on the exchange, still he exchanged them nevertheless, and his wallet became significantly fatter, which evidently gave him extreme pleasure. Finally he stopped in a shop selling various materials for ladies. Having negotiated purchases again for a splendid sum, Mr Golyadkin here too promised the merchant to drop by without fail, took the number of the shop and, to the question about a small deposit, again repeated that there would be a small deposit too at the right time. Then he visited several more shops as well; in all of them he struck deals, asked the prices of various small items, sometimes argued for a long time with the merchants, left the shops and returned three times or so to each – in short, displayed extraordinary activity. From Gostiny Dvor our hero set off to a certain well-known furniture shop where he negotiated for furniture for six rooms, admired a fashionable and very intricate lady's dressing table in the latest taste and, having assured the merchant that he would send for everything without fail, he left the shop according to his custom with the promise of a small deposit, then drove off somewhere else and negotiated for something else. In short, there was evidently no end to his business. Finally all this seemed to begin to get very tiresome for Mr Golyadkin himself. As a result of what, God knows, but out of the blue he even began to be tormented by pangs of conscience. Not for anything would he have consented to encounter, for example, Andrei Filippovich or even Krestyan Ivanovich now. Finally the city clock struck three in the afternoon. When Mr Golyadkin ultimately got into his carriage, of all the acquisitions he had made that morning, there turned out in reality to be just one pair of gloves and a bottle of perfume at one and a half roubles in notes. Since it was still quite early for Mr Golyadkin, he ordered his coachman to stop outside a certain well-known restaurant on Nevsky Avenue, of which he knew only by hearsay up until now, got out of the carriage and ran in to have a bite to eat, a rest and to wait out a certain time.

Having had a bite the way a man who has a rich banquet in prospect has a bite – that is, having had a snack with a view to, as they say, taking the edge off his hunger, and having drunk one glass of vodka – Mr Golyadkin sat down in an armchair and, looking modestly around, he settled himself down quietly with a tatty little national newspaper. After reading a couple of lines, he stood up, looked at himself in a mirror, spruced himself up and smoothed himself down; then he went over to the window and looked to see if his carriage was there… then he sat down in his place once more and picked up the newspaper. It was noticeable that our hero was extremely agitated. Glancing at the clock and seeing that it was still only a quarter past three and that consequently there still remained quite some while to wait, and at the same time reasoning that it was indecorous to sit like that, Mr Golyadkin ordered some chocolate to be served him, for which, however, he felt no great desire at that particular moment. After drinking the chocolate and noticing that time had moved on a little, he went out to pay. Suddenly somebody struck him on the shoulder.

He turned around and saw before him two of his colleagues and comrades, the same ones he had encountered on Liteinaya in the morning – still very junior lads both in years and in rank. Our hero was neither one thing nor the other with them, neither friendly, nor openly hostile. It goes without saying, decorum had been observed on both sides; but there had been no further intimacy, nor indeed could there have been. The encounter at this particular time was extremely unpleasant for Mr Golyadkin. He frowned a little and was for a moment embarrassed.

'Yakov Petrovich, Yakov Petrovich!' the Registrars both began to chirp, 'you're here? What's the…'

'Ah! It's you, gentlemen!' Mr Golyadkin interrupted them hurriedly, a little confused and scandalised by the astonishment of the clerks and at the same time by the familiarity of their manner, but still willy-nilly playing the free-and-easy young buck. 'You've deserted, gentlemen, hee-hee-hee!' At this point, so as not to demean himself and condescend to the office youth, with whom he always stayed within the proper bounds, he tried to slap one of the youngsters on the shoulder, but Mr Golyadkin did not succed with the popular touch in this instance, and instead of a respectably familiar gesture, something completely different was the result.

'Well, then, is that Bear of ours in the office?'

'Who's that, Yakov Petrovich?'

'Well, the Bear, as if you don't know who's called the Bear!…' Mr Golyadkin laughed and turned to the waiter to take his change from him. 'I'm talking about Andrei Filippovich, gentlemen,' he continued, having finished with the waiter and on this occasion addressing the clerks with a very serious air. The two Registrars exchanged meaningful winks with one another.

'He's still in the office and he's been asking for you, Yakov Petrovich,' one of them replied.

'Still there, eh! In that case, let him stay, gentlemen. And he's been asking for me, eh?'

'He has, Yakov Petrovich; but what's happened to you, all perfumed, all powdered, such a dandy?…'

'So, gentlemen, it's like that! Enough…' Mr Golyadkin replied, looking away and smiling tensely. Seeing that Mr Golyadkin was smiling, the clerks burst into laughter. Mr Golyadkin became a little sulky.

'I'll tell you, gentlemen, in a friendly way,' said our hero after a short silence, as though he had resolved (well, so be it) to reveal something to the clerks, 'you, gentlemen, all know me, but until now you've known only one side. There's no one to reproach in this respect, and in part, I confess, I have myself been to blame.'

Mr Golyadkin pursed his lips and glanced meaningfully at the clerks.

Again the clerks exchanged winks.

'You've not known me until now, gentlemen. To give explanations here and now wouldn't be entirely appropriate. I'll just tell you something briefly and in passing. There are men, gentlemen, who don't like devious ways and who mask themselves only for a masquerade. There are men who don't see mankind's prime purpose in an adroit ability to polish parquet with their boots. There are even those men, gentlemen, who won't say they're happy and live a full life when, for example, their trousers are a good fit. There are, finally, men who don't enjoy prancing and spinning to no purpose, flirting and sucking up and, most importantly, gentlemen, poking their noses into places they've not been asked at all... I've said almost everything, gentlemen; so allow me now to withdraw...'

Mr Golyadkin stopped. Since the gentlemen Registrars were now fully satisfied, both of them suddenly began rolling around laughing extremely impolitely. Mr Golyadkin flared up.

'Laugh, gentlemen, laugh for the time being! You wait and see,' he said with a sense of insulted dignity, picked up his hat and retreated to the doors.

'But I'll say more, gentlemen,' he added, addressing the gentlemen Registrars for the last time, 'I'll say more – you're both with me here eye to eye. These, gentlemen, are my rules: fail – and I take courage, succeed – and I hold on, and in any event I undermine no one. I'm not a schemer and I'm proud of it. I wouldn't do as a diplomat. They also say, gentlemen, that the bird flies to the hunter of its own accord. It's true and I'm prepared to agree; but who's the hunter here, and who's the bird? That's another question, gentlemen!'

Mr Golyadkin fell eloquently silent and with the most meaningful expression, that is, with eyebrows raised and lips pursed to the utmost, he made his bow to the gentlemen clerks and then went out, leaving them in extreme astonishment.

'Where do you want to go?' asked Petrushka quite sternly, probably already tired of dragging around in the cold. 'Where do you want to go?' he asked Mr Golyadkin, meeting the terrible, all-destroying gaze with which our hero had armed himself twice that morning already and to which he had now resorted for the third time, as he came down the stairs.

'To the Izmailovsky Bridge.'

'To the Izmailovsky Bridge! Drive on!'

'They'll start their meal no earlier than four or even at five o'clock,' thought Mr Golyadkin, 'is it too early now? Still, after all, I can arrive a little earlier; what's more it is a family meal. I can be *sans façon*[3], as respectable people put it. Why shouldn't I be *sans façon*? Our Bear was saying everything would be *sans façon* as well, so I too…' Thus thought Mr Golyadkin; but in the meantime his agitation was increasing more and more. It was noticeable that he was preparing for something very troublesome to say the least, whispering to himself, gesticulating with his right hand, continually glancing out of the carriage windows, so that, looking at Mr Golyadkin now, nobody would honestly have said that he was intending to have a good meal, without formality, and what's more within the family circle – *sans façon*, as respectable people put it. Finally, right by the Izmailovsky Bridge, Mr Golyadkin indicated a particular building; with a clatter the carriage drove through the gates and stopped by the entrance in the right-hand façade. Noticing a female figure at a first-floor window, Mr Golyadkin blew her a kiss. However, he did not know himself what he was doing, because at that moment he was positively petrified. He emerged from the carriage pale, bewildered; he went up onto the porch, took off his hat, straightened up his clothes mechanically, and, feeling, incidentally, a slight trembling in his knees, set off up the staircase.

'Olsufy Ivanovich?' he enquired of the servant who opened the door to him.

'At home, sir – that is, not, sir, he's not at home, sir.'

'What? What do you mean, my dear? I – I've come to dinner, old fellow. You know me, don't you?'

'How could I not know you, sir! I'm ordered not to receive you, sir.'

'You… old fellow, you… you're doubtless mistaken, old fellow. It's me. I'm invited, old fellow; I've come to dinner,' said Mr Golyadkin, throwing off his greatcoat and showing his clear intention of setting off into the rooms.

'Permit me, sir, you can't, sir. I'm ordered not to receive you, sir, I'm ordered to refuse you. That's how it is!'

Mr Golyadkin turned pale. At this very moment a door from the inner

24

rooms opened and out came Gerasimych, Olsufy Ivanovich's old valet.

'He wants to come in, Yemelyan Gerasimovich, and I…'

'And you're a fool, Alexeyich. Be off to the rooms and send that rogue Semyonych here. You can't, sir,' he said, addressing Mr Golyadkin politely, but resolutely. 'It's quite impossible, sir. He asks to be excused, sir, but he can't receive you, sir.'

'Did he say that, that he couldn't receive me?' asked Mr Golyadkin irresolutely. 'You'll excuse me, Gerasimych. But why is it quite impossible?'

'It's quite impossible, sir. I announced you, sir; but he said, "ask him to excuse me". He can't, he says, receive you.'

'But why? How can that be? How?…'

'Please, please!…'

'How can that be so, though? It can't be so! Announce me… How can that be so? I've come to dinner…'

'Please, please!…'

'Ah well, then, that's a different matter – he asks to be excused; but permit me, Gerasimych, how can that be, Gerasimych?'

'Please, please!' retorted Gerasimych, pushing Mr Golyadkin aside most resolutely with his arm and providing a wide passage for the two gentlemen who at this very moment were coming into the entrance hall. The gentlemen coming in were Andrei Filippovich and his nephew, Vladimir Semyonovich. Both of them looked at Mr Golyadkin in bewilderment. Andrei Filippovich was on the point of starting to say something, but Mr Golyadkin had already made up his mind; he was already leaving Olsufy Ivanovich's entrance hall with his eyes cast down, blushing, smiling, with an utterly lost expression.

'I'll drop by later, Gerasimych; I'll explain things; I hope all this won't delay a timely explanation,' he said from the threshold and in part from the stairs.

'Yakov Petrovich, Yakov Petrovich!' resounded the voice of Andrei Filippovich, who had followed Mr Golyadkin.

Mr Golyadkin was then already on the first landing. He turned around quickly to Andrei Filippovich.

'What do you want, Andrei Filippovich?' he said in quite a resolute tone.

'What's the matter with you, Yakov Petrovich? How is it you're here?...'

'I'm all right, Andrei Filippovich, sir. I'm my own man here. It's my private life, Andrei Filippovich.'

'What's that, sir?'

'I'm saying, Andrei Filippovich, that it's my private life, and that, so far as I can tell, there's nothing reprehensible to be found here as regards my official relations.'

'What! As regards official... What is the matter with you, sir?'

'Nothing, Andrei Filippovich, absolutely nothing; a cheeky young girl, nothing more...'

'What!... What?!' Andrei Filippovich was lost in astonishment. Mr Golyadkin, who, while conversing with Andrei Filippovich from the foot of the stairs, had until now been looking at him as if he were ready to go straight for his throat, on seeing that the head of department was somewhat perplexed, took, almost without knowing it himself, a pace forward. Andrei Filippovich drew back. Mr Golyadkin moved up one step, then another. Andrei Filippovich looked around anxiously. Mr Golyadkin suddenly moved quickly up the stairs. Even more quickly Andrei Filippovich jumped into the room and slammed the door behind him. Mr Golyadkin remained alone. His eyes grew dim. He had lost the plot completely and now stood in some muddle-headed meditative state, as though he had called to mind some event, also extremely senseless, that had occurred very recently. 'Oh dear! Oh dear!' he whispered, smiling from the strain. Meanwhile, voices and footsteps became audible on the staircase below, probably those of new guests invited by Olsufy Ivanovich. Mr Golyadkin came to his senses somewhat, rapidly raised his raccoon collar up higher, concealed himself behind it as far as possible, and began to go, hobbling, pattering, hurrying and stumbling down the stairs. He felt himself somehow weakened and numbed. He was confused to such a great degree that, emerging onto the porch, he did not even wait for his carriage, but went straight across the muddy courtyard to it. Going up to his vehicle and preparing to get into it, Mr Golyadkin mentally conceived the desire to be swallowed up by the earth or to hide, even in a mouse hole, together with the carriage. It seemed to him that everything there was in Olsufy Ivanovich's house was now just looking at him from every window. He knew he would certainly die right there on the spot if he were to turn back.

'What are you laughing about, you twit?' he rattled out at Petrushka, who was ready to help him into the carriage.

'What have I got to laugh about? I've done nothing; where are we going now?'

'Going home, go on…'

'Home!' cried Petrushka, perching on the footboard.

'He's got the voice of a carrion crow!' thought Mr Golyadkin. Meanwhile the carriage had already driven quite a distance beyond the Izmailovsky Bridge. Suddenly our hero pulled the cord with all his might and called to his coachman to turn back immediately. The coachman turned the horses and two minutes later drove once more into Olsufy Ivanovich's courtyard. 'There's no need, idiot, there's no need; back again!' shouted Mr Golyadkin – and it was as if the coachman had been expecting such an order: without objecting to a thing, without stopping by the entrance, and after driving in a circle all round the yard, he drove out again into the street.

Mr Golyadkin did not go home, but, after passing the Semyonovsky Bridge, he gave the order to turn into a side street and stop beside an inn of quite modest appearance. Getting out of the carriage, our hero settled up with the cabman and thus finally rid himself of his vehicle, ordered Petrushka to go home and await his return, while he himself entered the inn, took a private room and ordered dinner to be served. He felt himself to be very ill, and his head to be in utter disorder and chaos. He walked around the room in agitation for a long time; finally he sat down on a chair, propped his forehead up on his hands and began with all his might to try to consider and resolve something regarding his present situation…

4

The big day, the festive birthday of Klara Olsufyevna, the only daughter of State Councillor Berendeyev, Mr Golyadkin's benefactor in days of yore, a day commemorated by a brilliant, magnificent banquet – such a banquet as had long not been seen in the walls of the civil servants' apartments near the Izmailovsky Bridge and thereabouts, a banquet that more resembled some sort of Belshazzar's feast than a banquet, that had a flavour of something Babylonian as regards brilliance, luxury and decorum, with Clicquot champagne, with oysters and the fruits of Yeliseyev's and Milyutin's shops[4], with various fatted calves and the civil service Table of Ranks[5] – this festive day, commemorated with such a festive banquet, concluded with a brilliant ball, a small, intimate, family ball, but a brilliant one nonetheless as regards taste, educated manners and decorum. Of course, I entirely agree that such balls do take place, but rarely. Such balls, more reminiscent of joyous family events than of balls, can only be given in such houses as, for example, the house of State Councillor Berendeyev. I shall go further: I even doubt whether all State Councillors could give such balls. Oh, if I were a poet! It goes without saying, at least such a one as Homer or Pushkin; with a lesser talent you can't poke your nose in – I should without fail depict for you in vivid colours and with a broad brush, O readers, the whole of this most festive day. No, I should begin my poem with the banquet, I should apply myself in particular to the stunning and at the same time festive moment when the first toasting goblet was raised in honour of the princess of the feast. I should depict for you firstly these guests, sunk deep in reverential silence and expectation, more reminiscent of Demosthenic eloquence than silence. Next I should depict for you Andrei Filippovich as the senior guest, who even had a certain claim to primacy, adorned with silvery hair and the decorations befitting silvery hair, who rose from his seat and lifted above his head a toasting glass of sparkling wine, a wine specially imported from a distant kingdom to wash down moments like these, a wine more reminiscent of the nectar of the gods than wine. I should depict for you the guests and the happy parents of the princess of the feast, who followed Andrei Filippovich in also raising their glasses and turned towards him eyes filled with expectation. I should depict for you how this oft-mentioned Andrei Filippovich, after first dropping a tear into his glass, pronounced congratulations and good wishes, proposed a toast and drank to the health... But, I confess, I confess fully, I should not be able to depict all the solemnity of that moment when the princess of the feast herself, Klara Olsufyevna, blushing like a spring rose with the flush of bliss and modesty, fell in the plenitude of her emotions into the embrace of her tender mother – how the tender mother shed a tear, and how at this the father himself began to sob – the venerable elder and State Councillor Olsufy Ivanovich, who had lost the use of his legs in his lengthy career and had been recompensed by fate for this zeal with a little capital, a little home, some little estates and a beautiful daughter – how he began to sob like a child and proclaimed through his tears that His Excellency was a man of good deeds. Neither should I be able – indeed, specifically be able – to depict for you the universal firing of hearts that followed immediately after this moment, the firing that was clearly expressed even in the behaviour of one youthful Registrar (who at this moment resembled a State Councillor more than a Registrar), who also shed a tear while heeding Andrei Filippovich. Andrei Filippovich in his turn did not at all resemble at this solemn moment a Collegiate Councillor and a head of department in a certain Ministry, no, he seemed to be something else... I do not know precisely what; but not a Collegiate Councillor. He was higher! Finally... Oh! Why do I not possess the secret of elevated, powerful style, solemn style, for the depiction of all these fine and edifying minutes of human life which seem to have been specially arranged to prove how virtue sometimes triumphs over evil intentions, freethinking, vice and envy! I shall say nothing, but in silence – that will be better than any eloquence – shall point out to you the happy youth, entering his twenty-sixth spring, Vladimir Semyonovich, Andrei Filippovich's nephew, who in his turn rose from his seat, who in his turn proposes a toast and to whom are turned the moist eyes of the parents of the princess of the feast, the proud eyes of Andrei Filippovich, the modest eyes of the princess of the feast herself, the rapturous eyes of the guests and even the decorously envious eyes of certain young colleagues of this brilliant youth. I shall say nothing, although I cannot help but note that everything about this youth – who looks more like an elder than a youth, speaking in a respect advantageous to him – everything, from his blooming cheeks to the very rank of Assessor that lay upon him, everything at this solemn moment all but seemed to pronounce that it was to such an elevated degree that good behaviour can bring a man! I shall not describe how finally Anton Antonovich Setochkin, a head of section in a certain Ministry, a colleague of Andrei Filippovich and at one time of Olsufy Ivanovich, and at the same time an old friend of the household, Klara Olsufyevna's godfather – how the little old man, his hair as white as snow, when in his turn proposing a toast, crowed like a cockerel and recited some merry verse; how with such decorous forgetfulness of decorum, if one can express oneself thus, he reduced the entire company to tears of laughter, and how Klara Olsufyevna herself, at the behest of her parents, kissed him in return for such merriment and kindness. I shall say only that, finally, the guests who, naturally, after such a banquet must have felt themselves dear to one another and like brothers, rose from the table; how subsequently the old and middle-aged men, after a brief time spent on amicable conversation and even on, it goes without saying, very respectable and courteous revelations, passed in orderly fashion into another room and, without wasting precious time, dividing into groups, sat down with a sense of their own dignity at tables covered with heavy green cloth; how the ladies, having settled down in the drawing room, all suddenly became extraordinarily kind and began to talk about various matters; how, finally, the most esteemed master of the house himself, who had lost the use of his legs doing duty faithful and true and who had been recompensed for this by all that was mentioned above, began walking on crutches among his guests, supported by Vladimir Semyonovich and Klara Olsufyevna, and how, suddenly also becoming extra-ordinarily kind, he resolved to improvise a small, modest ball regardless of the expense; how to this end one smart youth (the very one who during the banquet was more like a State Councillor than a youth) was dispatched on a mission to find musicians; how subsequently the musicians arrived, a whole eleven in number, and how, finally, at exactly half-past eight there rang out the inviting sounds of a French quadrille and various other dances... It goes without saying that my pen is too weak, limp and blunt for a respectable depiction of the ball, improvised with extraordinary kindness by the silver-haired host. And how, I ask, how can I, the modest narrator of the adventures of Mr Golyadkin – albeit in their way very curious adventures – how can I depict this extraordinary and dignified mixture of beauty, brilliance, decorum, merriment, kind respectability and respectable kindness, playfulness, joyfulness, all these games and jests of all these civil servants' ladies, more like fairies than ladies – speaking in a respect advantageous to them – with their lilac-pink shoulders and faces, with their ethereal figures, with their playfully lively, homeopathic, to use the elevated style, feet? How shall I depict for you, finally, these brilliant civil service cavaliers, merry and respectable, youthful and middle-aged, joyous and decorously misty, those smoking pipes in the intervals between dances in a small, distant green room, and those not smoking pipes, cavaliers bearing from first to last a respectable rank and name, cavaliers profoundly imbued with a sense of beauty and of their personal dignity, cavaliers speaking for the most part in French with the ladies, but if in Russian, then in expressions of the most elevated tone, in compliments and profound phrases, cavaliers allowing themselves perhaps only in the smoking room certain courteous digressions from language of the highest tone, certain phrases of amicable and courteous intimacy such as, for example: 'Why, Petka, you son of a gun, that was a splendid polka you knocked off,' or 'why, Vasya, you son of a gun, you did whatever you wanted with your little lady.' For all this, as I have already had the honour to explain to you above, O readers, my pen is lacking, and for that reason I remain silent. Let us better turn to Mr Golyadkin, the sole true hero of our most truthful tale.

The thing is that he now finds himself in – to say the least – a very strange situation. He, gentlemen, is also here, not at the ball, that is, yet all but at the ball; he, gentlemen, is all right; although he's his own man, still at this moment he's standing on a road that's not entirely straight; he is now standing – it is strange even to say it – he is now standing in the entrance lobby on the back staircase to Olsufy Ivanovich's apartment. But it's all right that he's standing here; he's not too bad. He, gentlemen, is standing in a corner, huddled into a little spot that may not be relatively warm, but is on the other hand relatively dark, partly hidden by a huge cupboard and some old screens, amidst all sorts of rubbish, trash and junk, having concealed himself until the right moment, and for the time being only observing the progress of things in general in the capacity of a spectator on the sidelines. He, gentlemen, is only observing now; he, gentlemen, might go in as well, of course… so why not go in? He only has to take one step and he will be in, and be in very adroitly. Now – as he stood, incidentally, seeing out what was already his third hour in the cold between the cupboard and the screens amidst all sorts of trash, rubbish and junk – he was only quoting in his own justification a certain phrase of the French Minister of blessed memory Villèle[6], namely that 'everything will come in due course, if you have the gumption to wait for it'. Mr Golyadkin had read this phrase once in a completely – incidentally – irrelevant book, but now brought it to mind very appropriately. Firstly, the phrase suited his present situation very well, and secondly, what might not come into the head of a man who is awaiting the happy denouement of almost three whole hours he has spent in an entrance lobby, in the darkness and in the cold? Having quoted, as has already been said, very appropriately the former French Minister Villèle's phrase, Mr Golyadkin for an unknown reason immediately remembered about the former Turkish Vizir Martsimiris too, as well as about the beautiful Margravine Louisa, whose stories he had also once read in a book[7]. Then it came to mind that the Jesuits had even made it their rule to consider all means suitable, so long as the end could be achieved. Having reassured himself a little with a historical point like this, Mr Golyadkin said to himself, so to speak, what of the Jesuits? The Jesuits were the most utter fools to the very last man, he himself would outdo them all, if only the pantry (the room whose door opened directly into the entrance lobby, onto the back staircase and where Mr Golyadkin was now to be found) would empty just for a single moment, then he, regardless of all the Jesuits, would go and walk straight through, first from the pantry into the tearoom, then into the room where they were now playing cards, and then straight into the reception hall where they were now dancing a polka. And he would walk through, walk through without fail, walk through regardless of anything, would slip through – and that would be that, and no one would notice; and then he knew for himself what he should do. So that is the situation, gentlemen, in which we now find the hero of our completely truthful story, although it is difficult to explain, however, what precisely was happening to him at this particular time. The thing is that he had managed to get as far as the entrance lobby and the staircase for the reason that, as he put it, why shouldn't he get there, everybody gets there; but he did not dare to penetrate further, he clearly did not dare to do that… not because he did not dare to do something, but simply because he himself did not want to, because he preferred to be nice and quiet. And so here he is now, gentlemen, waiting for a quiet spell, and he has been waiting for it for exactly two and a half hours. And why not wait? Villèle himself waited. 'What's Villèle got to do with it!' thought Mr Golyadkin, 'who's this Villèle? The thing is, how am I now to, you know… go and penetrate?… Oh, you, you're such a nobody!' said Mr Golyadkin, pinching his frozen cheek with a frozen hand, 'you're such an idiot, you're such a Golyadka[8] – that's your name all right!…' This cajoling of his own person was, however, at this particular moment, nothing much, in passing, without any evident end. And then he was on the point of bursting in and he moved forward; the moment had arrived; the pantry had emptied and there was nobody in it; Mr Golyadkin could see all this through the little window; in two steps he found himself at the door and had already begun to open it. 'Should I go or not? Well, should I go or not? I'll go… why shouldn't I go? All roads are open to a bold man.' Reassuring himself in this way, our hero suddenly and quite unexpectedly retreated behind the screens. 'No,' he thought, 'and what if somebody came in? And there you are, somebody's come in; why did I delay when there was no one about? I could have gone and penetrated just like that!… No, what is it to penetrate when a man's got a character like that! What a vile tendency that is! Got cold feet, like a chicken. Getting cold feet, we can do that, that's what! Fouling up, we can always do that; you don't even have to ask us about that. Now you can just stand here like a blockhead, and that's that! I'd like to have a cup of tea at home now… It'd be so nice to have a cup of tea. Arrive any later and Petrushka will probably grumble. Should I go home? All this can go to the devil! I'm going, and that's that!' Having thus resolved his situation, Mr Golyadkin quickly moved forward, as if somebody had touched some spring inside him;

in two steps he found himself in the pantry, he threw off his greatcoat, took off his hat, hastily shoved it all into a corner, spruced himself up and smoothed himself down; then... then he moved into the tearoom, from the tearoom scampered into yet another room, slipped almost unnoticed between the now heated card players; then... then... at this point Mr Golyadkin forgot everything that was going on around him and entered, like a bolt from the blue, straight into the ballroom.

As if on purpose, at that moment there was no dancing. The ladies were strolling about the hall in picturesque groups. The men were huddling together in circles or darting around the room, engaging the ladies. Mr Golyadkin noticed none of this. He saw only Klara Olsufyevna; beside her Andrei Filippovich, then Vladimir Semyonovich, and also two or three officers, and also two or three young men, also very attractive, who promised much or had already, as could be seen at first glance, fulfilled a certain amount of promise... He saw certain other people too. Or no; he now saw nobody, looked at nobody... but driven by that same spring by means of which he had leapt uninvited into somebody else's ball, he moved forward, then forward again, and forward again; he stumbled in passing into some Councillor or other and trod on his foot; proceeded to step on the dress of a venerable old woman and tear it a little, he pushed a man with a tray, pushed someone else as well and, failing to notice all this or – to put it better – noticing it, but just as something coincidental, without looking at anyone, making his way further and further forward, he suddenly found himself facing Klara Olsufyevna herself. Without any doubt, without batting an eyelid, he would with the greatest pleasure have been swallowed up by the earth at this moment; but what had been done could not be undone... there is, after all, no way it can be undone. What was he to do then? Fail – take courage, succeed – hold on. Mr Golyadkin, it goes without saying, of course, was no schemer and was not skilled at polishing the parquet with his boots... That's just the way it happened. Moreover, the Jesuits had somehow got mixed up in it too... But still, Mr Golyadkin had no time for them! Everything that walked, made a noise, spoke, laughed, suddenly, as if in response to some gesture, fell silent and little by little crowded around Mr Golyadkin. It was as if Mr Golyadkin, however, heard nothing, saw nothing, he could not look... not for anything could he look; he lowered his eyes to the ground and just stood there like that, having promised himself in passing, incidentally, somehow or other to shoot himself that same night. Having made himself that promise, Mr Golyadkin said to himself mentally: 'What will be, will be!' – and, to his own utmost astonishment, he quite unexpectedly suddenly began to speak.

Mr Golyadkin began with congratulations and seemly good wishes. The congratulations went well; but at the good wishes our hero stumbled. He sensed that if he stumbled, everything would go to the devil straight away. And that was how it turned out – he stumbled and got stuck... he got stuck and blushed; he blushed and got confused; he got confused and raised his eyes; he raised his eyes and looked around; he looked around and – and froze... All stood, all was silent, all was waiting; a little further off all began whispering; a little closer by all began chuckling. Mr Golyadkin cast a submissive, lost look at Andrei Filippovich. Andrei Filippovich responded to Mr Golyadkin with such a look that if our hero had not already been utterly, completely destroyed, he would without fail have been destroyed a second time – if that had only been possible. The silence continued.

'This relates more to domestic circumstances and to my private life, Andrei Filippovich,' said the half-dead Mr Golyadkin in a scarcely audible voice, 'it's not an official event, Andrei Filippovich...'

'You should be ashamed, sir, ashamed!' said Andrei Filippovich in a low voice with an inexpressible look of indignation – he said it, took Klara Olsufyevna by the arm and turned away from Mr Golyadkin.

'I have nothing to be ashamed of, Andrei Filippovich,' Mr Golyadkin replied, also in a low voice, casting his miserable gaze around him, feeling lost, and trying as a result to seek out his milieu and social position in the bewildered crowd.

'Well, it's all right, well, it's all right, gentlemen! Well, what's the matter, then? Well, it could happen to anyone,' whispered Mr Golyadkin, beginning to shift little by little and trying to make his way out of the crowd surrounding him. He was allowed through. Our hero somehow passed between two rows of curious and wondering observers. Fate was carrying him along. Mr Golyadkin sensed this himself, the fact that fate was carrying him along. Of course, he would have given a lot for the opportunity to find himself now, without any breach of the proprieties, in his former parking place in the entrance lobby, beside the back staircase; but since that was definitely not possible, he began to try and slip away into a corner somewhere and just stand there – modestly, decorously, by himself, not bothering anyone, without attracting particular attention to himself, but at the same time having won the favourable disposition of the guests and the host. However, Mr Golyadkin felt as if something were urging him on, as if he were wavering, falling. Finally he reached a corner and stood in it like a rather indifferent outside observer, with his arms leaning on the backs of two chairs which he had thus taken completely into his possession, and trying as far as possible to glance with a cheerful gaze at those of Olsufy Ivanovich's guests who were gathered near him. Nearer to him than anyone stood some officer, a tall and handsome fellow, before whom Mr Golyadkin felt himself a real little insect.

'These two chairs are taken, Lieutenant: one's for Klara Olsufyevna, and the other's for Princess Chevchekhanova, who's dancing here too; I'm keeping them for them now, Lieutenant,' said Mr Golyadkin, gasping for breath and directing an imploring gaze at the gentleman lieutenant. In silence and with a murderous smile the lieutenant turned away. Having misfired in one place, our hero meant to have a go at trying his luck somewhere else and turned directly to a pompous Councillor with a significant decoration around his neck. But the Councillor measured him with such a cold gaze that Mr Golyadkin clearly sensed he had suddenly had an entire tub of cold water poured over him. Mr Golyadkin fell quiet. He resolved that it would be better to hold his tongue, not to start talking, to show that he was all right, that he was the same as everyone else, and that his position, so far as he could tell at least, was proper as well. To this end he riveted his gaze to the cuffs of his uniform coat, then raised his eyes and fixed them on a gentleman of most venerable appearance. 'That gentleman's wearing a wig,' thought Mr Golyadkin, 'and if the wig were removed, then there'd be a bald head, every bit as bald as the palm of my hand.' Having made such an important discovery, Mr Golyadkin remembered about the Arab emirs too, who, if the green turban they wear as a mark of their kinship with the prophet Muhammed were removed from their heads, would also be left with a bare, hairless head. Then, and probably because of the particular collision of ideas regarding Turks in his head, Mr Golyadkin arrived at Turkish slippers too, and at this point aptly remembered that Andrei Filippovich wore boots more like slippers than boots. It was noticeable that Mr Golyadkin had in part come to terms with his position. 'Now if that chandelier,' flashed through Mr Golyadkin's head, 'if that chandelier came loose now and fell on the company, I should immediately rush to save Klara Olsufyevna. Having saved her, I should say to her, "Don't worry, young lady; it's all right, but I'm the one that's your saviour." Then…' Here Mr Golyadkin turned his eyes to one side, seeking out Klara Olsufyevna, and caught sight of Gerasimych, Olsufy Ivanovich's old valet. Gerasimych, with the most solicitous, the most solemnly official look, was making his way straight towards him. Mr Golyadkin jumped and winced at some unaccountable and at the same time most unpleasant sensation. He looked around mechanically, the idea almost occurred to him to slip, to sidle off somehow out of harm's way, somewhere quite close, on the quiet, just to go and slip into the shade, that is, to act as if there were nothing the matter with him, as if he were not the point at all. However, before our hero had had the time to resolve upon anything, Gerasimych was already standing in front of him.

'You see, Gerasimych,' said our hero, addressing Gerasimych with a little smile, 'you go ahead and give the order – there, you see, the candle in the candelabrum there, Gerasimych, it'll fall over at any moment: so, you know, order it to be set right; it really will fall at any moment, Gerasimych…'

'The candle, sir? No, sir, the candle's quite straight, sir; but you, sir, there's someone here asking for you.'

'Whoever is it here asking for me, Gerasimych?'

'I really don't know, sir, who it is exactly, sir. A man come from somebody, sir. "Is Yakov Petrovich Golyadkin here," he says. "Then fish him out," he says, "on a most vital and urgent matter…" That's the way of it, sir.'

'No, Gerasimych, you're mistaken; you're mistaken here, Gerasimych.'

'That's doubtful, sir…'

'No, Gerasimych, it's not doubtful; there's nothing doubtful here, Gerasimych. Nobody's asking for me, Gerasimych, there isn't anybody to ask for me, and I'm at home here, that is, in my place, Gerasimych.'

Mr Golyadkin drew breath and looked around. So it was! All that there was in the hall, the eyes and ears of all were absolutely fastened on him in some sort of solemn expectation. The men were crowding closer and listening intently. Further away, the ladies were exchanging alarmed whispers. The host himself appeared at a distance not very far away from Mr Golyadkin, and although from the way he looked it was impossible to discern that he in his turn was playing a direct and immediate part in Mr Golyadkin's circumstances, because it was all being done on a tactful footing, nonetheless all this allowed the hero of our tale to sense clearly that for him the decisive moment had come. Mr Golyadkin saw clearly that the time had come for a bold blow, the time for the disgracing of his enemies. Mr Golyadkin was in agitation. Mr Golyadkin felt some sort of inspiration, and in a quavering, solemn voice he began anew, addressing the waiting Gerasimych:

'No, my friend, nobody is calling for me. You're mistaken. I'll say more, you were mistaken this morning too, when assuring me… daring to assure me, I say,' (Mr Golyadkin raised his voice) 'that Olsufy Ivanovich, my benefactor from time immemorial, who in a certain sense has taken the place of a father for me, would show me his door at a moment of familial and most solemn joy for his parental heart.' (Mr Golyadkin looked around in self-satisfaction, but deeply moved. Tears had appeared on his eyelashes.) 'I repeat, my friend,' our hero concluded, 'you were mistaken, you were cruelly, unforgivably mistaken…'

The moment was solemn. Mr Golyadkin felt that the effect was absolutely right. Mr Golyadkin stood, his eyes modestly cast down, and waited for Olsufy Ivanovich's embrace. Among the guests agitation and bewilderment were noticeable; even the unshakeable and terrible Gerasimych stumbled over the words 'doubtful, sir'… when suddenly the merciless orchestra burst without warning into a polka. All was lost, all was thrown to the winds. Mr Golyadkin jumped, Gerasimych staggered back, all that was in the hall became agitated like the sea, and Vladimir Semyonovich was already speeding along with Klara Olsufyevna in the first pairing, and so was the handsome lieutenant with Princess Chevchekhanova. The spectators crowded around curiously and excitedly to get a glimpse of those dancing the polka – an interesting, new, fashionable dance that was turning everyone's heads. For a time Mr Golyadkin was forgotten. But suddenly all was agitation, muddle, bustle; the music fell silent... a strange occurrence had taken place. Exhausted by the dance, Klara Olsufyevna, scarcely able to catch her breath from tiredness, with burning cheeks and her breast heaving deeply, fell at last into an armchair, her strength quite at an end. All hearts were directed towards the charming enchantress, all vied with one another in their eagerness to salute her and thank her for the pleasure she had given – and suddenly Mr Golyadkin came to be before her. Mr Golyadkin was pale, extremely upset; he also seemed to be in some sort of exhausted state, he scarcely moved. He was smiling for some reason, he was reaching his hand out in supplication. In her astonishment Klara Olsufyevna had no time to pull her hand away and she stood up mechanically at Mr Golyadkin's invitation. Mr Golyadkin lurched forward a first time, then a second time, then he raised a foot, then somehow clicked his heels, then stamped his foot, then tripped up... he too wanted to dance with Klara Olsufyevna. Klara Olsufyevna cried out; everybody rushed to free her hand from Mr Golyadkin's hand, and at once our hero was pushed aside by the crowd to a distance of almost ten paces. A little circle grouped itself around him too. There rang out the squeals and cries of two old ladies whom Mr Golyadkin had all but knocked over in his retreat. The commotion was terrible; all was questioning, all was shouting, all was arguing. The orchestra fell silent. Our hero was spinning around in his circle and mechanically, smiling a little, was muttering something to himself about 'so to speak, why on earth not, and, so to speak, the polka, so far as it seemed to him at least, was a new and very interesting dance, created for the amusement of the ladies... but that if that was the way things had gone, then he was certainly prepared to consent'. But nobody seemed to have asked for Mr Golyadkin's consent. Our hero felt that somebody's hand had suddenly fallen on his arm, that another hand had rather leant on his back, that he was being directed with some particular solicitude in some direction. At last he noticed that he was going straight towards the doors. Mr Golyadkin wanted to say something, to do something… But no, he no longer wanted anything. He was just mechanically laughing things off. Finally he felt that he was having his greatcoat put on him, that he had had his hat pulled down over his eyes; that finally he could feel himself in the entrance lobby, in the dark and the cold, finally on the staircase too. Finally he tripped up, it seemed to him that he was falling into an abyss; he wanted to cry out – and suddenly he found himself in the yard. He felt a breath of fresh air, just for a minute he stopped; at that very moment there came to him the sounds of the orchestra that had burst out anew. Mr Golyadkin suddenly remembered everything; all his lost strength seemed to return to him again. He broke away from the spot on which, as though rooted, he had hitherto been standing, and rushed off headlong somewhere into the open air, to liberty, wherever his nose led him…

5

On all the towers of St Petersburg that show and strike the hours, it struck exactly midnight as Mr Golyadkin, beside himself, ran out onto the Fontanka embankment right by the Izmailovsky Bridge, fleeing from his enemies, from persecution, from the hail of insults directed at him, from the cries of alarmed old ladies, from the oohing and ahing of women and from the murderous glances of Andrei Filippovich. Mr Golyadkin was dead – fully dead, in the full sense of the word – and if he had retained at the present moment the ability to run, it was only by some miracle, by a miracle in which he himself finally refused to believe. It was an awful November night – wet, misty, rainy, snowy, pregnant with gumboils, head colds, cold sores, sore throats, fevers of all possible types and kinds – in short, with all the gifts of November in St Petersburg. The wind howled in the deserted streets, raising the black water of the Fontanka higher than the mooring rings and plucking provocatively at the scrawny streetlights of the embankment which, in their turn, echoed its howls with the thin, piercing creaking which composed the endless, squeaking, tinkling concert so familiar to every resident of St Petersburg. It was raining and snowing all at once. Streams of rainwater with the wind ripping through them were gushing very nearly horizontally, as if from a fire hose, and pricked and whipped the face of the unfortunate Mr Golyadkin like thousands of pins and needles. Amidst the silence of the night, interrupted only by the distant rumble of carriages, the howling of the wind and the creaking of the streetlights, could be heard the doleful lashing and gurgling of the water streaming down from all the roofs, porches, gutters and cornices onto the granite surface of the pavement. There was not a soul about either near or far, and, indeed, it seemed there *could* not have been at such a time and in such weather. And so just Mr Golyadkin alone, alone with his despair, was trotting at this moment along the Fontanka pavement with his usual short and rapid little steps, hurrying to run as quickly as possible to his Shestilavochnaya Street, to his third floor, to his own apartment.

Although the snow, the rain and everything that does not even have a name when a blizzard blows up in the murk beneath the November sky in St Petersburg all at once suddenly attacked the unfortunate Mr Golyadkin, already dead as it was, showing him not the slightest mercy or respite, penetrating him to the bones, plastering over his eyes, blowing through him from all sides, knocking him off track and knocking out the last of his sense, although all this toppled onto Mr Golyadkin all at once, as if communicating and colluding with all his enemies on purpose to give him a splendid finish to the work of a nice day, evening and night – despite all this, Mr Golyadkin remained almost insensible to this final proof of fate's persecution: so greatly had he been shaken and stunned by all that had happened to him a few minutes before at the home of Mr State Councillor Berendeyev! If some dis-interested outside observer had now glanced, just like that, from the outside, at Mr Golyadkin's miserable gait, even he would at once have been pierced by all the terrible horror of his misfortunes and would without fail have said that Mr Golyadkin looked now as if he himself wanted to hide somewhere from himself, as if he himself wanted to escape some-where from himself. Yes, it really was so! We shall say more: Mr Golyadkin now not only wished to escape from himself, but even completely to annihilate himself, not to be, to turn to dust. At this particular moment he did not heed anything around him, he did not understand anything that was going on about him, and looked as if neither the unpleasant events of the foul night, nor the long road, nor the rain, nor the snow, nor the wind, nor all the severe weather really existed for him. The galosh that had come away from the boot on Mr Golyadkin's right foot remained just there in the mud and snow on the Fontanka pavement, and Mr Golyadkin did not even think of returning for it and did not notice its loss. He was so perplexed that several times, suddenly, regardless of anything around him, completely imbued with the idea of his recent terrible fall, he stopped, motionless, like a pillar, in the middle of the pavement; at these moments he was dying, disappearing; then suddenly he would break away from the spot like a madman and run, run without a backward glance, as if fleeing from somebody's pursuit, from some still more awful misfortune... The situation really was awful!... Finally, his strength at an end, Mr Golyadkin stopped, leant on the embankment railings in the pose of a man who has suddenly, quite unexpectedly, had a nosebleed, and began to stare at the turbid, black water of the Fontanka. It is not known precisely how much time he spent doing this. It is only known that at this moment Mr Golyadkin reached such despair, was so tormented, was so tortured, was so exhausted and so depressed in the already weak remnants of his spirit, that he forgot about everything: about the Izmailovsky Bridge, about Shestilavochnaya Street, and about his present... What, indeed? After all, it was all the same to him: the deed was done, finished, the decision signed and attached; what was it to him?... Suddenly... suddenly the whole of his body gave a start, and he involuntarily leapt a couple of paces to one side. In inexpressible disquiet he began gazing around; but there was nobody there, nothing in particular had happened – and yet... and yet it seemed to him that somebody was now, this very minute, standing here, near him, beside him, also leaning on the embankment railings, and – it was a wondrous thing! – had even said something to him, said something quickly, abruptly, not entirely comprehensibly, but about something very close to him, relevant to him. 'Well, did I imagine that or something?' said Mr Golyadkin, gazing around once more. 'And where is it I'm standing?... Oh dear, oh dear!' he concluded, shaking his head, and at the same time, with a worried, miserable feeling, even with fear, he began peering into the turbid, damp distance, straining his vision with all his might and trying with all his might to pierce with his myopic gaze the wet surroundings stretching out before him. However, there was nothing new, nothing in particular struck Mr Golyadkin. Everything seemed to be in order, as it ought – that is, the snow was falling even heavier, in bigger flakes and thicker; at a distance of twenty paces it was pitch black; the streetlights creaked even more piercingly than before, and the wind seemed to be striking up its depressing song still more mournfully, still more pitifully, like an importunate beggar pleading for a copper coin for sustenance. 'Oh dear, oh dear! What *is* the matter with me?' Mr Golyadkin repeated again, setting off on his way once more and still gazing around a little. But at the same time some new sensation echoed through Mr Golyadkin's entire being: not exactly anguish, not exactly fear… A feverish tremor ran through his veins. The moment was unbearably unpleasant! 'Well, it's all right,' he said to encourage himself, 'well, it's all right; perhaps it really isn't anything at all and doesn't sully anybody's honour. Perhaps that was how it had to be,' he continued, without himself understanding what he was saying, 'perhaps in good time it'll all turn out for the best, and there'll be nothing to complain about and everyone will be justified.' Talking in this way and giving himself some relief with the words, Mr Golyadkin shook himself down a little, shook off the snowflakes that had fallen in a thick crust onto his hat, onto his collar, onto his greatcoat, onto his tie, onto his boots and onto everything – but he could still not push away, throw off the strange feeling, his strange dark anguish. Somewhere far off the shot of a cannon rang out. 'What weather,' thought our hero, 'hark! Will there be a flood, I wonder? The water's clearly risen too much.' No sooner had Mr Golyadkin said or thought this than he saw ahead of him a passer-by walking towards him, probably like him too, also out late for some reason. A trifling, chance thing, it would have seemed; but for some unknown reason Mr Golyadkin became embarrassed and even felt scared, got a little flustered. Not that he was frightened of a bad man, it was just that, perhaps… 'Well, and who knows, this man out late,' flashed through Mr Golyadkin's head, 'perhaps he's the same too, perhaps he's more important than anything else here, and it's not for nothing he's coming, but with a purpose, crossing my path and knocking into me.' But perhaps Mr Golyadkin did not think exactly that, and only momentarily felt something of the sort and something very unpleasant. But there was no time to think or to feel; the passer-by was only a couple of paces away. Immediately, following his perpetual custom, Mr Golyadkin hastened to adopt a quite particular look – a look clearly expressing that he, Golyadkin, was his own man, that he was all right, that the road was wide enough for everyone and that after all he, Golyadkin, was not himself touching anybody. Suddenly he stopped, rooted to the ground, as though struck by lightning, and then quickly turned back after the passer-by, who had scarcely gone past him – turned, looking as if he had been jerked from behind, as if the wind had swung his weathercock. The passer-by was quickly disappearing in the snowy blizzard. He was also walking hurriedly, was also, like Mr Golyadkin too, clothed and bundled up from head to foot and, just like him too, was pattering and scurrying along the Fontanka pavement with short, rapid little steps, and a little bit of a trot. 'What, what's this?' whispered Mr Golyadkin, smiling distrustfully, and yet the whole of his body shuddered. A cold shiver ran down his spine. Meanwhile the passer-by had completely disappeared, already even his steps were no longer to be heard, but Mr Golyadkin still stood and gazed after him. Finally, however, little by little he came to his senses. 'But what on earth is it,' he thought in annoyance, 'have I really gone out of my mind or something?' He turned and went on his way, quickening and hurrying his steps more and more and trying his very best not to think of anything at all. To this end he finally even closed his eyes. Suddenly, through the howling of the wind and the noise of the weather, there again reached his ears the noise of someone's footsteps very nearby. He gave a start and opened his eyes. Ahead of him again, about twenty paces away from him, was the black shape of some little man rapidly approaching him. The little man was hastening, rushing, hurrying; the distance was quickly decreasing. Mr Golyadkin could already even see his new belated comrade perfectly clearly – he saw him clearly and cried out in astonishment and horror; his legs gave way. It was that same passer-by already familiar to him, whom he had allowed past him ten minutes or so before and who suddenly, quite unexpectedly, had now appeared before him again. But it was not this wonder alone that stunned Mr Golyadkin – and Mr Golyadkin was so stunned that he stopped, cried out, tried to say something – and set off to overtake the stranger, even shouted something to him, probably wishing to stop him the sooner. The stranger did indeed stop about ten paces from Mr Golyadkin, and in such a way that the light of a streetlamp standing nearby fell fully on the whole of his figure – he stopped, turned to Mr Golyadkin, and waited with an impatient, preoccupied look for what he had to say. 'Excuse me, I may have been mistaken,' said our hero in a quavering voice. In silence and annoyance the stranger turned and quickly went on his way, as if hastening to make up the two seconds lost with Mr Golyadkin. But as far as Mr Golyadkin was concerned, his every fibre began to tremble, his knees buckled, went weak, and with a groan he sat down on a kerbside bollard. Still, there really was good cause to fall into such a state of confusion. The thing was that this stranger now seemed somehow familiar to him. That would still have been all right. But he had recognised, almost completely recognised this man now. He had often seen him, this man, seen him at some time, very recently even; where could it have been? Could it have been yesterday? Still, yet again, the main thing was not that Mr Golyadkin had seen him often; and there was actually almost nothing in particular about this man – at first glance this man aroused absolutely nobody's particular attention. So, the man was like everybody else, respectable, it goes without saying, like all respectable people, and perhaps had some certain, even quite significant virtues – in short: was his own man. Mr Golyadkin did not even feel either hatred or hostility, nor even the slightest antipathy to this man, on the contrary even, it would have seemed – but at the same time (and it was this circumstance that was the most powerful thing), but at the same time not for any of the world's treasures would he have wished to meet with him, and particularly not to meet as now, for example. We shall say more: Mr Golyadkin knew this man fully; he even knew what he was called, what this man's surname was; but at the same time, not for anything, and, again, not for any treasure in the world, would he have wanted to name him, to agree to acknowledge that, so to speak, that's what he's called, that's his patronymic and that's his surname. Whether Mr Golyadkin's perplexity lasted long or not, whether it was really a long time he sat on the kerbside bollard, I cannot say – but, having finally come to a little, he suddenly set off at the double without a backward glance and with all the strength he could muster; he was breathless; he stumbled twice, almost fell – and at this occurrence Mr Golyadkin's second boot was orphaned, also abandoned by its galosh. Finally Mr Golyadkin reduced his pace a little to catch his breath, hurriedly looked around and saw that he had already run, without noticing it, the whole of his way along the Fontanka, he had crossed the Anichkov Bridge, covered part of Nevsky and was now standing at the turning into Liteinaya. Mr Golyadkin turned into Liteinaya. His situation at this moment resembled the situation of a man standing over a terrible precipice when the ground beneath him is breaking away, has already lurched, has already shifted, is swaying for the last time, falling, dragging him off into the abyss, but at the same time the unfortunate man has neither the strength, nor the firmness of spirit to leap back, to take his eyes off the yawning chasm; the abyss is drawing him, and finally he jumps into it himself, himself hastening the moment of his own destruction. Mr Golyadkin knew, sensed and was completely certain that something else bad was without fail going to happen to him on his way, that some other unpleasantness was going to break over him – that, for example, he was again going to meet his stranger; but it is an odd thing, he even wished for this meeting, considered it inevitable and asked only that it should all be over soon, that his situation should be resolved any way at all, provided it was soon. But at the same time he kept running and running, as if driven by some external force, for throughout the whole of his being there was a sort of weakening and numbing sensation; he could not think of anything, although his thoughts caught at everything like blackthorn. Some wretched stray dog, all wet and frozen, latched on to Mr Golyadkin and also ran along next to him, sidling, hurriedly, with its tail between its legs and ears laid back, glancing at him from time to time shyly and intelligently. Some distant, already long-forgotten thought – the memory of some event that had occurred long ago – now came into his head, knocked like a little hammer in his head, vexed him, would not leave him alone. 'Oh, that horrid little dog!' whispered Mr Golyadkin, himself not understanding himself. Finally he caught sight of his stranger at the turning into Italyanskaya Street. Only the stranger was now no longer coming towards him, but going in the same direction as him, and was also running, a few paces ahead. Finally they entered Shestilavochnaya. Mr Golyadkin had his breath taken away. The stranger stopped directly in front of the building in which Mr Golyadkin lodged. The ringing of a bell was heard and almost at the same time the creaking of a bolt. The gate opened, the stranger bent down, was visible for a moment and disappeared. Almost at the same moment Mr Golyadkin arrived too and flew, like an arrow, through the gates. Without listening to the yardman, who had begun to grumble, he ran panting into the courtyard and immediately caught sight of his interesting travelling companion, who had for a while been lost. The stranger was visible momentarily at the entrance to the staircase which led to Mr Golyadkin's apartment. Mr Golyadkin rushed after him. The staircase was dark, damp and dirty. At every turn a heap of the residents' rubbish was piled up so that a stranger, someone unfamiliar, coming upon this staircase in the dark, was compelled to spend about half an hour travelling up it, risking breaking his legs and cursing not only the staircase but his acquaintances too, who had taken up residence so inconveniently. But it was as if Mr Golyadkin's travelling companion was familiar with, as if he belonged in the building; he ran up easily, without difficulties and with perfect knowledge of the location. Mr Golyadkin was almost catching up with him; two or three times the hem of the stranger's greatcoat even struck him on the nose. His heart was skipping beats. The mysterious man stopped directly opposite the doors of Mr Golyadkin's apartment, knocked, and (something, incidentally, that would have surprised Mr Golyadkin at another time) Petrushka, as if he had been waiting and had not gone to bed, immediately opened the door and, with a candle in his hands, followed after the man who went in. Beside himself, the hero of our tale ran into his abode; without taking off his greatcoat or hat, he passed down the short corridor and, as if thunderstruck, stopped on the threshold of his room. All Mr Golyadkin's forebodings had been fully realised. Everything that he had feared and that he had foreseen had now happened in reality. His breathing broke off, his head began to spin. The stranger, also wearing his greatcoat and hat, sat before him on *his* bed, smiling slightly, and, squinting a little, he nodded to him amicably. Mr Golyadkin wanted to shout out, but could not, to protest in some way, but he did not have the strength. The hair on his head stood on end, and he squatted down on the spot, senseless, in horror. And, moreover, there was good cause. Mr Golyadkin had completely recognised his nocturnal friend. His nocturnal friend was none other than he himself – Mr Golyadkin himself, another Mr Golyadkin, but absolutely the same as he himself – in short, in all respects what is known as his double…

6

The next day at exactly eight o'clock Mr Golyadkin came to on his bed. Immediately all the unusual things of the previous day and the whole improbable, weird night with its almost impossible adventures, all at once, suddenly presented themselves to his imagination and memory in all their horrifying fullness. Such bitter, hellish malice on the part of his enemies and especially the final proof of this malice turned Mr Golyadkin's heart to ice. But at the same time it was all so strange, incomprehensible, weird, seemed so impossible, that it really was difficult to give credence to this whole business; Mr Golyadkin himself would even have been prepared to deem it all infeasible ravings, a momentary derangement of the imagination, a darkening of the mind, if he had not known, to his good fortune, from bitter experience of life, how far malice can sometimes lead a man – how far the embitterment of an enemy can sometimes go when avenging honour and self-respect. Moreover Mr Golyadkin's shattered limbs, his smoke-filled head, his broken back and a malignant head cold supported and bore powerful testament to the utter plausibility of the previous night's walk and, in part, of everything else that had happened during that walk too. Well, and finally, Mr Golyadkin had already known for a very long time that they had something in preparation, that they had someone else. So what then? Having thought it over thoroughly, Mr Golyadkin resolved to keep quiet, to submit and not to protest about this business until the time was right. 'Perhaps they just thought to give me a fright, but when they see that I'm all right, I'm not protesting and am quite resigned, am bearing it with resignation, then they'll give it up, they'll give it up themselves, and, what's more, will be the first to give it up.'

So these were the thoughts that were in Mr Golyadkin's head while, stretching in his bed and straightening out his shattered limbs, he waited on this occasion for the usual appearance of Petrushka in his room. He had already been waiting about a quarter of an hour; he could hear that sluggard Petrushka busy with the samovar on the other side of the partition, but at the same time he could not make up his mind to call him at all. We shall say more: Mr Golyadkin was even a little afraid of coming face to face with Petrushka now. 'I mean, God knows,' he thought, 'I mean, God knows how that scoundrel regards all this business now. He keeps his mouth tight shut, but he's no fool.' Finally the door creaked and Petrushka appeared with a tray in his hands. Mr Golyadkin cast a timid sidelong glance at him, waiting impatiently to see what would happen, waiting to see whether he would finally say anything regarding a certain circumstance. Yet Petrushka said nothing, and was, on the contrary, more taciturn, stern and cross than usual, looking at him askance from under his brows; all in all, it was evident that he was extremely displeased about something; not once did he even glance at his master, which, let it be said in passing, rather stung Mr Golyadkin; he put everything he had brought with him onto the table, turned round and went off in silence to the other side of his partition. 'He knows, he knows, he knows everything, the loafer!' grumbled Mr Golyadkin, starting on the tea. However, our hero asked his servant precisely nothing, although Petrushka subsequently came into his room several times for various reasons. Mr Golyadkin was in the most alarmed state of mind. Going to the office was terrifying too. He had a powerful presentiment that it was precisely there that something was wrong. 'I mean, off you'll go,' he thought, 'but what when you stumble upon something? Isn't it better to be patient now? Isn't it better to wait now? Let them do what they like there; but I should wait here today, get my strength up, recover, turn all this business over properly in my mind, then later I should find the right moment and be like a bolt from the blue for all of them, but act as if nothing had happened.' Pondering in this way, Mr Golyadkin smoked pipe after pipe; time was flying; it was almost half-past nine already. 'I mean, it's already half-past nine,' thought Mr Golyadkin, 'and it's too late to turn up. And what's more, I'm sick, of course I'm sick, sick without a doubt; who'll say I'm not? What's it to me! And if they send someone to check up, let an administrator come; and really, what on earth is it to me? My back's aching, I've got a cough, a cold; and finally, I can't go, I can't possibly go in this weather; I might fall ill, and then even die, perhaps; especially nowadays, the death rate is so…' With such arguments Mr Golyadkin finally salved his conscience completely and justified himself to himself in advance of the berating he expected from Andrei Filippovich for neglect of his work. In general, in all similar circumstances our hero was extremely fond of justifying himself in his own eyes with various incontrovertible arguments and in this way completely salving his conscience. And so, having now completely salved his conscience, he took up his pipe, filled it, and, when he had just begun to get it going decently – he leapt up quickly from the couch, tossed the pipe aside, rapidly washed, shaved, smoothed his hair down, pulled on his uniform jacket and all the rest, grabbed some documents and flew off to the office.

Mr Golyadkin entered his department timidly in tremulous expectation of something very bad – an expectation albeit unconscious, dark, still at the same time unpleasant too; timidly he sat down in his permanent place alongside the section head, Anton Antonovich Setochkin. Without looking at anything, without being distracted by anything, he investigated the content of the documents that lay before him. He resolved and promised himself to avoid as far as possible anything provocative, anything that might greatly compromise him: namely, immodest questions, anybody's little jokes and unseemly allusions regarding all the events of the previous evening; he resolved even to remain aloof from the usual courtesies with colleagues, that is, questions about health and so on. But it was also obvious that he could not remain like this, it was impossible. Anxiety and ignorance about anything that closely concerned him always tormented him more than the thing that concerned him itself. And that is why, despite the promise he had made to himself not to enter into anything, whatever might happen, and to avoid everything, whatever it might be, Mr Golyadkin occasionally, stealthily, ever so quietly, raised his head a little and glanced on the sly from side to side, to the right, to the left; he glanced into the faces of his colleagues and, judging by them, he then tried to conclude whether there was anything new and particular relating to him that was being concealed from him to some improper ends. He assumed an undoubted link between everything that had happened to him the previous day and everything that surrounded him now. Finally, in his anguish he began to wish that – God knows how – but that everything would just be settled soon, even if with some calamity – no matter! And, right on cue, fate caught Mr Golyadkin: he had scarcely had time to wish, when his doubts were suddenly settled, yet in the strangest and most unexpected way.

The door from the next room suddenly creaked quietly and timidly, as if announcing in this way that the person coming in was very insignificant, and somebody's figure, very familiar, incidentally, to Mr Golyadkin, appeared shyly in front of that very desk at which our hero was positioned. Our hero did not raise his head – no, he saw this figure only in passing, with the very slightest of glances, but already knew everything, understood everything, down to the smallest details. He burnt up from shame and buried his poor head in a document, having exactly the same objective with which an ostrich, pursued by a hunter, hides his head in the hot sand. The new arrival bowed to Andrei Filippovich, and after that a positively affectionate voice was heard, the sort the superiors in all workplaces use to speak to newly joined subordinates. 'Sit down just here,' said Andrei Filippovich, indicating Anton Antonovich's desk to the new man, 'just here, opposite Mr Golyadkin, and we'll give you some work to do straight away.' Andrei Filippovich concluded by making a quick gesture of decorous exhortation to the new arrival, and then immediately became absorbed in the contents of various documents, of which there was a whole pile in front of him.

Mr Golyadkin finally raised his eyes, and if he did not faint, it was solely because he had already had a premonition of the whole business from the beginning, he had already been forewarned about everything from the beginning, having divined the newcomer in his soul. Mr Golyadkin's first impulse was to look around quickly to see whether there was any whispering, whether any office wit was flowing on account of it, whether surprise, had contorted anyone's face – whether, finally, anybody had fallen under his desk in fright. But to Mr Golyadkin's very great surprise, nothing of the sort was to be found in anybody. The behaviour of Mr Golyadkin's gentlemen comrades and colleagues amazed him. It seemed beyond good sense. Mr Golyadkin even took fright at such unusual silence. Reality spoke for itself: it was a strange, disgraceful, weird business. There was good reason to stir. All this, it goes without saying, only flashed through Mr Golyadkin's head. Whereas he himself was burning on a low flame. And there was good cause, by the way. The man who was now sitting opposite Mr Golyadkin was Mr Golyadkin's horror, he was Mr Golyadkin's shame, he was Mr Golyadkin's nightmare of the day before, in short, he was Mr Golyadkin himself – not the Mr Golyadkin who now sat on his chair with his mouth agape and with his pen frozen in his hand; not the one who worked as assistant to his section head; not the one who liked to efface and bury himself in the crowd; not the one, finally, whose gait clearly pronounced: 'Don't touch me, and I won't touch you,' or 'Don't touch me, after all, I'm not knocking into you,' – no, this was a different Mr Golyadkin, a completely different one, but at the same time one completely like the first one too – the same height, the same build, dressed the same, with the same bald spot – in short, nothing, absolutely nothing, was forgotten for a perfect resemblance, so that if one were to go and stand them next to one another, then no one, absolutely no one, would take it upon himself to determine which precisely was the real Golyadkin and which the fake one, who the old and who the new, who the original and who the copy.

Our hero, if the comparison is possible, was now in the position of a man with whom some prankster is amusing himself by slyly bringing an incendiary lens to bear on him for a joke. 'What on earth is this, a dream or not,' he thought, 'the present or the continuation of yesterday's events? And how can it be? What right has all this to happen? Who allowed such a clerk, who gave anyone the right to do this? Am I asleep, am I dreaming?' Mr Golyadkin attempted to pinch himself, even attempted to conceive the idea of pinching somebody else... No, not a dream, and that's that. Mr Golyadkin sensed that the sweat was streaming off him, that what was happening to him was unprecedented and hitherto unseen and, for that very reason, to crown his misfortune, improper, for Mr Golyadkin understood and felt all the disadvantage of being the first example of such a disgusting business. Finally he even began to doubt his own existence, and although he was prepared in advance for anything and himself wished that his doubts could at least be settled one way or another, yet the very essence of the whole situation was of course still its unexpectedness. Anguish oppressed and tormented him. At times he completely lost both sense and awareness. Coming to after such a moment, he noticed that he was mechanically and unconsciously moving his pen over paper. Not trusting himself, he began to check all he had written – and could not understand a thing. Finally the other Mr Golyadkin, who until then had been sitting decorously and demurely, got up and disappeared through the doors into another section to get some file. Mr Golyadkin looked around – it was all right, all was quiet; only the scratching of pens could be heard, the noise of sheets of paper being turned and voices murmuring in the corners furthest away from Andrei Filippovich's seat. Mr Golyadkin glanced at Anton Antonovich, and since in all probability our hero's face fully echoed his present state and harmonised with the whole sense of the business, and was consequently in a certain respect very remarkable, kind Anton Antonovich, setting his pen aside, enquired with an unusual sort of concern after Mr Golyadkin's health.

'Thank God, Anton Antonovich, I,' said Mr Golyadkin, stammering, 'I'm perfectly well, Anton Antonovich; I'm all right now, Anton Antonovich,' he added irresolutely, not yet entirely believing what he kept on repeating to Anton Antonovich.

'Ah! And I got the impression you were unwell; still, it's not surprising, who knows? These days in particular there are always such epidemics. Do you know…'

'Yes, Anton Antonovich, I know there are such epidemics about… That, Anton Antonovich, isn't why I,' continued Mr Golyadkin, peering intently at Anton Antonovich, 'I don't even know, you see, Anton Antonovich, how, that is, I mean, where to begin this business, Anton Antonovich…'

'What, sir? I… you know… I confess, I don't understand so well;

you… you know, why don't you explain in more detail in what respect you're having difficulty here,' said Anton Antonovich, having a little difficulty himself when he saw that tears had even appeared in Mr Golyadkin's eyes.

'Truly, I… here, Anton Antonovich… there's a clerk here, Anton Antonovich…'

'Well, sir! I still don't understand.'

'I mean, Anton Antonovich, there's a newly arrived clerk here.'

'Yes, sir, there is, sir; with the same surname as you.'

'What?' cried Mr Golyadkin.

'I said: with the same surname as you; also Golyadkin. Is he your brother?'

'No, sir, Anton Antonovich, I…'

'Hm! Tell me, please, I had the impression that he must be a close relation of yours. There is, you know, a certain sort of family resemblance.'

Mr Golyadkin froze in astonishment and for a time he lost the power of speech. To treat so lightly such a disgraceful, unprecedented thing, a thing truly rare of its kind, a thing which would have stunned even the most disinterested observer, to talk of a family resemblance when here you could see, as in a mirror!

'Do you know what I advise you, Yakov Petrovich?' Anton Antonovich continued. 'You go to the doctor and get some advice. Do you know, you somehow *look* quite unwell. Your eyes are especially… you know, there's some special expression.'

'No, Anton Antonovich, sir, of course, I feel… that is, I still want to ask, how is it this clerk…?'

'Well, sir?'

'That is, have you noticed anything special about him, Anton Antonovich… anything too expressive?'

'That is?'

'That is, I mean, Anton Antonovich, such a striking resemblance to anyone, for example, that is, to me, for example. Just now, Anton Antonovich, you mentioned a family resemblance, made the remark in passing…You know, twins are sometimes like that – that is, absolutely like two peas in a pod so that they can't be told apart? Well, that's what I'm on about, sir.'

'Yes, sir,' said Anton Antonovich, having thought for a little, and as though struck for the first time by such a circumstance, 'yes, sir! That's right, sir. The resemblance is indeed striking, and your reasoning was faultless, so that one can indeed take one for the other,' he continued, opening his eyes more and more. 'And do you know, Yakov Petrovich, it's even a marvellous resemblance, a fantastic one, as they sometimes say, that is, it's absolutely, as you... Have you noticed, Yakov Petrovich? I myself even wanted to ask you for an explanation, but, I confess, I didn't pay due attention at first. A marvel, a marvel indeed! And do you know, Yakov Petrovich, you're not a local by birth, are you, I say?'

'No, sir.'

'After all, he isn't a local either. Perhaps from the same place as you. Dare I ask where your mother lived for the most part?'

'You said... You said, Anton Antonovich, that he's not a local?'

'No, sir, not from around here. And indeed, how wonderful it is,' continued the garrulous Anton Antonovich, for whom chatting about anything was a real treat, 'truly capable of exciting curiosity; but I mean, how often you might walk past, knock into him, push him, but not notice. Still, don't be embarrassed. It happens. Do you know – I'll tell you about it now – the same thing happened to my auntie on my mother's side; just before her death she saw two of herself as well...'

'No, sir, I – excuse my interrupting you, Anton Antonovich – I'd like to learn, Anton Antonovich, how is it this clerk, that is, on what basis is he here?'

'Come into the late Semyon Ivanovich's position, into the vacant position – the vacancy appeared, so a replacement was made. I mean, truly, the late Semyon Ivanovich, such a nice man, he left three children, they say, each smaller than the other. The widow fell at His Excellency's feet. They say she's concealing something, though: she's got a bit of money, but she's concealing it.'

'No, sir, Anton Antonovich, I'm still on about that circumstance.'

'That is? Well, yes! But why is it you're so interested in that? I'm telling you: don't you be embarrassed. It's all just for a time to some extent. Well, then? After all, it's not your fault; that's the way the Lord God Himself arranged it, it was His will, and it's a sin to grumble about it. His wisdom can be seen in it. And you, Yakov Petrovich, so far as I can tell, aren't a bit to blame for it. How many marvels are there in the world? Mother Nature is generous; and you won't be asked to answer for this, you won't answer for it. I mean, to give an example, apropos, you've heard, I hope, how they, what do you call them, yes, the Siamese twins, their backs grew together, and that's how they live, and they eat and sleep together; they make a lot of money, they say.'[9]

'Allow me, Anton Antonovich…'

'I understand you, I understand! Yes! So what, then? It's all right! I tell you, to my mind at least, there's no reason to get embarrassed here. So what? He's a clerk like any other; seems to be a businesslike man. Says he's Golyadkin; not from around here, he says, a Titular Councillor. Explained himself in person to His Excellency.'

'Well, and how was that, then, sir?'

'All right, sir; they say he gave a good enough explanation, presented arguments; it's like this, Your Excellency, he says, and I've no assets, and I wish to work and particularly under your flattering command… well, and then all that was proper, you know – he expressed everything neatly. Must be a clever man. Well, and came with a reference, it goes without saying; can't do without, can you…'

'Well, sir, from whom, sir… that is, I mean, who precisely has got his hand mixed up in this shameful business?'

'Yes, sir. A good reference, they say; His Excellency had a laugh with Andrei Filippovich, they say.'

'Had a laugh with Andrei Filippovich?'

'Yes, sir; just smiled and said that it was fine, and if you please, and that he for his part didn't mind, as long as he served faithfully…'

'Well, sir, go on, sir. You're reviving me somewhat, Anton Antonovich; I implore you – go on, sir.'

'Permit me, again, somehow, I… Well, sir, yes, sir; well, and it's all right, sir; a simple thing; I'm telling you, don't be embarrassed, and there's nothing dubious to be found in this…'

'No, sir. That is, I'd like to ask you, Anton Antonovich – what, His Excellency added nothing more… regarding me, for example?'

'That is, how do you mean? Yes, sir! Well, no, nothing; you can be perfectly at ease. Of course, you know, it goes without saying, it's quite a striking thing and at first... well I, for example, hardly even noticed at first. I really don't know why I didn't notice until you alerted me. But still, you can be perfectly at ease. Nothing in particular, he said precisely nothing,' added nice, kind Anton Antonovich, getting up from his seat.

'Well, I, Anton Antonovich, sir...'

'Ah, if you'll excuse me, sir. I've chattered on about trifles as it is, but there's an important, urgent matter. Needs to be dealt with.'

'Anton Antonovich!' rang out the courteously summoning voice of Andrei Filippovich, 'His Excellency has been asking.'

'Straight away, straight away, Andrei Filippovich, I'm coming straight away, sir.' And Anton Antonovich, taking a small pile of papers in his arms, flew first to Andrei Filippovich and then into His Excellency's office.

'So how's that?' thought Mr Golyadkin to himself. 'So that's what sort of game we have! So that's the sort of wind we've got blowing now... That's not bad; and so that's the most pleasant turn matters have taken,' said our hero to himself, rubbing his hands and not feeling the chair beneath him in his joy. 'So this business of ours is an ordinary business. So it all ends in trifles, nothing is the result. Indeed, nothing from anybody, not a peep out of them, the ruffians – they're sitting and getting on with their work; splendid, splendid! I like a good man, I always have and am always ready to respect... Still, after all, it's, you know, if you think about it, that Anton Antonovich... I'm afraid to trust him; too many grey hairs, and he's gone downhill rather. But the most splendid and enormous thing is the fact that His Excellency said nothing and let it pass just like that: that's good! I approve! But why ever is Andrei Filippovich getting involved here with his chuckling? What's this to him? The old stirrer! Always in my way, always like a black cat trying to run across a man's path, always crossing and spiting a man; spiting and crossing a man...'

Mr Golyadkin looked around again, and again hope revived him. He felt, however, that there was, all the same, a certain remote thought troubling him, a bad sort of thought. The idea almost even came into his own head to make up to the clerks somehow, to run ahead like a hare, even (while on the way out from work somehow or by going up to them as though for files) to allude in the middle of a conversation to the fact that, so to speak, gentlemen, it's like this, there's this striking resemblance, a strange thing, a disgusting comedy – that is, to mock it all himself, and in this way to take soundings of the depth of the danger. 'After all, still waters run deep otherwise,' concluded our hero in his head. However, Mr Golyadkin only thought about it; but then he had second thoughts in time. He realised that this meant looking too far ahead. 'That's your nature!' he said to himself, giving himself a light smack on the forehead with his hand, 'you'll be over the moon in a minute, you're so pleased, you simple soul! No, better if you and I are patient, Yakov Petrovich, if we wait and are patient!' Nonetheless, and as we have already mentioned, Mr Golyadkin was regenerated in full hope, as though he had risen from the dead. 'Never mind,' he thought, 'it's as if ten tons had fallen off my chest! I mean, there's a thing! And the casket opened simply after all[10]. Krylov's right too. Krylov's right too... he's an authority, a sly one, that Krylov, and a great fable writer! And as for that one, let him work, let him work to his heart's content, so long as he isn't in anyone's way and doesn't bother anyone; let him work – I give my consent and approbation!'

But in the meantime hours were passing, flying, and, unnoticed, it struck four o'clock. The office closed; Andrei Filippovich took up his hat and, as is the custom, everyone followed his example. Mr Golyadkin lingered a little, the necessary time, and went out on purpose after everybody, the very last one, when all had gone their different ways. Going out into the street, he felt as if he were in heaven, so that he even sensed the desire to go for a stroll down Nevsky, even if it meant a detour. 'There's fate, after all!' said our hero, 'an unexpected turn for the whole business. And the weather's cleared up, and there's a nice frost and sleighs. And the frost suits a Russian, a Russian gets on splendidly with the frost! I like the Russians. And there's the nice snow, and the first sprinkling, as a hunter would say; how nice it would be to chase a hare across the newly fallen snow here! Ah! Well, never mind!'

That was how Mr Golyadkin's delight expressed itself, but at the same time something was still tickling inside his head, not really anguish – yet at times there was such a gnawing in his heart that Mr Golyadkin did not know how to comfort himself. 'Anyway, let's give it a day. And then we'll rejoice. But anyway, what is it, after all? Well, let's discuss it, let's see. Well, let's have a discussion, my young friend – well, let's have a discussion. Well, a man just the same as you, in the first place, absolutely the same. Well, what's wrong in that? If he's a man like that, do I have to cry then? What's it to me? I'm out of it; I whistle away and that's that! If that's the way he wants it, then that's that! Let him work! Well, a marvel and an oddity, the Siamese twins, they say… Well, and why them, the Siamese? Suppose they're twins, but I mean, even great men have sometimes looked odd. It's well known from history even, that the renowned Suvorov crowed like a cockerel[11]… Well and he did it all because of politics… still, who cares about generals? But then I'm my own man, and that's that, and I don't want to know anyone, and in my innocence I despise my enemy. I'm no schemer and I'm proud of it. Pure, straightforward, tidy, pleasant, mild-mannered…'

Suddenly Mr Golyadkin fell silent, stopped short and began trembling like a leaf, even closed his eyes for a moment. Hoping, however, that the object of his fear was simply an illusion, he finally opened his eyes and timidly gave a sidelong glance to the right. No, not an illusion!… Alongside him pattered his acquaintance of the morning, he was smiling, looking him in the face, and seemed to be waiting for the opportunity to start a conversation. A conversation did not start, however. They both walked some fifty paces in this way. All Mr Golyadkin's effort went into wrapping himself as tight as possible, burying himself in his greatcoat and pulling his hat down over his eyes to the last possible degree. To complete the insult, even his friend's greatcoat and hat were exactly the same, as though removed that minute from Mr Golyadkin's shoulders.

'My dear sir,' our hero finally pronounced, trying to speak almost in a whisper and not looking at his foe, 'it seems we're taking different roads… I'm even certain of it,' he said after a short silence. 'Finally, I'm certain that you've understood me perfectly,' he added quite sternly in conclusion.

'I should like,' Mr Golyadkin's friend finally said, 'I should like… you'll probably be magnanimous and excuse me… I don't know who to turn to here… my circumstances – I hope you'll excuse my imper-tinence – it even seemed to me that, moved by compassion, you took an interest in me this morning. For my part, at first sight I felt attracted to you, I…' At this point Mr Golyadkin mentally wished the earth would open up beneath his new colleague. 'If I dared hope that you, Yakov Petrovich, would be so kind as to hear me out…'

'We – here we – we… we'd better go to my place,' replied Mr Golyadkin, 'we'll cross to the other side of Nevsky now, it'll be more convenient for us there, and then by a side street… better if we take a side street.'

'Very well, sir. Perhaps we should take a side street, sir,' said Mr Golyadkin's meek companion timidly, as though hinting by the tone of the reply that he could not be expected to decide, and that in his position he was prepared to make do even with a side street. And as far as Mr Golyadkin was concerned, he did not understand what was happening to him at all. He did not trust himself. He had still not come to his senses after his astonishment.

7

He came to his senses a little on the staircase at the entrance to his apartment. 'Ah, I've got the brain of a sheep!' he scolded himself mentally, 'well, where am I taking him? I'm putting my own head in the noose. Whatever will Petrushka think, seeing us together? What will that scoundrel dare to think now? And he's suspicious…' But it was already too late to repent; Mr Golyadkin knocked, the door opened, and Petrushka began removing the greatcoats from his master and the guest. Mr Golyadkin slipped in a look, just threw a passing glance at Petrushka, trying to penetrate his physiognomy and divine his thoughts. But to his very great surprise he saw that his servant was not even thinking of being surprised and it was even as if, on the contrary, he had been expecting something of the kind. Of course, now he too was scowling, squinting sideways, and seemed to be intending to devour somebody. 'Has somebody put a spell on them all today,' thought our hero, 'some little devil done the rounds? There must definitely be something special about all these people today. Damn it, what torture it is!' And keeping on thinking and pondering in this way, Mr Golyadkin led the guest into his room and humbly invited him to sit down. The guest was evidently in extreme confusion, was very timid, humbly followed all his host's movements, tried to catch his looks and from them, it seemed, guess his thoughts. There was a downtrodden, cowed, dispirited look about all his gestures, so that, if the comparison can be permitted, he was quite reminiscent at this moment of a man who, not having his own clothes, has put on someone else's; the sleeves climb upwards, the waist is almost at the back of his head, but he keeps on either adjusting the short little waistcoat every minute, or stands sideways on, keeps out of the way, or attempts to hide somewhere, or gazes into everyone's eyes and listens intently to hear whether people are saying anything about his circumstances, whether they are laughing at him, whether they are ashamed of him – and the man blushes, and the man gets muddled and his self-respect suffers... Mr Golyadkin stood his hat on the windowsill; an incautious movement sent his hat flying off onto the floor. The guest immediately rushed to pick it up, cleaned off all the dust, stood it solicitously on its former spot and stood his own on the floor beside the chair on the edge of which he himself had meekly found a place. This minor event opened Mr Golyadkin's eyes somewhat; he realised that his guest was in great need, and for that reason he no longer had any difficulty knowing where to begin with him, and left everything, as he should have done, to him himself. But the guest, for his part, did not begin anything either, whether being timid, feeling a little ashamed, or waiting out of courtesy for his host to begin is unknown, it was difficult to make out. At this point Petrushka came in, stopped in the doorway and fixed his eyes in the direction diametrically opposite to that in which both his master and the guest were located.

'Do you want me to get two portions of dinner?' he said offhandedly in a rather hoarse voice.

'I, I don't know... you – yes, get two portions, my good fellow.'

Petrushka left. Mr Golyadkin glanced at his guest. His guest blushed to the roots of his hair. Mr Golyadkin was a kind man, and for that reason, out of the goodness of his heart, he immediately drew up a theory. 'A poor man,' he thought, 'and he's been in his job only one day; he's probably suffered in his time; perhaps the only thing he's got is a decent set of clothes, but he hasn't anything to feed himself on. Look at him, how cowed he is! Well, never mind; it's even better to some extent…'

'Excuse me,' began Mr Golyadkin, 'for… incidentally, permit me to learn what I should call you?'

'I… I… Yakov Petrovich,' his guest all but whispered, as though conscience-stricken and ashamed, as if begging forgiveness for the fact that he was also called Yakov Petrovich.

'Yakov Petrovich!' our hero repeated, unable to conceal his embarrassment.

'Yes, sir, exactly so, sir… Your namesake, sir,' replied Mr Golyadkin's meek guest, taking the liberty of smiling and saying something a little light-hearted. But straight away he sat back, adopting the most serious look and, incidentally, a little embarrassed, noticing that his host was not in the mood for jokes just now.

'You… permit me then to ask you, to what do I owe the honour…'

'Knowing your generosity and your virtues,' his guest interrupted him quickly, but in a timid voice, and rising a little from his chair, 'I've taken the liberty of turning to you and asking for your… acquaintance and protection…' concluded his guest, obviously having difficulties with his expressions, and selecting words not overly flattering or denigrating, so as not to compromise himself with regard to self-respect, and yet not so bold as to have a ring of unseemly equality. In general, it can be said that Mr Golyadkin's guest behaved like a noble beggar in a darned tailcoat and with a noble passport in his pocket, who has not yet practised holding out his hand properly.

'You're confusing me,' replied Mr Golyadkin, examining himself, his walls and the guest, 'how on earth could I… that is, I mean to say, in what respect precisely can I be of service to you in anything?'

'I, Yakov Petrovich, felt attracted to you at first glance and – be generous and forgive me – I have put my hope in you – have taken the liberty of putting my hope, Yakov Petrovich. I… I am a forsaken man here, Yakov Petrovich, poor, I've suffered very much, Yakov Petrovich, and here once more anew. Learning that you, with the usual, innate qualities of your fine soul, have the same surname as me…'

Mr Golyadkin winced.

'Have the same surname as me and are from the same place as me by birth, I resolved to turn to you and set my difficult position out for you.'

'Very well, sir, very well, sir; truly, I don't know what to say to you,' replied Mr Golyadkin in a confused voice, 'now, after dinner, we'll have a talk…'

The guest bowed; dinner arrived. Petrushka laid the table – and the guest together with the host set about sating themselves. Dinner did not last long; they were both in a hurry – the host because he was not his usual self, and moreover was ashamed that the dinner was poor – was ashamed in part because he wanted to feed his guest well, and partly because he wanted to show he did not live like a beggar. For his part, the guest was in extreme embarrassment and was extremely confused. Having taken some bread once and eaten his slice, he was now afraid to reach out his hand for another slice, was ashamed to take the best pieces and asserted at every moment that he was not at all hungry, that the meal was fine and that he for his part was completely satisfied and would appreciate all this to the grave. When the food was finished, Mr Golyadkin lit his pipe, offered another, acquired for a friend, to his guest, both settled down opposite one another, and the guest began relating his adventures.

Mr Golyadkin junior's tale lasted three or four hours. The story of his adventures was, incidentally, composed of the most trivial, of the most scanty, if it can be said, circumstances. It was about working in a Chamber of Justice somewhere in the provinces, about procurators and court presidents, about some office intrigues, about the depraved soul of one of the court officials, about a government inspector, about a sudden change of superiors, about how Mr Golyadkin had suffered completely innocently; about his aged aunt, Pelageya Semyonovna; about how, through the various intrigues of his enemies, he had lost his post and arrived on foot in St Petersburg; about how he had pined and led a dog's life here in St Petersburg, how he had spent a long time fruitlessly looking for a job, had run out of money, been spent out, lived all but on the street, eaten stale bread and washed it down with his tears, slept on the bare floor and, finally, how some kind person had taken it upon himself to do something for him, recommended him and generously settled him in his new job. Mr Golyadkin's guest cried as he told the story and wiped the tears away with a blue check handkerchief which was very like oilcloth. He concluded by opening up to Mr Golyadkin completely and admitting that not only did he have nothing to live on or with which to get decently settled for the time being, but that he did not even have the money to fit himself out with uniform properly; he also mentioned that he could not even stump up the money for a wretched pair of boots, and that his uniform coat had been borrowed from somebody just for a short time.

Mr Golyadkin was emotional, was truly moved. Moreover, and even despite the fact that his guest's story was the most trivial story, every word of this story fell on his heart like manna from heaven. The thing was that Mr Golyadkin forgot his last doubts, released his heart to freedom and joy and, finally, committed himself mentally to the rank of idiot. Everything was so natural! And was there any reason to get distressed, to sound the alarm? Well, there is, there really is one ticklish thing – but that's no problem, after all; it cannot sully a man, stain his self-respect and ruin his career, when the man is not to blame, when nature itself has got mixed up in it. What is more, his guest was asking for protection, his guest was crying, his guest was denouncing fate, he seemed so uncomplicated, without malice or cunning, pitiful, insignificant, and seemed himself to be ashamed now – although, perhaps, in a different respect – of the strange resemblance of his own face to the face of his host. He behaved with inconceivable devotion, always looking to please his host, and looked as a man looks who is tortured by pangs of conscience and feels he is at fault before another man. If, for example, they began discussing some dubious point, the guest immediately concurred with Mr Golyadkin's opinion. And if somehow or other, by mistake, his opinion ran contrary to Mr Golyadkin's, and he noticed that he had gone astray, then he immediately adjusted his speech, explained himself and rapidly let it be known that he understood everything in exactly the same way as his host, thought just as he did and looked at everything with absolutely the same eyes as he did. In short, the guest made every possible effort to 'get in' with Mr Golyadkin, so that Mr Golyadkin finally decided that his guest must be a very amiable man in all respects. By the by, tea was served; it was after eight. Mr Golyadkin felt himself to be in excellent spirits, he cheered up, got excited, relaxed bit by bit and finally entered into the most lively and absorbing conversation with his guest. Mr Golyadkin, when in good cheer, sometimes enjoyed recounting something interesting. And so it was now: he told his guest a lot about the capital, about its amusements and beauties, about the theatre, about the clubs, about Bryullov's painting[12]; about how two Englishmen came to St Petersburg from England especially to look at the railings of the Summer Garden and immediately left; about work, about Olsufy Ivanovich and about Andrei Filippovich; about how from hour to hour Russia was moving towards perfection, and that here

The literary world is now in bloom;

about a little anecdote recently read in *The Northern Bee*[13], and that in India there is a boa constrictor of extraordinary strength; finally about Baron Brambeus[14], etc, etc. In short, Mr Golyadkin was fully satisfied, firstly because he was perfectly calm; secondly because he was not only unafraid of his enemies, but was now even ready to challenge them all to the most decisive battle; thirdly because he was himself in his own person giving protection and, finally, doing a good deed. In his heart, however, he was conscious that he was still not entirely happy at this minute, that there was still one little worm lurking inside him, although a very tiny one, and gnawing even now at his heart. He was tormented in the extreme by the memory of the previous evening at Olsufy Ivanovich's. He would have given a great deal now if certain things that had happened the day before had not happened. 'Still, I mean, it's all right!' our hero finally concluded, and resolved firmly in his soul to behave well in future and not to fall into similar error. Since Mr Golyadkin was now fully relaxed and had suddenly become almost perfectly happy, he took it into his head even to lead a bit of a gay life. Petrushka brought rum, and a punch was made up. The host and his guest drained a glass each and then another. The guest proved even more amiable than before, and on his part gave more than one proof of his straightforwardness and his happy character, he entered fully into Mr Golyadkin's pleasure, seemed to rejoice in his joy alone and looked upon him as his true and his sole benefactor. Taking a pen and a small sheet of paper, he asked Mr Golyadkin not to look at what he was going to write, and then, when he had finished, he himself showed his host all he had written. It turned out to be a quatrain, written with some sensitivity and, anyway, in a fine style and handwriting – a composition, as was evident, of the amiable guest himself. The verse was as follows:

If thou were me to forget
Still should I not forget thee;
Much might happen yet in life,
Do not thou then forget me! [15]

With tears in his eyes Mr Golyadkin embraced his guest and, finally completely and deeply moved, he himself let his guest into certain secrets and confidences of his own, with the strong emphasis of what was said falling on Andrei Filippovich and Klara Olsufyevna. 'Well, you know, Yakov Petrovich, you and I'll get together,' said our hero to his guest, 'you and I, Yakov Petrovich, we'll live like a fish with water, like brothers; we, my great friend, we'll be sly, we'll be sly as one; on our part we'll carry on an intrigue to spite them… just to spite them we'll carry on an intrigue. And don't you put your trust in any of them. I mean, I know you, Yakov Petrovich, and I understand your character; I mean, you'll tell them absolutely everything, you honest soul! You avoid them all, brother.' The guest concurred fully, thanked Mr Golyadkin and finally shed a few tears too. 'Do you know, Yasha,' continued Mr Golyadkin in a quavering, weak voice, 'you move in with me, Yasha, for a time, or move in with me for good. We'll get on. What do you think, brother, eh? And don't you be embarrassed, and don't grumble about the strange situation between us here now: it's a sin to grumble; it's nature! But Mother Nature's generous, that's what, brother Yasha! Loving you, loving you as a brother, I'm speaking. And you and I, Yasha, we'll be sly, and on our part we'll carry on plotting and put their noses out of joint.' The punch finally reached the third and fourth glasses per brother, and then Mr Golyadkin began to experience two sensations: one that he was extraordinarily happy, and the other – that he could no longer stand up. His guest, it goes without saying, was invited to spend the night. A bed was made up somehow or other out of two rows of chairs. Mr Golyadkin junior declared that

66

under a friendly roof even a bare floor is soft to sleep on, that for his part he would fall asleep wherever he had to, with humility and gratitude; that he was now in heaven, and that, finally, in his time he had borne misfortunes and grief, had seen everything, had suffered everything and – who knew the future? – perhaps would suffer yet. Mr Golyadkin senior protested against this and began to demonstrate that all hope needed to be put in God. His guest concurred fully and said that, of course, no one was like God. Here Mr Golyadkin senior remarked that the Turks were right in one respect, calling on God's name even in their sleep. Then, without concurring, incidentally, with certain scholars in certain aspersions directed at the Turkish prophet Muhammed, and acknowledging him to be a great politician in his way, Mr Golyadkin went on to a very interesting description of an Algerian barber's shop, about which he had read in a miscellany in some book. The guest and his host laughed a lot at the artlessness of the Turks; could not fail, however, to pay due tribute in amazement to their fanaticism, aroused by opium... The guest finally began getting undressed, and Mr Golyadkin, partly out of the kindness of his heart, thinking that perhaps he did not even have a decent shirt, went out behind the partition so as not to embarrass a man who had already suffered as it was, and partly in order to satisfy himself so far as possible about Petrushka, to test him out, to cheer him up, if possible, and be nice to the man, so that absolutely everyone would be happy, and no spilt salt would be left on the table. It should be noted that Petrushka still embarrassed Mr Golyadkin a little.

'You go to bed now, Pyotr,' said Mr Golyadkin meekly, going into his servant's area, 'you go to bed now, and you wake me up tomorrow at eight o'clock. Do you understand, Petrusha?'

Mr Golyadkin spoke unusually softly and affectionately. But Petrushka was silent. At that moment he was busy by his bed and did not even turn around to his master, which he ought to have done, incidentally, out of respect for him alone.

'Did you hear me, Pyotr?' Mr Golyadkin continued. 'You go to bed now, and tomorrow, Petrusha, you wake me up at eight o'clock; do you understand?'

'Of course I remember, what's so hard about that!' grumbled

Petrushka under his breath.

'Well, all right, Petrusha; I'm only talking like this so that you're calm and happy too. Here we are all happy now, so that you're calm and happy too. And now I wish you a good night. Go to sleep, Petrusha, go to sleep; we must all labour… You know, brother, don't think anything…'

Mr Golyadkin was going to begin, but stopped. 'Won't that be too much,' he thought, 'haven't I gone too far? It's always the same; I always overdo it.' Our hero left Petrushka, feeling very dissatisfied with himself. What is more, he was a little offended by Petrushka's rudeness and intractability. 'Making up to a good-for-nothing, a master doing honour to a good-for-nothing, and he doesn't appreciate it,' thought Mr Golyadkin. 'Still, that's the villainous tendency of all of that type!' Rocking a little, he returned to his room and, seeing that his guest had gone to bed completely, he sat down for a minute on his bed. 'But still, Yasha, admit it, you villain,' he began in a whisper, his head nodding, 'you're at fault before me, aren't you? I mean, my namesake, you know…' he continued, teasing his guest in a quite familiar way. Finally, after bidding him an amicable goodnight, Mr Golyadkin went off to bed. In the meantime the guest began to snore. Mr Golyadkin in his turn began getting into bed, but in the meantime, having a little laugh, he whispered to himself, 'You're drunk today, you know, my dear Yakov Petrovich, you villain, you, you Golyadka, you – that's your name!! Well, what are you so pleased about? Tomorrow you'll be in tears, you know, you cry-baby, you: what am I to do with you?' Here a rather strange sensation was felt throughout Mr Golyadkin's being, something resembling doubt or repentance. 'How carried away I got,' he thought, 'I mean, now there's a noise in my head and I'm drunk; and you couldn't restrain yourself, you idiot, you! Spouted a whole heap of nonsense, and were meaning to be sly, you villain. Of course, to forgive and forget injuries is the very first virtue, but still it's a bad thing, that's how it is!' Here Mr Golyadkin half-rose, picked up the candle and went once more on tiptoe to take a look at his sleeping guest. He stood over him for a long time, deep in thought. 'Not a pretty picture! A caricature, the purest caricature, and there's an end to it!'

Finally Mr Golyadkin went to bed completely. There was a noise in his head, a cracking, a ringing. He began dozing off, dozing off… he made the effort to think about something, to remember something very interesting, to settle something very important, some ticklish business – but he could not. Sleep swooped down upon his poor head, and he fell asleep the way that people usually sleep when, unused to it, they have suddenly taken five glasses of punch at some friendly party.

8

Mr Golyadkin woke up the next day at eight o'clock as usual; and having woken up, he immediately recalled all the occurrences of the previous evening – recalled and winced. 'Oh dear, how I acted the fool yesterday!' he thought, raising himself a little from the bed and glancing at his guest's bed. But how great was his surprise to find that not only the guest, but even the bed on which the guest had slept was not in the room! 'What on earth is this?' Mr Golyadkin all but cried out, 'what on earth could it be? What on earth does this new thing mean now?' While the bewildered Mr Golyadkin was looking open-mouthed at the deserted space, the door creaked and Petrushka entered with a tea tray. 'Where on earth, where on earth?' said our hero in a scarcely audible voice, pointing his finger at the place assigned the day before to his guest. At first Petrushka made no reply, did not even look at his master, but turned his eyes into the corner on the right so that Mr Golyadkin was himself compelled to glance into the corner on the right. However, after a certain silence Petrushka replied in a rather hoarse and coarse voice that 'the master isn't at home'.

'You're a fool; I mean, I'm your master, Petrushka,' said Mr Golyadkin in a breaking voice and staring wide-eyed at his servant.

Petrushka made no reply, but gave Mr Golyadkin such a look that the latter blushed to the roots of his hair – a look of a sort of insulting reproach that resembled abuse, pure and simple. Mr Golyadkin even lost heart, as they say. Finally Petrushka announced that *the other one* had already been gone about an hour and a half and had not wanted to wait. Of course, the reply was probable and plausible; it was apparent that Petrushka was not lying, that his insulting look and the phrase *the other one* that he had used were only the consequence of the whole familiar vile situation; yet he understood, nonetheless, albeit but dimly, that something was wrong here and that fate was preparing another treat of some sort for him, and not an entirely pleasant one. 'Very well, we'll see,' he thought to himself, 'we shall see, we'll get to the bottom of all this in good time… Oh, my good Lord!' he groaned in conclusion, already in a quite different voice, 'and why was it I invited him, to what end did I do it all? I mean, I really am sticking my own head into their thieves' noose, I'm tying the noose myself. Oh, what a head, what a head! I mean, you just can't resist giving yourself away like some little boy, some clerk, like some rankless scum, some dishcloth, some rotten rag, gossip that you are, old woman that you are!… Oh, my holy saints! Even wrote some verse, the good-for-nothing, and declared his love for me! How am I, you know… How can I show him the door with reasonable decorum, the good-for-nothing, if he returns? It goes without saying, there are lots of various turns of phrase and methods. It's like this, so to speak, with my limited salary… Or else scare him somehow with, so to speak, having taken this and that into consideration, I'm compelled to express myself… you must pay half for the apartment and board and give me the money in advance. Hm! No, damn it, no! That sullies me. It's not entirely tactful! Only if it could be somehow done like this: go and give Petrushka the idea that Petrushka might somehow treat him badly, be somehow neglectful of him, be rude to him, and get rid of him like that? Set them against one another that way… No, damn it, no! It's dangerous, and again, if you look from a certain point of view – well, it's not at all good! Not at all good! And what if he doesn't come? Will that be a bad thing too? I gave myself away to him yesterday evening!… Ah, it's bad, bad! Ah, it's pretty bad, our business is! Oh, what a head I've got, what an accursed head! You can't cram what you need to in there, you can't knock any sense in there! Well, how will he come and refuse? But God grant he should come! I'd be very pleased if he came; I'd give a great deal if he came…' Thus Mr Golyadkin reasoned, swallowing his tea and continually glancing at the wall clock. 'It's a quarter to nine now; I mean, it's already time to go now. But what will happen; what will happen here? I'd like to know what it is precisely that's hidden here that's so special – you know, the objective, the direction and the various catches. It'd be good to learn what it is precisely all these people are aiming for and what their first step will be…' Mr Golyadkin could not stand it any longer, he abandoned his unfinished pipe, got dressed and set off for work, wanting to cover the danger, if possible, and satisfy himself of everything by his personal presence. And there was danger: he knew that for himself, that there was danger. 'But now we'll go and… get to the bottom of it,' said Mr Golyadkin, taking off his greatcoat and galoshes in the hallway, 'now we'll go and penetrate into all these matters.' Having resolved in this manner to act, our hero put his clothing in order, assumed a respectable and formal air, and was just meaning to penetrate into the next room when suddenly, right in the doorway, he was bumped into by his acquaintance, friend and chum of the day before. Mr Golyadkin junior seemed not to notice Mr Golyadkin senior, although he did meet with him almost nose to nose. Mr Golyadkin junior seemed to be busy, was hurrying somewhere, was out of breath; he had such an official, such a businesslike air that anyone, it seemed, could have read directly on his face – 'dispatched on a special mission…'

'Ah, it's you, Yakov Petrovich!' said our hero, grabbing his guest of the previous day by the arm.

'Later, later, excuse me, tell me later,' shouted Mr Golyadkin junior, tearing forward.

'Permit me, however; you seemed, Yakov Petrovich, to want, you know, sir…'

'What, sir? Explain quickly, sir.' Here Mr Golyadkin's guest of the previous day stopped, as if forcing himself and against his will, and put his ear right up to Mr Golyadkin's nose.

'I tell you, Yakov Petrovich, I'm surprised at the reception… a reception such as I evidently couldn't have expected at all.'

'There is a certain form, sir, for everything. Go and see His Excellency's secretary and then apply properly to the gentleman office manager… Do you have a request?…'

'I don't know, Yakov Petrovich! You simply amaze me, Yakov Petrovich! You probably don't recognise me or you're joking, in accordance with the innate gaiety of your character.'

'Ah, it's you!' said Mr Golyadkin junior, as if having only just now

71

made out Mr Golyadkin senior, 'so it's you? Well, then, did you sleep well?' Here Mr Golyadkin junior, smiling a little – smiling officially and formally, though not at all as he should have done (because, after all, he in any event did owe a debt of gratitude to Mr Golyadkin senior) – and so, smiling officially and formally, he added that he for his part was very glad that Mr Golyadkin had slept well; then he bent a little, took a few little pattering steps on the spot, looked to the right, to the left, then lowered his eyes to the ground, took aim at a side door, and, whispering rapidly that he was on a special mission, he darted away into the next room. He was gone in a flash.

'Well, there's a thing for you,' whispered our hero, rooted to the ground for a moment, 'there's a thing for you! So that's the situation here!…' At this point Mr Golyadkin sensed that for some reason his flesh had begun to creep. 'Still,' he continued, making his way to his department, 'still, after all, I've been talking about a circumstance like this for a long time now; I've long had a premonition that he was on a special mission – just yesterday I was saying that the man was certainly being used on some special mission…'

'Have you finished your document from yesterday, Yakov Petrovich?' asked Anton Antonovich Setochkin of Mr Golyadkin, who had settled down beside him. 'Have you got it here?'

'Here,' whispered Mr Golyadkin, looking at his section head with a somewhat lost air.

'Look out, sir. I'm saying this because Andrei Filippovich has already asked twice. Before you know it, His Excellency will be demanding it…'

'No, sir, it's finished, sir…'

'Well, sir, good, sir.'

'Anton Antonovich, I think I've always carried out my duties properly and I take pains, sir, over the matters entrusted to me by my superiors, I deal with them assiduously.'

'Yes, sir. Well, sir, what do you mean by that, sir?'

'I don't mean anything, Anton Antonovich, sir. I only want to explain, Anton Antonovich, that I… that is, I wanted to state that sometimes disloyalty and envy spare no person whatsoever in their search for their repulsive daily food, sir…'

'Excuse me, I don't fully understand you. That is to say, to what individual are you now alluding?'

'That is to say, I only meant, Anton Antonovich, that I go by the direct route, and I despise going by the roundabout route, that I'm not a schemer and that, if I'm only allowed to express myself, I can be very justly proud of it...'

'Yes, sir, it's all so, sir, and, to my mind at least, I do full justice to your argument; but do allow me too, Yakov Petrovich, to remark to you that personal comments aren't entirely permissible in good society; that I, for example, am prepared to put up with them behind someone's back – because who isn't abused behind his back? – but to his face, say what you like, I too, my good sir, for example, won't permit myself to be rude. I, my good sir, have grown grey in service to the state and won't permit myself, sir, to be rude in my old age...'

'No, sir, I, Anton Antonovich, sir, you, do you see, Anton Antonovich, you seem, Anton Antonovich, not to have fully comprehended me, sir. But I, pardon me, Anton Antonovich, I, for my part, can only count it an honour, sir...'

'Well, and I beg forgiveness for us too, sir. We've been schooled in the old way, sir. And it's too late for us to be schooled in your way, the new way. In service to the fatherland we seem to have had sufficient understanding up until now. I, my good sir, as you know yourself, have a decoration for twenty-five years' irreproachable service, sir...'

'I appreciate it, Anton Antonovich, I for my part appreciate it all perfectly, sir. But it wasn't about that, sir, I was talking about a mask, Anton Antonovich, sir...'

'About a mask, sir?'

'That is, again you... I'm afraid that here too you'll take the other side of the sense, the sense of my words, that is, as you yourself say, Anton Antonovich. I'm only developing the theme, that is, putting out the idea, Anton Antonovich, that people wearing a mask have become not uncommon, sir, and that it's difficult now to recognise a man beneath a mask, sir...'

'Well, sir, do you know, sir, it's not even entirely difficult, sir. Sometimes it's even quite easy, sir, sometimes you don't even have to go far to seek, sir.'

'No, sir, do you know, sir, Anton Antonovich, I'm speaking, sir, speaking for myself, that I, for example, put on a mask only when there's a need for it, that is, solely for a carnival and merry gatherings, speaking in the direct sense, but that I don't mask myself in front of people daily, speaking in a different, more secretive sense, sir. That's what I meant, Anton Antonovich, sir.'

'Well, we'll leave all this for the moment; I haven't even got the time, sir,' said Anton Antonovich, rising a little from his seat and gathering some papers for a report to His Excellency. 'Your business, I assume, will not delay your explaining in good time. You'll see for yourself whom you should blame and whom you should accuse, and then I beg you most humbly to free me from further private explanations and gossip that are harmful for work, sir...'

'No, sir, Anton Antonovich, I,' began a now rather pale Mr Golyadkin in the wake of the departing Anton Antonovich, 'I, you know, sir, Anton Antonovich, did not even think, sir. What on earth is it?' continued our hero, now to himself as he remained alone. 'What on earth are these winds that are blowing here, and what does this new catch signify?' At the very time when our lost and half-dead hero was preparing to solve this new question, a noise became audible in the next room, some businesslike movement was apparent, the door opened, and Andrei Filippovich, who just prior to this had been absent on matters of business in His Excellency's office, appeared in the doorway and called Mr Golyadkin. Knowing what the matter was and not wishing to make Andrei Filippovich wait, Mr Golyadkin leapt up from his seat and immediately, for all he was worth, began making a real fuss, finishing off the preparation and tidying the book that was being demanded, and also preparing to set off himself in the wake of the book and Andrei Filippovich into His Excellency's office. Suddenly, and almost from under the arm of Andrei Filippovich, who was standing right in the doorway at the time, into the room darted Mr Golyadkin junior, fussing, breathless and tired out from work, with an important, resolutely formal air, and rolled straight up to Mr Golyadkin senior, who was least of all expecting an attack like this...

'The papers, Yakov Petrovich, the papers... His Excellency has been so good as to ask if you have them ready?' twittered Mr Golyadkin senior's friend rapidly in a low voice. 'Andrei Filippovich is waiting for you…'

'I know he's waiting for me without your telling me,' said Mr Golyadkin senior, also rapidly and in a whisper.

'No, Yakov Petrovich, I didn't mean that; I didn't mean that at all, Yakov Petrovich; I sympathise, Yakov Petrovich, and am moved by heartfelt concern.'

'From which I most humbly beg you to deliver me. If you please, if you please, sir…'

'It goes without saying, you'll put them in a folder, Yakov Petrovich, and put a bookmark in at the third page, if you please, Yakov Petrovich…'

'If *you* please, finally…'

'But there's an ink blot here, you know, Yakov Petrovich, had you noticed the ink blot?…'

Here Andrei Filippovich called Mr Golyadkin a second time.

'Straight away, Andrei Filippovich; I'm just, just a little, just here… My dear sir, do you understand Russian?'

'It'll be best to get it off with a penknife, Yakov Petrovich, better to rely on me: better not to touch it yourself, Yakov Petrovich, but rely on me – with a penknife just here a little I'll…'

Andrei Filippovich called Mr Golyadkin for a third time.

'But, pardon me, where is there a blot here? I mean, there doesn't seem to be a blot here at all?'

'But it's a huge blot, here it is! Here, allow me, I saw it here; here, allow me… just allow me, Yakov Petrovich, with a penknife here a little, out of concern, Yakov Petrovich, and with a penknife from the bottom of my heart, I'll… like that, and there's an end to it…'

Here, and quite unexpectedly, Mr Golyadkin junior suddenly, without warning, overpowering Mr Golyadkin senior in the momentary struggle that arose between them, and in any event completely against the latter's will, took possession of the document demanded by his superiors and, instead of scraping it a little with a penknife from the bottom of his heart as he had treacherously assured Mr Golyadkin senior, he quickly rolled it up, poked it under his arm, in two bounds was beside Andrei Filippovich – who had not noticed a single one of his tricks – and flew with him into the director's office. Mr Golyadkin senior remained as if rooted to the spot, holding a penknife in his hands and apparently preparing to scrape something with it...

Our hero did not yet fully understand his new situation. He had not yet come to his senses. He had felt a blow, but thought that it was something unimportant. In terrible, indescribable anguish he finally broke away from where he was standing and rushed straight into the director's office, praying to heaven, incidentally, on the way that it would all somehow be sorted out for the best and would be all right... In the last room before the director's office he ran absolutely nose to nose into Andrei Filippovich and his namesake. They were both already returning: Mr Golyadkin stood aside. Andrei Filippovich was speaking cheerfully, with a smile. Mr Golyadkin senior's namesake was smiling too, fussing and pattering at a respectful distance from Andrei Filippovich and whispering something in his ear with an admiring look, to which Andrei Filippovich was nodding his head in the most favourable way. At once our hero understood the whole state of affairs. The thing is that his work (as he learnt later) almost exceeded His Excellency's expectations and really was ready by the deadline and in good time. His Excellency was extremely pleased. It was even said that His Excellency had said thank you to Mr Golyadkin junior, a warm thank you; said that he would remember this when the opportunity offered and would certainly not forget... It goes without saying that Mr Golyadkin's first business was to protest, to protest to the utmost with all his might. Almost beside himself and pale as death, he rushed to Andrei Filippovich. But Andrei Filippovich, hearing that Mr Golyadkin's business was a private matter, refused to listen, remarking resolutely that he did not have a single free moment even for his own needs...

The dryness of his tone and the sharpness of his refusal stunned Mr Golyadkin. 'Better if I somehow from another angle... better if I go to Anton Antonovich.' To Mr Golyadkin's ill fortune, Anton Antonovich was not available either: he too was busy with something somewhere. 'So it wasn't for nothing then that he asked to be spared explanations and gossip!' thought our hero. 'That's what he was driving at – the old stirrer! In that case I shall simply be so bold as to entreat His Excellency.'

Still pale and feeling his head to be in complete disorder, very much perplexed about what precisely he ought to resolve upon, Mr Golyadkin sat down on a chair. 'It would be much better if all this were just unimportant,' he continually thought to himself. 'Such a murky business was really even quite improbable. In the first place, it was nonsense, and secondly it couldn't happen either. It probably got imagined somehow, or it came out as something different, and not what really happened; or it must have been me that went myself... and I somehow took myself for someone else entirely... in short, it's a completely impossible business.'

No sooner had Mr Golyadkin decided that it was a completely impossible business than suddenly into the room flew Mr Golyadkin junior with documents in both hands and under his arm. Having said two vital words of some sort to Andrei Filippovich in passing, having spoken to somebody else as well, having paid a compliment to someone and having made familiar comments to someone else, Mr Golyadkin junior, who evidently did not have spare time to be spent pointlessly, already seemed to be intending to leave the room, but, to Mr Golyadkin senior's good fortune, he stopped right in the doorway and began speaking in passing with two or three young clerks who happened to be there too. Mr Golyadkin senior rushed straight towards him. No sooner had Mr Golyadkin junior seen Mr Golyadkin senior's manoeuvre than he immediately began looking around him with great anxiety to see where he could slip off to quickly. But our hero was already holding onto the sleeves of his guest of the previous day. The clerks standing around the two Titular Councillors parted and waited to see what would happen with curiosity. The old Titular Councillor understood very well that good opinion was not now on his side, understood very well that intrigues were being carried on against him: all the more was it necessary to support himself now. The moment was a decisive one.

'Well, sir?' said Mr Golyadkin junior, looking at Mr Golyadkin senior rather impertinently.

Mr Golyadkin senior was scarcely breathing.

'I don't know, my dear sir,' he began, 'how to explain to you now the strangeness of your behaviour with me.'

'Well, sir. Continue, sir.' Here Mr Golyadkin junior looked around and winked his eye at the clerks surrounding them, as though letting them know it was right now that the comedy would begin.

'The impertinence and shamelessness of your tricks with me in the present instance, my dear sir, expose you even more... than all my words. Don't hope for anything from your game: it's not a very good one...'

'Well, Yakov Petrovich, now come on, tell me, how did you sleep?' replied Golyadkin junior, looking Golyadkin senior straight in the eyes.

'You forget yourself, my dear sir,' said the utterly lost Titular Councillor, scarcely feeling the floor beneath him, 'I hope you'll change your tone...'

'My dear!!' said Mr Golyadkin junior, pulling a rather indecent face at Mr Golyadkin senior, and suddenly, quite unexpectedly, in the guise of a caress he seized him with two fingers by the rather chubby right cheek. Our hero flared up like fire... As soon as Mr Golyadkin senior's friend noticed that his adversary, shaking in every limb, dumb with rage, red as a lobster and finally brought to the end of his tether, might even resolve on a genuine attack, he immediately, and in the most shameless way, forestalled him in his turn. Having tugged on his cheek another couple of times, having tickled him another couple of times, having toyed with him, immobile and mad with fury, for another few seconds in this way, to the no little delight of the young men surrounding them, Mr Golyadkin junior, with infuriating shamelessness, flicked Mr Golyadkin senior in closing on his sloping belly and, with the most poisonous smile that hinted at much, he said to him, 'Misbehaving, brother, Yakov Petrovich, you're misbehaving! You and I'll act on the sly, Yakov Petrovich, on the sly.' Then, and before our hero had managed to recover in the slightest degree from the latest attack, Mr Golyadkin junior suddenly (having given just a little preliminary smile to the spectators surrounding them) assumed the most busy, the most businesslike, the most formal air, lowered his eyes to the ground, huddled up, shrank, and, saying quickly 'on a special mission', kicked out with his short little leg and nipped into the next room. Our hero could not believe his eyes and was still in no state to come to his senses...

Finally he did come to his senses. Having recognised in a single moment that he was lost, had been in a certain sense annihilated, that he had sullied himself and stained his reputation, that he had been ridiculed and spat upon in the presence of third parties, that he had been treacherously desecrated by the man he had only the day before considered his number one and most reliable friend, that he had come a cropper, finally, like nothing on earth – Mr Golyadkin rushed off in pursuit of his foe. At the present moment he no longer even wanted to think about the witnesses of his desecration. 'It's all in agreement one with another,' he said to himself, 'One stands up for another and one sets another upon me.' However, after ten paces our hero clearly saw that all pursuit was pointless and in vain, and for that reason he returned. 'You won't get away,' he thought, 'you'll be trumped in good time, the wolf will have to pay for the sheep's tears.' With furious sangfroid and with the most energetic resolution Mr Golyadkin reached his chair and settled down on it. 'You won't get away,' he said again. It was not a matter now of some sort of passive resistance: it smacked of the decisive, of the offensive, and whoever saw how Mr Golyadkin at that moment, flushing and scarcely containing his agitation, stabbed his pen into the inkwell, and with what fury he set about scribbling on the paper, might already have decided in advance that the matter would not pass off lightly and could not be concluded simply in some sort of girly way. In the depths of his soul he put together a certain decision, and in the depths of his heart he swore to execute it. In truth, he did not yet know fully how he should act – that is, it would be better to say, did not know at all; but all the same, that was all right! 'But with imposture and shamelessness, my dear sir, in this day and age you don't succeed. Imposture and shamelessness, dear sir of mine, lead to no good, but rather lead to the noose. Grishka Otrepyev[16] was the only one, my dear sir that you are, who succeeded with imposture, deceiving the blind people, but even then not for long.' In spite of this last circumstance Mr Golyadkin proposed waiting until the masks should fall from certain faces and something should be laid bare. For this to happen it was necessary firstly for the working day to end as soon as possible, and until that time our hero proposed not to undertake anything. And then, when the working day ended, he would take a certain measure. And then he knew how he should act, having taken this measure, how to arrange the whole plan of his actions so as to shatter the horn of pride and crush the snake that bit the dust in the scorn of impotence. But Mr Golyadkin could not allow himself to be soiled like a rag on which dirty boots are wiped. He could not consent to this, and particularly in the present instance. Had there not been this last disgrace, perhaps our hero would even have resolved to brace himself, perhaps he would even have resolved to keep quiet, to submit and not to protest too persistently; he would just have argued and complained a little, demonstrated that he was within his rights, then would have conceded a little, then perhaps he would have conceded a little more, then he would have consented fully, then, and particularly when the opposition had solemnly acknowledged that he was within his rights, then perhaps he would even have made peace, would even have been a little touched, even – who could know – perhaps a new friendship would have been reborn, a strong, warm friendship, even more expansive than the friendship of the day before, so that this friendship might have completely eclipsed, finally, the unpleasantness of the rather indecent resemblance of the two men, so that both Titular Councillors would have been extremely glad and would have lived, finally, to a ripe old age, etc. Let us finally say everything: Mr Golyadkin was even beginning to repent a little of standing up for himself and for his rights, as a result of which he had straight away had some unpleasantness. 'Had he submitted,' thought Mr Golyadkin, 'said he'd been joking – I'd have forgiven him, would have forgiven him even more if only he'd admitted it loudly. But I won't let myself be soiled like a rag. I've not let myself be soiled by bigger people than him, still less will I allow a man who's corrupt to have a try at it. I'm not a rag; I, good sir, am not a rag!' In short, our hero was resolved. 'You yourself, my good sir, are to blame!' He was resolved to protest, and to protest to the utmost with all his might. That's the sort of man he was! He could not possibly consent to allow himself to be bullied, and still less permit himself to be soiled like a rag, and, finally, permit a completely corrupt man all that. No arguing, however, no arguing. Perhaps if someone had wanted, if someone had, for example, really felt like absolutely without fail turning Mr Golyadkin into a rag, then he would have turned him, would have turned him without resistance and unpunished (Mr Golyadkin sensed this himself at times) and the result would have been a rag, and not Golyadkin – just a vile, dirty rag would have been the result, but this rag would not have been an ordinary one, this rag would have been one with self-respect, this rag would have been one with animation and feelings, even if only with unspoken self-respect and with unspoken feelings, concealed far away in the dirty creases of the rag, but with feelings nonetheless…

The day lasted an incredibly long time; finally it struck four. After a little everyone got up and moved off in the wake of their superior to their respective homes. Mr Golyadkin mixed himself in with the crowd; his eye was alert and did not let the man he needed out of sight. Finally our hero saw that his friend had run up to the office watchmen who were handing out greatcoats and, as was his vile habit, was fidgeting around them while awaiting his. The moment was a decisive one. Somehow Mr Golyadkin pushed his way through the crowd and, not wishing to fall behind, also began to make a fuss about getting his greatcoat. But Mr Golyadkin's friend and acquaintance was handed his greatcoat first, since here too he had managed in his own special way to make himself popular, be on good terms, cast his spell, behave like a scoundrel.

Throwing his greatcoat on, Mr Golyadkin junior glanced ironically at Mr Golyadkin senior, thus acting openly and impertinently to spite him; then, with his characteristic insolence, he looked around, did a final little bit of pattering – probably to leave an advantageous impression of himself – around the clerks, said a word to one, exchanged whispers about something with another, exchanged respectful kisses with a third, addressed a smile to a fourth, gave his hand to a fifth and darted cheerfully down the stairs. Mr Golyadkin senior was after him and, to his indescribable pleasure, actually overtook him on the last step and seized the collar of his greatcoat. Mr Golyadkin junior seemed to be a little dumbfounded and he looked around with a lost air.

'What do you mean by this?' he finally whispered to Mr Golyadkin in a weak voice.

'My dear sir, if you are but a noble man, then I hope you will remember our friendly relations of yesterday,' said our hero.

'Ah, yes. Well, then? Did you sleep well, sir?'

For a moment fury took away Mr Golyadkin senior's tongue.

'I did sleep well, sir… But do permit me to tell you too, my dear sir, that your game is extremely complicated…'

'Who says that? It's my enemies who say that,' replied the one who called himself Mr Golyadkin curtly, and with these words he unexpectedly freed himself from the weak hands of the real Mr Golyadkin. Having freed himself, he rushed down the stairs, glanced around and, seeing a cabman, he ran up to him, got onto the droshky, and in a single moment disappeared from Mr Golyadkin senior's sight. The despairing Titular Councillor, abandoned by all, glanced around, but there was no other cab. He tried to run, but his legs buckled. With face cast down, with mouth agape, annihilated, shrunken, impotent, he leant up against a lamp-post and remained that way for several minutes in the middle of the pavement. It seemed that all was lost for Mr Golyadkin…

9

Everything, apparently, and even nature itself, seemed up in arms against Mr Golyadkin; but he was still on his feet and unbeaten; he sensed it, that he was unbeaten. He was ready to fight. He rubbed his hands with such feeling and with such energy when he came to after his initial amazement, that from the look of Mr Golyadkin alone it was already possible to conclude that he would not concede. Danger, however, was near at hand, was obvious; Mr Golyadkin sensed that too; but how should it be tackled, this danger? That was the question. For a moment the idea even flashed through Mr Golyadkin's head, 'well, then, so to speak, shouldn't I just leave it all as it is, shouldn't I just give it all up without any fuss? Well, then? Well, all right. I'll keep out of it, as if it's not me,' thought Mr Golyadkin, 'I let everything pass; it's not me, and that's that; he keeps out of it too, maybe he'll give it up. That's how it is! I'll succeed by using humility. And where's the danger? Well, what danger? I'd like someone to show me the danger in this business? It's a trivial business! An ordinary business!…' Here Mr Golyadkin stopped short. The words froze on his tongue; he even cursed himself for this thought; right away he even found himself guilty of baseness, of cowardice for this thought; however, his business nevertheless failed to get under way. He sensed that it was completely impossible for him to resolve upon anything at the present moment; he even sensed that he would have given a lot to anyone who could tell him upon what precisely he ought to resolve. Well, how could he guess, after all? Anyway, there was no time for guessing. Just in case, so as not to lose time, he hired a cab and flew home. 'So, how do you feel now?' he thought inside himself. 'How are you so good as to feel now, Yakov Petrovich? What will you do? What will you do now, scoundrel that you are, rogue that you are? You've driven yourself to the utmost, and now you're crying, and now you're snivelling!' Thus did Mr Golyadkin tease himself, bobbing up and down in his cabby's bumpy vehicle. Teasing himself and thereby rubbing salt in his wounds was a sort of profound delight for Mr Golyadkin at that particular moment – all but voluptuousness even. 'Well,' he thought, 'if some magician were to come along now, or something official happened somehow, and they said, "Give up a finger from your right hand, Golyadkin – and we'll be quits; there won't be another Golyadkin, and you'll be happy, only you'll be missing one finger", then I'd give up the finger, I'd give it up for sure, I'd give it up without pulling a face. The devil take it all!' the despairing Titular Councillor finally cried out, 'well, why all this? Well, all this had to happen; without fail, this, precisely this, as if nothing else would have done! And everything was fine at first, everyone was content and happy; but then no, this had to happen! Still, you won't achieve anything with words, after all. You need to act.'

And so, having almost resolved upon something, Mr Golyadkin, on entering his apartment and without the least delay, grabbed hold of his pipe and, sucking on it for all he was worth, scattering wisps of smoke to left and right, began in extreme agitation to run back and forth about the room. Meanwhile Petrushka started laying the table. Finally Mr Golyadkin was completely resolved, he suddenly tossed down his pipe, threw on his greatcoat, said he would not be dining at home, and ran off out of the apartment. Petrushka, panting, caught him on the stairs, holding in his hands the hat he had forgotten. Mr Golyadkin took the hat, was on the point in passing of justifying himself a bit in Petrushka's eyes, so that Petrushka did not think anything in particular – that there was this situation, so to speak, that there he was forgetting his hat, etc. – but since Petrushka did not even want to look at him and left straight away, Mr Golyadkin too put on his hat without further explanations, ran down the stairs and, muttering that everything would perhaps be for the best and that the business would somehow be settled – although he felt, by the way, a chill even in his heels – he went out into the street, hired a cab and flew to Andrei Filippovich. 'Still, wouldn't it be better tomorrow?' thought Mr Golyadkin, taking hold of the bell cord at the doors of Andrei Filippovich's apartment, 'and what on earth will I say in particular? There's nothing in particular here. It's such a minor business, and it really is, in the end, minor, trivial, that is, almost a trivial business… I mean, there it is, what is it all, this situation…' Suddenly Mr Golyadkin tugged at the bell; the bell rang, from within someone's footsteps were heard… At this point Mr Golyadkin even cursed himself somewhat for his hastiness and audacity. The recent unpleasant events, about which Mr Golyadkin had all but forgotten because of his business, and his falling out with Andrei Filippovich immediately came to mind. But it was already too late to flee: the door opened. Fortunately for Mr Golyadkin, he was told that neither had Andrei Filippovich come home from work, nor was he dining at home. 'I know where he's dining: he's dining by the Izmailovsky Bridge,' thought our hero, and was terribly pleased. To the servant's question as to what message should be given, he said, 'I, my friend, am fine,' and 'I'll be back, my friend, later,' and ran down the stairs even with a certain cheerfulness. Going out into the street, he resolved to let the vehicle go and settle up with the cabman. And when the cabman asked for extra, saying, 'I waited a long time, sir, and didn't spare the horse for your honour,' he gave five kopeks extra too, and even with great willingness; and he himself set off on foot.

'It's such a business, it's true,' thought Mr Golyadkin, 'that it really can't be left as it is; however, if you reason thus, reason sensibly like this, then why should one make a fuss here? Well, no, however, I'll keep on talking about the question of why I should make a fuss. Why should I toil, struggle, suffer, kill myself? Firstly, the deed's done and you can't turn it back… you can't turn it back, after all! Let's reason like this: a man appears – a man appears with sufficient recommendation, so to speak, he's a capable civil servant of good conduct, only he's poor and has suffered various sorts of unpleasantness, such scrapes… well, and after all, poverty isn't a crime; so that it's not my fault. Well really, what nonsense is this? Well, he suited, got fixed up, the man got fixed up by nature itself in such a way that he's as like another man as two peas, he's a perfect copy of another man: so then why shouldn't he be taken into the Ministry?! If it's fate, if it's fate alone, if blind fortune alone is to blame here – then should he be soiled like a rag, then shouldn't he be allowed to work… and where will justice be here after that? He's a poor, lost, frightened man; there's heartache here, compassion demands he should be given charity here! Yes indeed! Our superiors would be a lot of good if they reasoned as I, a hothead, do! I mean, that bonce of mine! There's foolishness enough for ten there at times! No, no! They did well and deserve thanks for giving charity to a poor victim of misfortune… Well, and suppose, for example, that we're twins, that there we were, born in such a way that we were twin brothers, and that's that – there's a thing! Well, what then? Well, that's all right! All the clerks can be trained… and surely no outsider coming into our Ministry would find anything improper and insulting in such a circumstance. There's even something touching here; in that, here's a thought then, so to speak: in that, divine Providence, so to speak, created two men absolutely alike, and the beneficent authorities, recognising divine Providence, gave shelter to the two twins. It would, of course,' continued Mr Golyadkin, drawing breath and lowering his voice a little, 'it would, of course… it would, of course, have been better if there'd been none of this touching stuff, and if there'd been no twins either… The devil take it all! And why was it all necessary? And what sort of particular need was there here that would suffer no delay? Oh, Lord God! My goodness, what a mess the devils have cooked up, haven't they! I mean, though, he has such a character too, he's got such a playful, nasty manner – he's so vile, so frivolous, a crawler, a lickspittle, he's such a Golyadkin! He may behave badly too and sully my name, the scoundrel. So now keep an eye on him and look after him! My goodness, I mean, what a punishment! Still, what then? Well, there's no need! Well, he's vile – well, let him be vile, but then the other one's honest. Well, so he'll be vile, and I'll be honest – and they'll say that that Golyadkin there is vile – don't look at him, and don't confuse him with the other one; but that one's honest, virtuous, meek, mild, very reliable at work and worthy of promotion; that's how it is! Well, all right... but when, you know... But when they go and, you know... and mix things up! I mean, anything can happen with him involved! Oh, my dear Lord God!... And he'll replace a man, replace him, such a vile fellow – and when he replaces a man with a rag he won't even consider that a man isn't a rag. Oh, my dear Lord God! My, what a misfortune!...'

So in this way, reasoning and lamenting, Mr Golyadkin ran on, without making out his route and scarcely knowing where he was going. He came to on Nevsky Avenue, and then only on account of bumping into some passer-by so good and solidly that he simply saw stars. Without raising his head, Mr Golyadkin mumbled an apology, and only when the passer-by, after growling something not too complimentary, had already moved on a considerable distance, did he lift his nose up and look around to see where he was and how things were. Having looked around and noted that he was right beside the restaurant in which he had had a rest while preparing for the banquet at Olsufy Ivanovich's, our hero suddenly felt some tweaking and twitching in his stomach, remembered he had had no dinner and there was no banquet imminent anywhere, and for that reason, without wasting his precious time, he ran up the stairs into the restaurant, hurrying as best he could to have a quick bite to eat and not to hang around. And although everything was rather dear in the restaurant, this minor circumstance did not stop Mr Golyadkin on this occasion; and there was no time now to stop over such trifles. In a brightly lit room, by a counter on which there lay a varied pile of everything consumed by respectable people as hors d'oeuvres, there stood quite a dense crowd of customers. The assistant scarcely had the time to pour, serve, hand the food out and take the money. Mr Golyadkin waited his turn and, having waited, reached his hand out modestly for a pie. Having moved away into a corner, turned his back on those present and eaten hungrily, he returned to the assistant, put his plate down on the table, took out ten silver kopeks, as he knew the price, and put the coin on the counter, catching the assistant's eye to point out to him that the money was there; so to speak, one pie, etc.

'That'll be one rouble ten kopeks,' the assistant let through his teeth.

Mr Golyadkin was pretty amazed.

'Are you talking to me? I... I believe I had one pie.'

'You had eleven,' retorted the assistant confidently.

'You... so far as it seems to me... you seem to be mistaken... Really, I believe I had one pie.'

'I was counting; you had eleven of them. And if you had them, you've got to pay; you don't get anything for nothing here.'

Mr Golyadkin was stupefied. 'What is this, some sort of magic being practised on me or something?' he thought. Meanwhile, the assistant was awaiting Mr Golyadkin's decision; Mr Golyadkin was surrounded; Mr Golyadkin was already on the point of delving into his pocket to take out a silver rouble and settle up at once, to be out of harm's way. 'Well, if it's eleven, it's eleven,' he thought, turning as red as a lobster, 'well, what is there in that, if eleven pies have been eaten? Well, a man's hungry, so he's eaten eleven pies; well, and let him eat to his heart's content; well, there's nothing to wonder at here and nothing to laugh about...' Suddenly it was as if something had pricked Mr Golyadkin; he raised his eyes and – all at once he understood the mystery, understood all the magic; all at once all the difficulties were resolved... In the doorway into the next room, almost directly behind the assistant's back and facing Mr Golyadkin, in the doorway which, incidentally, our hero had up to this point taken to be a mirror, stood a little man – *he* stood, Mr Golyadkin himself stood – not the old Mr Golyadkin, not the hero of our tale, but the other Mr Golyadkin, the new Mr Golyadkin. The other Mr Golyadkin was evidently in superb spirits. He was smiling at the first Mr Golyadkin, nodding to him, winking his little eyes, pattering his feet a little and looking as though as soon as anything happened – he'd be off into the shadows, he'd be off into the next room, and then probably out by the back way, and that would be that... and all pursuit would be in vain. In his hands was the last piece of the tenth pie, which, before Mr Golyadkin's very eyes, he dispatched into his mouth, smacking his lips with pleasure. 'Passed himself off, the villain!' thought Mr Golyadkin, flaring up like fire in shame, 'felt no shame in a public place! Can they see him? Nobody seems to notice…' Mr Golyadkin dropped a silver rouble as if he had burnt all his fingers on it and, not noticing the assistant's meaningfully insolent smile, a smile of triumph and calm power, he fought his way out of the crowd and rushed off without a backward glance. 'My thanks for at least not compromising a man utterly!' thought Mr Golyadkin senior. 'My thanks to the brigand, both to him and to fate, that everything was settled all right anyway. But the assistant was rude. But still, he was within his rights after all! One rouble ten was owed, so he was within his rights. Nobody gets anything here without money, he said! But he could have been a bit more civil, the ne'er-do-well!…'

Mr Golyadkin said all this as he was going down the stairs to the porch. However, on the last step he stopped, as if rooted to the ground, and suddenly blushed in such a way that tears even appeared in his eyes from the paroxysm of mortified self-respect. After standing like a pillar for about thirty seconds he suddenly stamped his foot decisively, leapt in a single bound from the porch onto the street and, without a backward glance, gasping for breath, not feeling his tiredness, he set off for home, to Shestilavochnaya Street. At home, without even taking off his outdoor clothes, contrary to his habit of dressing informally when he was in, without even picking up his pipe as a preliminary, he settled down immediately on the couch, moved his inkstand closer, took up his pen, got out a sheet of notepaper and set about scribbling down with a hand trembling from inner agitation the following missive:

My dear sir, Yakov Petrovich!
I should not have taken up the pen at all if my circumstances and you yourself, my dear sir, had not forced me to it. Believe me, necessity alone has forced me to enter into explanations of this sort with you, and thus I request you first and foremost to consider this my measure not a deliberate intention, my dear sir, to insult you, but an essential consequence of the circumstances now linking us.

'Doesn't that seem good, proper, polite, and yet not without strength and firmness?… There doesn't seem to be any cause for offence there. What's more, I'm within my rights,' thought Mr Golyadkin, reading over what he had written.

Your unexpected and strange appearance, my dear sir, on a stormy night, after a coarse and unseemly act against me by my enemies, whose names I pass over in silence out of contempt for them, was the germ of all the misunderstandings that exist at the present time between us. Your stubborn desire, dear sir, to have your own way and to enter forcibly into the circle of my being and all my relations in practical life goes even beyond the bounds demanded by mere courtesy alone and simple life in a community. I think there is no reason to refer here to your theft, my dear sir, of my document and of my own honest name in order to gain the favour of superiors – favour that you do not deserve. Nor is there any reason to refer here to your deliberate and offensive evasions of the necessary explanations on this account. Finally, so that everything should be said, nor do I refer here to your last strange, one might say, incomprehensible action against me in the coffee house. I am far from lamenting my futile loss of a silver rouble; yet I cannot help but manifest all my indignation at the memory of your blatant infringement, dear sir, to the detriment of my honour and in addition in the presence of several persons, albeit not known to me, yet at the same time of very good tone...

'Am I not going too far?' thought Mr Golyadkin. 'Won't it be too much; isn't it too sensitive – that allusion to good tone, for example?... Well, never mind! I need to show him firmness of character. Anyway, to soften it, I can flatter and butter him up a bit at the end like this. So now we'll see.'

But I would not have thought, my dear sir, of tiring you with my letter, if I had not been absolutely certain that the nobility of heartfelt emotions and your open, straightforward character would indicate to you yourself the means to put right all the omissions and to restore everything to the way it was before.

In full hope I dare to remain certain that you will not take my letter in a manner offensive to you, nor at the same time will you decline to explain yourself adequately on this account in written form through the mediation of my servant.

In expectation, I have the honour to be, dear sir,

your most humble servant
Y. Golyadkin.

'Well, that's all fine, then. The deed's done; it's even gone as far as being written down. But then who's to blame? He himself is to blame: he himself drives a man to having to demand written documents. And I'm within my rights…'

After reading through the letter a final time, Mr Golyadkin folded it, sealed it and called Petrushka. Petrushka appeared, as was his custom, with sleepy eyes and extremely angry about something.

'You'll take this letter here, old fellow… do you understand?'

Petrushka was silent.

'You'll take it and go to the Ministry; there you'll find the duty officer, Provincial Secretary Vakhrameyev. Vakhrameyev's on duty today. Do you understand that?'

'I understand.'

' "I understand"! Can't you say, "I understand, sir"? You'll ask for the clerk Vakhrameyev and tell him that it's like this – you'll say, the master, you'll say, ordered you to pay respects and humbly ask you to check in our Ministry address book – where, you'll say, does Titular Councillor Golyadkin live?'

Petrushka remained silent and, as it seemed to Mr Golyadkin, smiled.

'Well, so, Pyotr, you'll ask him the address and find out: where, you'll say, does the new clerk Golyadkin live?'

'Very well.'

'You'll ask the address and take this letter to that address; do you understand?'

'I understand.'

'If there… where you take the letter – that gentleman you give the letter to, Golyadkin… Why are you laughing, blockhead?'

'Why should I be laughing? What's it to me! I'm all right, sir. The likes of me have nothing to laugh at…'

'Well, right then… if that gentleman asks and says how's your master, how is he there, says, what's he, you know… well, if he pumps

90

you about anything – you keep quiet and reply: my master's all right, you'll say, but he's asking for a reply from you, you'll say, in your own hand. Do you understand?'

'I understand, sir.'

'Well, right then, you'll say, my master, you'll say, is all right, you'll say, and he's well, and he's getting ready, you'll say, to go visiting now; and from you, you'll say, he requests a written reply. Do you understand?'

'I understand.'

'Well, off you go.'

'I mean, it's hard work with that blockhead too! Laughs to himself and nothing but. What's he laughing at? Now I've ended up in a mess, look what a mess I've ended up in! Still, perhaps it'll all take a turn for the better. That rogue will probably be dragging himself about for a couple of hours now, he'll just disappear off somewhere. I can't send him anywhere. Oh dear, I mean, what a mess!... I mean, oh dear, what a mess I'm in!...', he thought.

Thus in full appreciation of the mess he was in, our hero resolved upon a two-hour passive role waiting for Petrushka. He walked around the room smoking for about an hour of the time, then he dropped his pipe and sat down with some book, then lay down on the couch, then took up his pipe again, then again started running around the room. He would have liked to do a bit of reasoning, but he could not reason about anything at all. Finally the agony of his passive state grew to the final degree, and Mr Golyadkin resolved to take a certain measure. 'Petrushka will arrive in another hour,' he thought, 'I can give the key to the yardman, while in the meantime I, you know... I'll investigate the matter, I'll investigate my part of the matter.' Without losing time and hurrying to investigate the matter, Mr Golyadkin took his hat, left the room, locked the apartment, dropped in on the yardman, handed him the key together with a ten-kopek coin – Mr Golyadkin had become unusually generous somehow – and set off to where he needed to go. Mr Golyadkin set off on foot, first to the Izmailovsky Bridge. About half an hour passed in walking. Reaching the objective of his journey, he went straight into the courtyard of the building he knew and glanced at the windows of State Councillor Berendeyev's apartment. Besides the three windows with their red curtains drawn, the remainder were all dark. 'Olsufy Ivanovich probably has no guests today,' thought Mr Golyadkin, 'they're probably all sitting at home now by themselves.' After standing outside for some time, our hero already wanted to resolve on something. But a resolution was evidently not fated to be reached. Mr Golyadkin changed his mind, gave it up as a bad job and went back into the street. 'No, I shouldn't have come here. Whatever am I going to do here?... But now it'd be better if I, you know... and I'll investigate the matter personally.' Having taken this decision, Mr Golyadkin set off to his Ministry. The journey was not a short one, and in addition it was terribly muddy, and the thickest flakes of wet snow were falling heavily. But at the present time there did not seem to be any difficulties for our hero. As far as getting soaked was concerned, he had got soaked, it is true, and had also got not a little muddy, 'well so be it, but at the same time the objective has been achieved'. And indeed, Mr Golyadkin was already approaching his objective. The dark mass of the huge government building had already loomed black in the distance before him. 'Wait!' he thought, 'where am I going, and what am I going to do here? Suppose I find out where he lives; but in the meantime Petrushka's probably already returned and brought me a reply. I'm just wasting my precious time, I've just wasted my time like this. Well, never mind; it can all still be put right. However, shouldn't I really just drop in on Vakhrameyev? Well, no! I'll do it later... Oh, there was no need to come out at all. No, I've just got that sort of character! It's a knack, whether it's necessary or not, I always manage to run on ahead somehow... Hm... what's the time? It's nine, for sure. Petrushka may arrive and not find me at home. I've done an utterly stupid thing, coming out... Oh dear, what a job this is!'

Thus sincerely acknowledging that he had done an utterly stupid thing, our hero ran back to his home on Shestilavochnaya. He got back tired and worn out. What is more, he learnt from the yardman that Petrushka had not even thought of appearing. 'Well, then! I had a presentiment of this,' thought our hero, 'and in the meantime it's already nine o'clock. Ah, what a good-for-nothing he is! He's always getting drunk somewhere! Lord God of mine! I mean, what a day it's turned out to my hapless lot!' Reflecting and lamenting in this way,

Mr Golyadkin unlocked his apartment, got some light, got completely undressed, smoked a pipe, and, exhausted, tired, jaded, hungry, he lay down on the couch to wait for Petrushka. The candle burnt down dimly, the light flickered on the walls... Mr Golyadkin gazed and gazed, thought and thought, and he finally fell asleep like a dead man.

He awoke when it was already late. The candle had burnt down almost completely, it was smoking and was ready to go out entirely at any moment. Mr Golyadkin leapt up, shook himself and remembered everything, absolutely everything. Behind the partition Petrushka's heavy snoring rang out. Mr Golyadkin rushed to the window – not a light anywhere. He opened the transom – it was quiet; it was as if the city had become deserted, was sleeping. It was about two or three o'clock then; so it was: the clock behind the partition strained itself and struck two. Mr Golyadkin rushed behind the partition.

Somehow, and moreover after lengthy efforts, he shook Petrushka awake and managed to sit him up on the bed. During this time the candle went out completely. Some ten minutes passed before Mr Golyadkin managed to find another candle and light it. During this time Petrushka managed to fall asleep once again. 'You're such a swine, you're such a good-for-nothing!' said Mr Golyadkin, shaking him awake once more, 'will you get up, will you wake up?' After half an hour's efforts Mr Golyadkin managed, however, to rouse his servant completely and to drag him out from behind the partition. Only at this point did our hero see that Petrushka was, as they say, dead drunk and could scarcely stay on his feet.

'You're such a ne'er-do-well!' shouted Mr Golyadkin. 'You're such a brigand! You've done for me! Good Lord, what can he have done with the letter? Alas! Oh, my Creator, well, how is it... And why did I write it? And I just had to write it! I got carried away, idiot, with self-respect! Went off after self-respect! There's self-respect for you, you villain, you, there's self-respect for you!... Well, you! What on earth have you done with the letter, you brigand, you? Who on earth have you given it to?...'

'I haven't given any letter to anyone; and I never had any letter... there!'

Mr Golyadkin wrung his hands in despair.

'Listen, Pyotr... you listen, you listen to me...'

'I'm listening…'

'Where did you go? Answer…'

'Where did I go?… I went to see some good people! What else?'

'Oh, my Lord God! Where did you go first? Were you at the Ministry?… You listen, Pyotr; perhaps you're drunk?'

'Me, drunk? May I be struck dead on the spot, with a hey nonny no – there…'

'No, no, it's all right that you're drunk… I was just asking; it's good that you're drunk; I've nothing against it, Petrushka, I've nothing against… Perhaps you've just forgotten for a bit, but still remember. Come on, try and remember, did you see Vakhrameyev, the clerk – did you or didn't you?'

'I didn't, and there never was any such clerk. Even now…'

'No, no, Pyotr! No, Petrusha, I mean, I've nothing against it. I mean, you can see I've nothing against… Well, what's so bad? Well, it's cold out, damp, well, a man had a bit to drink, well, that's all right… I'm not angry. I've had a drink today myself, old fellow… Now own up, try and remember, old fellow: did you see the clerk Vakhrameyev?'

'Well, since that's the way it's gone now, then, to tell the truth, then I did, even now…'

'Well, that's good, Petrusha, that's good that you did. You see, I'm not angry… Well, well,' our hero continued, coaxing his servant still more, patting him on the shoulder and smiling at him, 'well, you had a little drop, you swine… had a drop for ten kopeks, did you? What a rascal you are! Well, that's all right; well, you can see I'm not angry… I'm not angry, old fellow, I'm not angry…'

'No, as you wish, sir, but I'm not a rascal… I just dropped in on some good people, but I'm not a rascal, and never have been a rascal…'

'Oh, no, Petrusha, no! You listen, Pyotr: I've nothing against it, have I? I'm not criticising you when I call you a rascal, am I? I'm saying it to comfort you, aren't I? I'm saying it in the noble sense. That means, Petrusha, it can be flattering to a person if you say to him that he's a real sly one, a crafty chap, that he's nobody's fool and won't let anyone deceive him. Some people like that… Well, well, it's all right! Well, you just tell me, Petrusha, frankly now, candidly, as to a friend… well, did you see the clerk Vakhrameyev and did he give you the address?'

'Gave the address too, also gave the address too. A good clerk! And your master, he says, is a good man too, a very good man, he says; I, he says, tell him, he says, pay my respects, he says, to your master, thank him and tell him that I, he says, like him; that, he says, is how much I respect your master! For the fact, he says, that you, your master, he says, Petrusha, is a good man, he says, and you, he says, are a good man as well, Petrusha – there…'

'Oh, my Lord God! And the address, the address, you Judas, you?' Mr Golyadkin uttered these last words almost in a whisper.

'And the address… and he gave the address.'

'He did? Well, where does he live then, Golyadkin, Golyadkin the civil servant, the Titular Councillor?'

'And you'll find Golyadkin, he says, in Shestilavochnaya Street. As you go, he says, into Shestilavochnaya, then to the right, up the stairs, to the third floor. And that's where, he says, you'll find Golyadkin…'

'You scoundrel, you!' shouted our hero, who had finally lost his patience. 'You brigand, you! I mean, that's me; I mean, you're talking about me. But then there's the other Golyadkin; I'm talking about the other one, you scoundrel, you!'

'Well, as you wish! What's it to me! As you wish – there!…'

'And the letter, the letter…'

'What letter? There wasn't any letter, and I didn't see any letter.'

'But what on earth have you done with it – you blackguard, you?!'

'Handed it over, handed the letter over. Pay my respects, he says, thank him; your master's a good man, he says. Pay my respects, he says, to your master.'

'But who was it that said it? Was it Golyadkin said it?'

Petrushka was silent for a little and gave the broadest grin, looking his master straight in the eye.

'You listen, you brigand, you!' began Mr Golyadkin, choking, losing control in his fury, 'what have you done to me? You tell me, what have you done to me? You've done for me, you villain, you! Taken the head from my shoulders, you Judas, you!'

'Well, as you wish now! What's it to me?' said Petrusha in a decisive tone, retreating behind the partition.

'Come here, come here, you brigand, you!…'

'I won't come to you now, I won't come at all. What's it to me? I'll go to good people… And good people live in honesty, good people live without falsity and they never come in twos…'

Mr Golyadkin's hands and feet turned to ice and his breath was taken away.

'Yes, sir,' continued Petrushka, 'they never come in twos, they don't upset God and honest men…'

'You ne'er-do-well, you're drunk! You go to sleep now, you brigand, you! But you'll catch it tomorrow,' said Mr Golyadkin in a barely audible voice. And as for Petrushka, he mumbled something else; then he could be heard lying down on his bed in a way that made the bed crack, yawning protractedly, stretching, and finally starting to snore in the sleep, as they say, of the innocent. Mr Golyadkin was neither dead nor alive. Petrushka's behaviour, his hints, very strange, albeit vague, over which there was consequently no cause to get angry, all the more since it was a drunk talking, and, finally, the whole malignant turn the matter had taken – all this had rocked Mr Golyadkin to his foundations. 'What possessed me to give him a talking to in the middle of the night?' said our hero, his whole body trembling from some morbid sensation. 'And I was foolish enough to get involved with a drunk! What sense can you expect from a drunk? Every word's a lie. Still, what was it he was hinting at, brigand that he is? Lord God! And why did I write all those letters, I, murderer; I, suicide that I am! I can't keep quiet! I had to give myself away! I mean, so what! You die, you're like a rag, but oh, no, off you go with self-respect, my honour's injured, I say, I need to go and save my honour, I say! Suicide that I am!'

Thus spoke Mr Golyadkin, sitting on his couch and not daring to stir in his terror. Suddenly his eyes fixed on an object that excited his attention in the highest degree. In terror – was the object that had excited his attention not an illusion, not a trick of the imagination? – he reached out his hand to it with hope, with timidity, with indescribable curiosity… No, not a trick! not an illusion! A letter, definitely a letter, certainly a letter, and addressed to him… Mr Golyadkin picked the letter up from the table. His heart was beating terribly. 'That scoundrel must have brought it,' he thought, 'and put it down here and then forgotten; it must have all happened like that; it must have all happened just like that…' The letter was from the clerk Vakhrameyev, a young colleague and at one time friend of Mr Golyadkin's. 'Anyway, I had a premonition of it all in advance,' thought our hero, 'and also a premonition of everything that will now be in the letter…' The letter ran as follows:

Dear sir, Yakov Petrovich!
Your man is drunk and you'll get nothing sensible out of him; for this reason I prefer to reply in writing. I hasten to inform you that the commission laid upon me by yourself and consisting in the transfer of a letter through my hands to a person known to you, I consent to fulfil in all faith and exactitude. This person, very well known to you, and who for me has now taken the place of a friend and whose name I herein pass over in silence (for the reason that I do not wish to blacken unjustly the reputation of a perfectly innocent man), is lodging here with us, in Karolina Ivanovna's apartment, in that very room where previously, during your stay here, the visiting infantry officer from Tambov was lodged. However, this person you can find anywhere among men honest and sincere in heart, which cannot be said for some. My contacts with you I intend to cease from this day forward; it is not possible for us to continue in an amicable tone and in the former harmonious air of our comradeship, and for that reason I request you, my dear sir, immediately upon receipt of this my candid letter, to send the two silver roubles owing to me for the razors of foreign manufacture I sold to you on credit, if you will be so good as to recall, seven months ago during the period of your residence here at Karolina Ivanovna's, whom I respect with all my soul. I am acting in this way because you, according to the accounts of discerning people, have lost your self-respect and reputation and have become a danger to the morality of innocent and untainted people, for certain persons live other than by the truth and, moreover, their words are false and their loyal air suspect. People capable of intervening over the insult to Karolina Ivanovna, who has always been of good conduct and, secondly, an honest woman, and, in addition, a spinster, albeit not young in years, yet at the same time

of good foreign family, can be found anytime and anywhere, a fact to which certain persons asked me to refer in this my letter in passing and speaking for myself. In any event you will learn everything in good time, if you have not learnt yet, despite the fact that, according to the accounts of discerning people, you have given yourself a bad name in every corner of the capital and, consequently, might already have been given in many places, dear sir, appropriate information about yourself. In conclusion to my letter I inform you, my dear sir, that the person known to you, whose name I do not mention here for obvious noble reasons, is highly respected by right-thinking people; moreover, is of a cheerful and pleasant disposition, is successful both at work and also among all judicious people, is true to his word and friendship, and does not insult behind their backs those with whom, when face to face, he enjoys friendly relations.

In any event I remain
Your humble servant
N. Vakhrameyev.

P.S. Get rid of your man: he's a drunkard and in all probability causes you a lot of trouble, and take on Yevstafy, who used to work for us and who now finds himself without a position. Your present servant is not only a drunkard, but, moreover, a thief, for last week he sold a pound of sugar in lump form to Karolina Ivanovna at a reduced price, which, in my opinion, he could not have done other than by having thieved from you in a cunning manner, bit by bit and at various times. I write this to you, wishing you well, despite the fact that certain persons know only how to insult and deceive everybody, and primarily those who are honest and of good character; moreover, they revile them behind their backs and represent them in an inverted way, solely out of envy and because they cannot call themselves the same.

V.

After reading Vakhrameyev's letter, our hero remained for a long time yet in an immobile pose on his couch. Some new light was breaking through all the unclear and mysterious fog which had been surrounding him for two days now. Our hero was beginning in part to understand… He meant to try and get up from the couch and take a turn or two about the room, in order to refresh himself, somehow to collect his shattered thoughts, direct them at a certain object and then, having put himself to rights a little, to give his position mature reflection. But no sooner did he mean to rise a little than immediately, in feebleness and impotence, he fell back again into his former place. 'Of course, I had a premonition of all this in advance; however, the way he writes, and what's the direct sense of these words? Suppose I know the sense; but where will it lead? If he'd said it straight: here, so to speak, it's like this and like this, you must do this and this, and I'd have carried it out. The shape, the turn this business has taken is becoming so unpleasant! Ah, if only I could get to tomorrow more quickly and more quickly get down to business! For now I know what to do. It's like this, so to speak, I'll say, I agree with the arguments, I shan't sell my honour, but, you know… if you will; incidentally, him, this certain person, this inauspicious figure, how did he get mixed up in it? And why precisely did he get mixed up in it? Ah, if only I could get to tomorrow quickly! They'll give me a bad name until then, they're scheming, working to spite me! The main thing is, I mustn't lose any time, and now, for example, I can at least get a letter written and just let it be known that there's this and this, I'll say, and I agree to that and that. And first thing tomorrow I'll send it off, and I'll get going early myself, you know… and I'll move against them from the opposite direction and forestall them, the darlings… They'll give me a bad name, and that's that!'

Mr Golyadkin shifted his paper, picked up his pen and wrote the following missive in response to Provincial Secretary Vakhrameyev's letter:

> *Dear sir, Nestor Ignatyevich!*
> *With surprise, grievous to my heart, did I read your letter, so insulting to me, since I clearly see that in referring to certain improper persons and certain people with false loyalty you mean me. With true sorrow I see what far-reaching roots slander has developed so quickly and successfully to the detriment of my*

prosperity, my honour and my good name. And all the more grievous and insulting is it that even honest people, with a truly noble mode of thought and, most importantly, endowed with a direct and open character, withdraw from the interests of noble people and affix themselves with the best qualities of their heart to noxious lice – which in our difficult and immoral times have unfortunately multiplied greatly and extremely disloyally. In conclusion I shall say that the debt of mine you mention, two silver roubles, I shall consider it a sacred duty to return to you in all its fullness.

So far as your allusions are concerned, my dear sir, regarding a certain person of the female sex, regarding the intentions, calculations and various designs of that person, I shall tell you, my dear sir, that I dimly and vaguely understood all those allusions. Allow me, my dear sir, to preserve unstained the noble mode of my thoughts and my honest name. In any event I am prepared to condescend to explanations in person, preferring the reliability of the personal to the written, and, moreover, I am prepared to enter into various peaceable and, it goes without saying, reciprocal agreements. To this end I request you, my dear sir, to convey to this person my readiness for a personal agreement and, moreover, to request the person to appoint a time and place of meeting. It was bitter for me to read, my dear sir, allusions to the effect that I had insulted you, had betrayed our long-standing friendship and spoken ill of you. I ascribe all this to misunderstanding, the foul slander, envy and ill-will of those whom I can justly call my most bitter enemies. But they probably do not know that innocence is already strong in its innocence alone, that certain persons' shamelessness, insolence and outrageous familiarity will sooner or later earn them the universal stigma of scorn, and that those persons will perish of nothing other than their own impropriety and corruptness of heart. In conclusion I request you, my dear sir, to convey to those persons that their strange pretension and ignoble, fantastical desire to try to oust others from the limits occupied by those others by virtue of their existence in this world, and to occupy their place, are deserving of amazement, scorn, pity and, moreover, the madhouse; that, moreover, such relations are strictly forbidden by the laws, something which, in my opinion, is perfectly just, since all men should be content with their own places. There are limits to everything, and if this is a joke, then it is an improper joke – I shall say more: an utterly immoral one, for I dare to assure you, my dear sir, that my ideas propagated above regarding their places are purely moral.

> *In any event I have the honour to be*
> *Your humble servant*
> *Y. Golyadkin.*

10

All in all, it can be said that the occurrences of the previous day had shaken Mr Golyadkin to the foundations. Our hero slept very badly, that is, he was quite unable to get to sleep properly even for five minutes: it was as if some prankster had sprinkled something prickly into his bed. He spent the entire night in some sort of half-sleeping, half-waking state, turning over from side to side, from flank to flank, moaning, groaning, falling asleep for a minute, waking up again a minute later – and all this was accompanied by some strange anguish, vague recollections, shocking visions – in short, by everything unpleasant that one could possibly find... At times there would appear before him in some strange, mysterious half-light the figure of Andrei Filippovich – a dry figure, an angry figure, with a dry, harsh gaze and with a callously courteous reprimand... And no sooner did Mr Golyadkin begin to try to approach Andrei Filippovich in order, somehow, in one way or another, to justify himself before him and prove to him that he was not at all as his enemies had painted him – that he was like this and like that, and even possessed, above and beyond his ordinary, innate qualities, this one and that one – than there appeared at this point a figure known for his improper tendencies and by some most outrageous means immediately ruined all Mr Golyadkin's attempted initiatives, and here, almost before Mr Golyadkin's very eyes, he thoroughly blackened his reputation, trampled his self-respect into the dirt and then immediately occupied his place at work and in society. At other times Mr Golyadkin's head was stinging from some recently received and humiliatingly accepted slap, given either in social life or somehow in the course of his duties, against which slap it was hard to protest... And while Mr Golyadkin was beginning to rack his brains over the question why precisely it was hard to protest even against a slap like this – this same idea about the slap was meanwhile flowing imperceptibly into some other form – into the form of some particular vile act, minor or quite significant, that he had seen, heard, or himself recently carried out – and often carried out not even on a vile basis, not even out of some vile motive, but for no good reason – sometimes, for example, out of delicacy, another time because of his utter defencelessness, well, and, finally, for the reason... for the reason, in short, Mr Golyadkin knew very well, *why*! Here Mr Golyadkin blushed in his sleep and, suppressing his flush, mumbled to himself that, so to speak, here, for example, one could show strength of character, in this instance one could show significant firmness of character... and then he went and concluded that, 'so to speak, what's the use of firmness of character!... why remember it now!...' But most of all Mr Golyadkin was infuriated and irritated by the way that here, and at precisely such a moment, whether he was summoned or not, there appeared the figure known for the disgraceful and defamatory nature of his tendencies, and also, despite the fact that the business already seemed to be clear – also, there too, he mumbled with an improper little smile: 'so to speak, what on earth has firmness of character to do with anything, what, so to speak, firmness of character do you and I have, Yakov Petrovich!...' At times Mr Golyadkin dreamed that he was in a splendid group of people, known for its wit and for the noble tone of all those of whom it was composed; he dreamed that Mr Golyadkin in his turn excelled in respect of charm and wit, that everybody came to like him, even some of his enemies who were here too came to like him, which was very pleasant for Mr Golyadkin; he dreamed that everybody gave him precedence, and that, finally, Mr Golyadkin himself pleasantly overheard the host there and then, while taking one of the guests aside, praising Mr Golyadkin... and suddenly, out of the blue there again appeared the figure known for his disloyalty and bestial motives in the form of Mr Golyadkin junior, and straight away, at once, in a single moment, with his appearance alone, Golyadkin junior ruined all the triumph and all the glory of Mr Golyadkin senior, himself eclipsed Golyadkin senior, trampled Golyadkin senior into the dirt and, finally, clearly proved that the senior and at the same time genuine Golyadkin was not genuine at all, but fake, and that he was genuine, that, finally, Golyadkin senior was not at all what he seemed, but this and that, and consequently ought not, and had no right to belong to the society of people loyal and of good tone. And all this was done so quickly that Mr Golyadkin senior did not even have time to open his mouth before everybody devoted themselves body and soul to the disgraceful and fake Mr Golyadkin and with the deepest contempt rejected him, the genuine and innocent Mr Golyadkin. Not a person remained whose opinion could not have been altered by the disgraceful Mr Golyadkin in his own particular way in a single moment. Not a person remained, not even the most insignificant of the whole group, to whom the worthless and false Mr Golyadkin could not have sucked up in his own particular way, in the most sickly manner, to whom he would not have crawled up in his own particular way, before whom he would not have smoked, as was his custom, something most pleasant and sweet, so that the person being enveloped in smoke only sniffed and sneezed until tears came into his eyes as a mark of his extreme pleasure. And, most important, all this was done in a moment: the quickness of movement of the suspect and worthless Mr Golyadkin was amazing! He would scarcely have the time, for example, to suck up to one, to earn his favour – before in the twinkling of an eye he was already with a second. He would lick and lick surreptitiously with the second, extract a little smile of goodwill, kick out with his short, rounded, quite, incidentally, coarse little leg, and there he already was with a third, and was now courting the third, with him too he would lick in the manner of a friend; you would not have time to open your mouth, you would not have time to register astonishment – before he was already with a fourth, and with the fourth already on the same terms – terrible: nothing less than sorcery! And all are pleased to see him, and all like him, and all praise him, and all proclaim in unison that his charm and the satirical tendency of his mind are better by far than the charm and satirical tendency of the genuine

Mr Golyadkin, and they put the genuine and innocent Mr Golyadkin to shame with this, and reject the truth-loving Mr Golyadkin, and now they drive the loyal Mr Golyadkin away with blows, and now they rain slaps down on the genuine Mr Golyadkin, known for his love for his neighbour!... In anguish, in horror, in fury, the suffering Mr Golyadkin ran out into the street and started trying to hire a cab so as to fly straight to His Excellency, and if not to him, then at the very least to Andrei Filippovich, but – it was awful! – the cabmen would not agree to take Mr Golyadkin at all, saying: 'we can't take two absolutely similar people, master; a good man strives to live honestly, Your Honour, and not just any old how, and never appears in twos.' In a paroxysm of shame the perfectly honest Mr Golyadkin looked around and did indeed satisfy himself with his own eyes that the cabmen and Petrushka, who was in cahoots with them, were all within their rights; for the corrupt Mr Golyadkin was indeed there too, beside him, not a great distance from him, and, following the vile customs of his morals, even here, even in this critical instance, was without fail preparing to do something very improper and by no means displaying the particular nobility of character which is normally acquired during one's education – the nobility in which the repulsive Mr Golyadkin the Second so gloried at every convenient opportunity. Beside himself, in shame and despair, the mortified and absolutely just Mr Golyadkin rushed where his nose led him, into the hands of fate, wherever he might be carried; but with his every step, with every blow of his foot on the granite of the pavement, there leapt out, as if from beneath the ground, a Mr Golyadkin exactly identical, utterly similar and repulsive in the corruptness of his heart. And immediately upon their appearance, all these utterly similar ones set off running, one after another and in a long chain, like a string of geese, stretched out and stumping along behind Mr Golyadkin senior so that there was nowhere to flee from the utterly similar ones – so that Mr Golyadkin, worthy of pity in every way, had his breath taken away in horror – so that in the end there came into being a terrible multitude of the utterly similar ones – so that in the end the entire capital was filled to overflowing with utterly similar ones, and a police officer, seeing such a violation of propriety, was forced to take all these utterly similar ones by the scruff of the neck and set them in the sentry box that happened to be close at hand... Turning rigid and ice-cold with fear, our hero woke up and, turning rigid and ice-cold with fear, he sensed that even in the real world the time was spent scarcely any more cheerfully... Hard, tortuous it was... Such anguish was coming upon him, it was as if someone were eating the heart out from his breast...

Finally Mr Golyadkin could bear it no longer. 'It simply won't happen!' he cried, resolutely rising a little from the bed, and, following this exclamation, he came to completely.

The day had evidently already begun long ago. It was unusually bright in the room somehow; rays of sunlight were filtering densely through the panes of the frost-covered windows and scattering abundantly around the room, which surprised Mr Golyadkin not a little; for only at midday perhaps did the sun look in on him in its course; previously there had almost never been such exceptions in the flow of the heavenly body, so far, at least, as Mr Golyadkin himself could recall. Our hero had only just had the time to wonder at this when the wall clock behind the partition began to buzz and, in this way, prepared itself fully to strike. 'Ah, there,' thought Mr Golyadkin, and in anxious expectation prepared to listen... But, to Mr Golyadkin's complete and final defeat, his clock exerted all its effort and struck just once. 'What sort of business is this?' exclaimed our hero, leaping out of bed completely. As he was, not believing his ears, he rushed behind the partition. The clock really did show one. Mr Golyadkin glanced at Petrushka's bed; but there was not even a sniff of Petrushka in the room: his bed had evidently been tidied and left long before; neither were his boots anywhere – an undoubted sign that Petrushka really was out. Mr Golyadkin rushed to the doors: the doors were locked. 'Where on earth is Petrushka?' he continued in a whisper, all in terrible agitation and feeling a quite significant trembling in all his limbs... Suddenly a thought flew through his head... Mr Golyadkin rushed to his table, examined it, rummaged around – so it was! His letter of the day before to Vakhrameyev was not there... Neither was Petrushka behind the partition at all; the wall clock showed one, and in Vakhrameyev's letter of the day before some new points had been introduced, at first glance actually very vague points, but which were now perfectly explicable. Even Petrushka was, in the end, evidently a bribed Petrushka! Yes, yes, it was so!

'So it's there that the main knot was being tied!' exclaimed Mr Golyadkin, striking himself on the forehead, 'So it's in the nest of that miserly German woman that the main evil now all lurks! So she was just creating a strategic diversion, therefore, in directing me to the Izmailovsky Bridge – distracting my attention, confusing me (the worthless witch!) and thus carrying on her underhand plotting!!! Yes, it's so! If you just take a look at the business from this point of view, it'll all indeed be precisely so! And the appearance of the swine is now also fully explained: it's all one thing added to another. They've been keeping him for a long time now, preparing and storing him up for a rainy day. So that's how it is now, is it, how everything's turned out! How everything's been resolved! Ah well, never mind! The time is not yet lost!...' Here Mr Golyadkin remembered in horror that it was already after one o'clock in the afternoon. 'What if they've already had the time...' A groan burst out from his chest... 'But no, they're lying, they've not had the time – we'll see...' Somehow or other he got dressed, seized paper, a pen and dashed off the following missive:

> *My dear sir, Yakov Petrovich!*
>
> *Either you or me, but we can't go on together! And for that reason I declare to you that your strange, ridiculous and at the same time impossible desire to seem to be my twin and to pass yourself off as such will serve nothing other than your utter dishonour and defeat. And for that reason I request you, for your own good, to step aside and give way to men truly noble and with loyal objectives. Otherwise I am prepared to resolve even upon the most extreme measures. I lay down my pen and await... Anyway, I remain ready to be at your service – and to use pistols.*
>
> *Y. Golyadkin*

Our hero rubbed his hands energetically when he had finished the note. Then, pulling on his greatcoat and putting on his hat, he unlocked the apartment with a second, spare key and set off for the Ministry. He reached the Ministry, but could not make up his mind to go in; it really was too late already; Mr Golyadkin's watch showed half-past two. Suddenly an apparently very unimportant event resolved some of Mr Golyadkin's doubts: from around the corner of the Ministry building there suddenly appeared a panting and flushed little figure and stealthily, with the gait of a rat, it sneaked onto the porch and then immediately into the lobby. It was the scribe Ostafyev, a man very familiar to Mr Golyadkin, a man somewhat needy and prepared to do anything for a ten-kopek coin. Knowing Ostafyev's weak point and grasping that, after an absence on his vital personal business he had probably become even more than ever susceptible to ten kopeks, our hero resolved not to spare them and immediately sneaked onto the porch and then into the lobby too in Ostafyev's wake, called to him and with a mysterious air invited him to one side, into a secluded corner behind a huge iron stove. Having led him in there, our hero began his questioning.

'Well, then, my friend, how're things up there, you know... you know what I mean?...'

'Yes, sir, Your Honour, I wish Your Honour good health.'

'Good, my friend, good; and I'll show you my gratitude, dear friend. Well, do you see, how are they then, my friend?'

'What are you so good as to be asking, sir?' Here Ostafyev used his hand to give a little support to his mouth, which had accidentally fallen open.

'I'm, do you see, my friend, I, you know... but don't you go thinking anything... Well, then, is Andrei Filippovich here?...'

'Here, sir.'

'And the clerks are here?'

'And the clerks as well, sir, as they should be, sir.'

'And His Excellency as well?'

'And His Excellency as well, sir.' Here for a second time the scribe once again gave some support to his mouth, which had again fallen open, and he looked curiously and strangely somehow at Mr Golyadkin. At least so it seemed to our hero.

'And there's nothing in particular going on, my friend?'

'No, sir, not at all, sir.'

'And so, my dear friend, there isn't anything up there about me, you know, anything just… eh? It's for no reason, my friend, you understand?'

'No, sir, there's still nothing to be heard for the time being.' Here the scribe again gave some support to his mouth and again glanced strangely somehow at Mr Golyadkin. The thing is that our hero was now trying to penetrate Ostafyev's physiognomy, to read something in it, to see whether anything was being concealed. And it was, indeed, as if something were being concealed; the thing is that Ostafyev was becoming somehow more and more rude and dry and was now no longer entering into Mr Golyadkin's interests with the same sort of concern as at the start of the conversation. 'He's within his rights in part,' thought Mr Golyadkin, 'after all, what am I to him? Perhaps he's already even had something from the other side and that's why he was out on his vital personal business. But now I'll give him something too…' Mr Golyadkin realised the time for ten-kopek coins had come.

'There you are, dear friend…'

'I'm deeply grateful to Your Honour.'

'I'll give you still more.'

'Yes, Your Honour.'

'I'll give you still more now, this minute, and when the business is over I'll give you just as much again. Understand?'

The scribe was silent, standing to attention and looking fixedly at Mr Golyadkin.

'Well, tell me now: is there nothing to be heard about me?…'

'There still seems, for the time being… you know, sir… there's nothing for the time being, sir.' Ostafyev replied slowly and deliberately, also, like Mr Golyadkin too, observing a rather mysterious air, twitching his eyebrows a little, looking at the ground, trying to find the appropriate tone and, in short, trying with all his might to earn what had been promised, because what had been given he already considered his own and definitively acquired.

'And nothing has come up?'

'Not for the time being, sir.'

'But listen… you know… perhaps something will come up?'

'Later on, it goes without saying, perhaps something will come up, sir.'

'That's bad!' thought our hero.

'Listen, here's another one for you, my dear.'

'I'm deeply grateful to Your Honour.'

'Was Vakhrameyev here yesterday?'

'He was, sir.'

'And was there anybody else?… Can you remember, old fellow?'

The scribe rummaged in his recollections for a minute and did not remember anything appropriate.

'No, sir, there wasn't anybody else, sir.'

'Hm!' A silence ensued.

'Listen, old fellow, here's another one for you; tell me everything, all the ins and outs.'

'Yes, sir.' Ostafyev now stood there as good as gold: that was what Mr Golyadkin needed.

'Explain to me now, old fellow, what footing is he on?'

'Not a bad one, sir – a good one, sir,' replied the scribe, looking wide-eyed at Mr Golyadkin.

'That is, how good?'

'That is, all right, sir.' Here Ostafyev twitched his eyebrows meaningfully. However, he was becoming decidedly nonplussed and did not know what else he should say.

'That's bad!' thought Mr Golyadkin.

'Is there anything further between him and Vakhrameyev?'

'Well, everything's as it was before, sir.'

'Have a think, now.'

'There is something, so they say, sir.'

'Well, and what is it?'

Ostafyev gave his mouth some support with his hand.

'Is there a letter for me from that quarter?'

'Well, the watchman Mikheyev went to Vakhrameyev's apartment, sir, over there to that German woman of theirs, sir, so I'll go and ask, if that's what you want.'

'Do me the kindness, old fellow, for God's sake!… It's for no reason… Don't go thinking anything, old fellow, it's for no reason. And you ask around, old fellow, find out if anything's being prepared there on my account. How is it he's acting? That's what I need to know; so you find that out, dear friend, and later on I'll show my gratitude, dear friend…'

'Yes, sir, Your Honour, and Ivan Semyonych has taken your seat today, sir.'

'Ivan Semyonych! Ah! Yes! Surely not?'

'Andrei Filippovich directed him to sit there, sir…'

'Surely not? To do with what? Find that out, old fellow, for God's sake, find that out, old fellow; find it all out – and I'll show you my gratitude, my dear; that's what I want… But don't you go thinking anything, old fellow…'

'Yes, sir, yes, sir, I'll come down here straight away, sir. So aren't you coming in today then, Your Honour?'

'No, my friend; I'm only – I mean, I'm only – I've just come to have a look, dear friend, and later on I'll show you my gratitude too, my dear.'

'Yes, sir.' The scribe ran up the stairs quickly and zealously, and Mr Golyadkin remained on his own.

'This is bad,' he thought. 'Oh dear, this is bad, bad! Oh dear, this little business of ours… how bad it's looking now! What could it all mean? What precisely did some of that drunkard's hints mean, for example, and whose trickery is it? Ah! Now I know whose trickery it is. That's the sort of trickery it is. They probably found out and then they put… Still, what do I mean – *they* put? It was Andrei Filippovich that put him there, that Ivan Semyonovich; and anyway, why was it he put him there and with what precise aim did he put him there? They probably found out… That's Vakhrameyev's work; that is, not Vakhrameyev's, he's as thick as two short planks, that Vakhrameyev; but they're all working on his behalf, and they set that scoundrel loose here to the same end; and the one-eyed German's complained! I always suspected this whole intrigue wasn't so straightforward and there was definitely something in all this women's, this old women's gossip; I said as much to Krestyan Ivanovich too, "They've sworn,' I said, "to murder a man, speaking in the moral sense, and they've seized upon Karolina Ivanovna." No, there are experts at work here, it's clear! Here, my dear sir, the hand of an expert is at work, and not Vakhrameyev's. I've already said that Vakhrameyev's stupid, and this is… now I know who's working on behalf of them all here: it's the scoundrel working, the impostor! And it's to this alone he's clinging, which partly confirms his successes in high society too. But I really would like to know what footing he's on now… what is he to them? Only why on earth have they gone and taken Ivan Semyonovich? Why the devil did they need Ivan Semyonovich? As if they couldn't possibly have got anybody else. Still, whoever they sat there it would have been the same; but what I do know is that for a long time I've found him suspect, that Ivan Semyonovich, for a long time I've been taking note of him: such a vile little old man, horrible – they say he lends money and charges extortionate rates of interest. But it's all the Bear's handiwork of course. The Bear's mixed up in this whole business. That's how it started. It started at the Izmailovsky Bridge; that's how it started…' Here Mr Golyadkin pulled a face as though he had bitten into a lemon, probably having remembered something very unpleasant. 'Well, never mind anyway!' he thought. 'But all this time I've been wrapped up in my own thoughts. Now why is it that Ostafyev doesn't come? He's probably having a sit down or been held up somehow. It's even partly a good thing, you know, that I'm scheming like this and carrying on intrigues for myself. I only have to give Ostafyev ten kopeks and he's, you know… and he's on my side. Only the thing is this: is he definitely on my side; perhaps for their part they're also… and for their part, having reached an agreement with him, they're carrying on an intrigue. I mean, he looks a brigand, the villain, a pure brigand! He's concealing things, the rogue! "No, nothing," he says, and "I'm deeply, so to speak," he says, "grateful to you, Your Honour." You brigand, you!'

A noise was heard… Mr Golyadkin shrank down and jumped behind the stove. Somebody had come down the stairs and gone out into the street. 'Who could that have been setting off now?' thought our hero to himself. A minute later somebody's footsteps were heard again… Here Mr Golyadkin could not resist and poked the tiniest little end of his nose out from behind his parapet – poked it out and immediately whipped back, as though somebody had pricked his nose with a pin. On this occasion it was clear who was passing – that is, the rogue, the schemer and the profligate – he was passing according to his custom with his vile, quick little steps, pattering and throwing out his little legs as if he were intending to kick somebody. 'Villain!' said our hero to himself. Still, Mr Golyadkin could not help but notice that under the villain's arm was a huge green portfolio that belonged to His Excellency. 'Again he's on a special mission,' thought Mr Golyadkin, flushing and shrinking even more than before in annoyance. No sooner had Mr Golyadkin junior flashed past Mr Golyadkin senior without noticing him at all, than for a third time somebody's footsteps were heard, and on this occasion Mr Golyadkin guessed that the footsteps were a scribe's. And the little figure of a scribe with greased-down hair did indeed glance in behind the stove at him; however, the little figure was not Ostafyev's, but that of another scribe nicknamed Scriblet. This astonished Mr Golyadkin. 'Why on earth has he involved others in the secret?' thought our hero. 'Such barbarians! They hold nothing sacred!'

'Well, what is it, my friend?' he said, addressing Scriblet. 'Who are you from, my friend?...'

'Well, sir, about your little matter, sir. There's no news from anyone for the time being, sir. But if there is anything, we'll let you know, sir.'

'And Ostafyev?...'

'He can't possibly make it, Your Honour. His Excellency has passed through the department twice already, and I've not got the time now either.'

'Thank you, my dear, thank you... Only you tell me...'

'Honest to God, there's no time, sir... They're asking for us every minute, sir... But you be so good as to stand here a little longer, sir, then if there's anything regarding your little matter, sir, then we'll let you know, sir...'

'No, my friend, you tell me...'

'Permit me, sir; I've not got the time, sir,' said Scriblet, pulling away from Mr Golyadkin, who had seized him by his coat flap, 'truly, I can't, sir. You be so good as to stand here a little longer, sir, then we'll let you know.'

'One moment, one moment, my friend! One moment, my friend! This is what, now; here's a letter, my friend; and I'll show you my gratitude, my dear.'

'Yes, sir.'

'Try and give it, my dear, to Mr Golyadkin.'

'Golyadkin?'

'Yes, my friend, to Mr Golyadkin.'

'Very well, sir; as soon as I clear off, I'll take it. And you stand here for the time being. No one'll see you here…'

'No, I, don't you go thinking, my friend… I mean, I'm not standing here so that I won't be seen by anyone. And I'll be somewhere else now, my friend… I'll be over there in the side street. There's a coffee house there; well, I'll be waiting there, and you, if anything happens, you let me know about everything, understand?'

'Very well, sir. Only please let me go; I understand…'

'And I'll show you my gratitude, my dear!' Mr Golyadkin called after Scriblet, who had finally freed himself… 'Seems a rogue, got ruder later on,' thought our hero, stealthily emerging from behind the stove. 'There's another catch here. That's clear… At first he was "yes, sir, no sir"… Still, he really was in a hurry; perhaps there's a lot of work up there. And His Excellency has walked around the department twice… What might that be in connection with?… Oof! Well, never mind! Perhaps it's all right anyway, but now we shall see…'

Here Mr Golyadkin was on the point of opening the door and already meant to go out into the street, when suddenly, at that very moment, His Excellency's carriage made a clatter by the porch. Mr Golyadkin had not had time to collect himself before the carriage doors opened from within and the gentleman who had been sitting inside it jumped out onto the porch. The new arrival was none other than that same Mr Golyadkin junior who had left some ten minutes before. Mr Golyadkin senior remembered that the director's apartment was a stone's throw away. 'He was on his special mission,' thought our hero to himself. Meanwhile, Mr Golyadkin junior, grabbing from the carriage the fat green portfolio and some other papers too, and giving, finally, some order to the coachman, opened the door, almost hitting Mr Golyadkin senior with it, and, deliberately not noticing him and consequently acting in this way to spite him, he set off at a rapid pace up the Ministry staircase. 'This is bad!' thought Mr Golyadkin, 'oh dear, what's our little matter got mixed up with now! Look at him, Good Lord!' Our hero stood motionless for about another half a minute; finally he made up his mind. Without thinking for long, and feeling, moreover, a powerful palpitation in his heart and a trembling in all his limbs, he ran up the staircase after his friend. 'Ah! What will be, will be; what's it to me, then? I'm not to blame in this business,' he thought, taking off his hat, greatcoat and galoshes in the hallway.

When Mr Golyadkin entered his department it was already fully dusk. Neither Andrei Filippovich nor Anton Antonovich was in the room. They were both in the director's office with reports; and the director, as was known from rumours, was in his turn hurrying to get to his superior. As a result of these circumstances, and also because the dusk had stirred itself in here too and the working day was drawing to a close, some of the clerks, and primarily the youngsters, were, at the very moment when our hero entered, busy with a sort of inactivity, getting together, conversing, talking, laughing – and some of the most youthful, some of the most unofficial officials, that is, were surreptitiously, and to the accompaniment of the general hum, making up a game of pitch-and-toss in the corner by the window. Aware of decorum and feeling at this particular time a sort of special need to achieve some gain and 'get in', Mr Golyadkin immediately approached one or two people with whom he was on better terms to wish them good day, etc. But his colleagues replied to Mr Golyadkin's greeting strangely somehow. He was unpleasantly struck by a sort of universal coldness, dryness, even, it might be said, by a sort of sternness of reception. Nobody gave him their hand. Some simply said 'hello' and moved off; others only nodded, one or two simply turned away, indicating that they had noticed nothing; finally, some – and what was most hurtful to Mr Golyadkin, some of the most unofficial youngsters – lads who, as Mr Golyadkin justly expressed himself about them, knew only how to play pitch-and-toss, given the opportunity, and hang about the place – little by little surrounded Mr Golyadkin, grouped around him and almost barred his way out. They all looked at him with a sort of insulting curiosity.

It was a bad sign. Mr Golyadkin sensed this and prudently prepared for his part to notice nothing. Suddenly an utterly unexpected event completely, as they say, finished off and annihilated Mr Golyadkin.

In the little crowd of young colleagues surrounding him and, as if on purpose at the most anguished moment for Mr Golyadkin, there appeared Mr Golyadkin junior, cheerful as ever, with a little smile as ever, frivolous as ever too, in short, a mischievous one, a frisky one, a crawly one, a chuckling one, light of tongue and foot, as always, as before, just as yesterday, for example, at a very unpleasant moment for Mr Golyadkin senior. Grinning, fidgeting, pattering, with a little smile that simply said to everyone 'good evening', he wormed his way into the crowd of clerks, shook one by the hand, patted another on the shoulder, gave a third a little hug, explained to a fourth for precisely what purpose he had been used by His Excellency, where he had gone, what he had done, what he had brought back with him; a fifth, and probably his best friend, he gave a smacking kiss right on the lips – in short, everything was happening exactly as in Mr Golyadkin senior's dream. Having had his fill of jumping about, and having done with everyone in his own particular way, having dealt with them all to his own advantage, whether it was necessary or not, having smooched to his heart's content with them all, Mr Golyadkin junior suddenly, and probably by mistake, still not yet having had time to notice his oldest friend, reached out his hand to Mr Golyadkin senior too. Probably also by mistake, although actually he had had quite enough time to notice the ignoble Mr Golyadkin junior, our hero immediately and greedily seized the hand stretched out to him so unexpectedly and shook it in the firmest, most friendly manner, shook it with some strange, completely unexpected inner impulse, with some lachrymose feeling. Whether our hero was deceived by the first impulse of his improper enemy, or whether he was simply at a loss, or felt and realised in the depths of his soul the full degree of his defencelessness, is difficult to say. But the fact is that Mr Golyadkin senior, in full health, by his own free will and in front of witnesses, solemnly shook the hand of the man he had called his mortal enemy. But what then was the astonishment, the frenzy and the fury, what then was the horror and shame of Mr Golyadkin senior, when his foe and mortal enemy, the ignoble Mr Golyadkin junior, noticing the mistake of the persecuted, innocent man he had treacherously deceived, without any shame, without feelings, without compassion and conscience, suddenly, with unendurable effrontery and rudeness, tore his hand free of Mr Golyadkin senior's hand; what is more, he gave his hand a shake as though it had been soiled by all this in something altogether unpleasant; what is more, he spat to one side, accompanying everything with the most insulting gesture; what is more, he took out his hand-kerchief and on the spot, in the most unseemly way, used it to wipe each one of his fingers that had rested for a moment in the hand of Mr Golyadkin senior. Acting in this way, Mr Golyadkin junior, as was his vile little custom, deliberately looked around, made sure that everyone had seen his behaviour, looked everyone in the eye and evidently sought to inspire in everyone all that was most unfavourable regarding Mr Golyadkin. The behaviour of the repugnant Mr Golyadkin junior seemed to arouse the universal indignation of the surrounding clerks; even the empty-headed youngsters demonstrated their displeasure. All around arose the murmuring of voices. The general impulse could not escape Mr Golyadkin senior's ears; but meanwhile, suddenly, a timely little joke came boiling up on Mr Golyadkin junior's lips and shattered, annihilated our hero's last hopes, tipping the balance once more in favour of his mortal and worthless enemy.

'This is our Russian Faublas[17], gentlemen; allow me to recommend young Faublas to you,' squeaked Mr Golyadkin junior, pattering and winding his way between the clerks and indicating to them the frozen, and at the same time frenzied, real Mr Golyadkin. 'Give us a kiss, dear!' he continued with unendurable familiarity, moving towards the man he had traitorously insulted. The worthless Mr Golyadkin junior's little joke seemed to have found a response where it was intended, all the more as it contained a crafty allusion to a certain circumstance, evidently already public and known to all. Our hero felt the hand of his enemies heavy upon his shoulders. However, he had already made up his mind. With a burning gaze, with a pale face, with a fixed smile, he somehow struggled out of the crowd and with uneven, quickened steps made his way directly to His Excellency's office. In the penultimate room he met with Andrei Filippovich, who had just left His Excellency, and although here in the room there were a fair number of various other people, completely extraneous for Mr Golyadkin at the present moment, still our hero did not even think of paying any attention to such a circumstance. Directly, resolutely, boldly, almost amazing himself and inwardly praising himself for boldness, without losing time he made a direct assault on Andrei Filippovich, who was pretty astonished at such an unexpected attack.

'Ah!... What do you... what do you want?' asked the head of department, not listening to Mr Golyadkin, who had stumbled over some of his words.

'Andrei Filippovich, I... may I, Andrei Filippovich, have now, immediately and eye to eye, a conversation with His Excellency?' said our hero volubly and distinctly, fixing the most resolute gaze on Andrei Filippovich.

'What, sir? Of course not, sir.' Andrei Filippovich measured Mr Golyadkin from head to toe with his gaze.

'I say all this, Andrei Filippovich, as I'm surprised that no one here will denounce an impostor and a villain.'

'Wha-at, sir?'

'A villain, Andrei Filippovich.'

'And to whom does it please you to refer in such a way?'

'To a certain person, Andrei Filippovich. I am alluding, Andrei Filippovich, to a certain person; I'm within my rights... I think, Andrei Filippovich, that high-ranking officials should encourage such impulses,' Mr Golyadkin added, evidently forgetting himself, 'Andrei Filippovich... you can probably see for yourself, Andrei Filippovich, that this noble impulse signifies my good intent in its various forms – so far as accepting a superior as a father goes, Andrei Filippovich – I accept, so to speak, my beneficent superiors as fathers and entrust them blindly with my fate. It's like this, so to speak... that's how it is...' Here Mr Golyadkin's voice began to quaver, his face went all red, and two tears ran onto both his sets of eyelashes.

Listening to Mr Golyadkin, Andrei Filippovich was so surprised that he somehow involuntarily staggered a pace or two backwards. Then he looked around in disquiet... It is hard to say how the matter would have ended... But suddenly the door of His Excellency's office opened, and he himself came out, accompanied by some officials. Behind them stretched everybody who was in the room. His Excellency called Andrei Filippovich over and set off alongside him, striking up a conversation about some business matters. When everyone had moved off and left the room, Mr Golyadkin came to his senses too. Falling quiet, he took shelter under the wing of Anton Antonovich Setochkin, who was in his turn stumping along last of all and, as it seemed to Mr Golyadkin, with the sternest and most preoccupied air. 'I've said too much here as well,' he thought to himself, 'oh well, never mind.'

'I hope that you at least, Anton Antonovich, will consent to listen to me and investigate my situation,' he said quietly and in a voice that was still quavering a little from agitation. 'Rejected by all, I turn to you. I'm still perplexed now as to the meaning of Andrei Filippovich's words, Anton Antonovich. Explain them to me, if you can…'

'Everything will be explained in good time, sir,' replied Anton Antonovich sternly and deliberately and, as it seemed to Mr Golyadkin, with an air that let it be clearly known that Anton Antonovich had no desire whatsoever to continue the conversation. 'You'll learn everything in the near future, sir. This very day you'll be formally notified about everything.'

'What on earth is this "formally", Anton Antonovich? Why so specifically "formally", sir?' asked our hero timidly.

'It's not for us, Yakov Petrovich, to discuss how our superiors decide things.'

'But why our superiors, Anton Antonovich,' said Mr Golyadkin, becoming still more timid, 'but why our superiors? I can see no reason why our superiors need to be troubled here, Anton Antonovich… Perhaps you want to say something regarding what happened yesterday, Anton Antonovich?'

'Not at all, sir, not what happened yesterday, sir; there's something else here where you're not up to scratch, sir.'

'What is it that's not up to scratch, Anton Antonovich? It doesn't seem to me, Anton Antonovich, that there's anything about me that's not up to scratch.'

'And who were you intending to be sly with?' Anton Antonovich sharply cut in on the utterly dumbfounded Mr Golyadkin. Mr Golyadkin winced and turned as white as a sheet.

'Of course, Anton Antonovich,' he said in a scarcely audible voice, 'if one pays heed to the voice of slander and listens to one's enemies, without accepting justification from the other side, then, of course… of course, Anton Antonovich, then one can indeed suffer, Anton Antonovich, suffer innocently and for nothing.'

'Quite so, sir; and your improper action to the detriment of the reputation of the noble young woman of that virtuous, esteemed and well-known family that was a benefactor to you?'

'What action is that, Anton Antonovich?'

'Quite so, sir. And regarding another young woman – poor, maybe, yet still of honest foreign origin, don't you know, sir, of your praiseworthy action there either?'

'Allow me, Anton Antonovich… do me the kindness, Anton Antonovich, of hearing me out…'

'And your treacherous action and slander of another person – accusing another person of what you've been guilty of yourself? Eh? What do you call that?'

'I didn't drive him out, Anton Antonovich,' said our hero, beginning to tremble, 'and didn't teach Petrushka, my man, that is, anything of the sort, sir… He ate my bread, Anton Antonovich, he enjoyed my hospitality,' added our hero expressively and with deep feeling, so that his chin began to twitch a little and tears were ready to well up once more.

'You're only *saying* that he ate your bread, Yakov Petrovich,' replied Anton Antonovich with a grin, and such cunning could be heard in his voice that Mr Golyadkin felt a pang of anxiety in his heart.

'Permit me to ask you most humbly once more, Anton Antonovich: is His Excellency aware of this whole business?'

'What do you think, sir! Anyway, you must let me go now, sir. I haven't the time for you now… You'll learn everything that you ought to know today, sir.'

'Please, for God's sake, another minute, Anton Antonovich…'

'You can tell me later, sir…'

'No, Anton Antonovich, sir; you see, sir, I, sir, just listen, Anton Antonovich… I'm not at all freethinking, Anton Antonovich, I shun freethinking; I'm perfectly prepared for my part and have even voiced the idea…'

'Very well, sir, very well, sir. I've heard it already, sir…'

'No, sir, this you haven't heard, Anton Antonovich. This is something else, Anton Antonovich, this is a good thing, truly good, and pleasant to hear… I've voiced the idea, as I explained earlier, Anton

Antonovich, that Divine Providence has created two perfectly similar men, and the beneficent authorities, seeing Divine Providence, have given shelter to the two twins, sir. That's a good thing, Anton Antonovich. You can see that that's a very good thing, Anton Antonovich, and that I'm far from freethinking. I accept the beneficent authorities as a father. It's like this, so to speak, beneficent authorities, and you, you know… so to speak… a young man needs to work… . Give me your support, Anton Antonovich, stand up for me, Anton Antonovich… I'm all right, sir… Anton Antonovich, for God's sake, one more little word… Anton Antonovich…'

But Anton Antonovich was already a long way away from Mr Golyadkin… And our hero did not know where he was standing, what he had heard, what he had done, what had been done to him, and what else would be done to him – so confused was he and shaken by all that he had heard and all that had happened to him.

With an imploring gaze he tried to seek out Anton Antonovich in the crowd of clerks so as to justify himself still more in his eyes and say something to him extremely loyal and very noble and pleasant regarding himself… However, little by little, a new light was beginning to break through Mr Golyadkin's confusion – a new, terrible light, which illuminated before him suddenly, all at once, a whole vista of until now utterly unknown and even completely unsuspected circumstances… At this moment somebody nudged our utterly worn-down hero in the side. He looked around. Before him stood Scriblet.

'A letter, Your Honour, sir.'

'Ah!… Have you already come back, my dear?'

'No, it was this morning as early as ten o'clock it was brought here, sir. Sergei Mikheyev, the watchman, brought it, sir, from Provincial Secretary Vakhrameyev's apartment.'

'Very well, my friend, very well, and I'll show you my gratitude, my dear.'

After saying this, Mr Golyadkin put the letter away into the side pocket of his uniform jacket and did up all the buttons; then he looked around and, to his surprise, noticed that he was already in the entrance lobby of the Ministry, in a little crowd of clerks pressing towards the exit, for the working day had finished. Not only had Mr Golyadkin not noticed this last detail until now, he had not even noticed, and how it had happened he did not remember, that he had suddenly come to be wearing his greatcoat and galoshes and holding his hat in his hands. All the clerks were standing motionless and waiting respectfully. The thing was that His Excellency had stopped at the bottom of the stairs, waiting for his vehicle, which had for some reason been delayed, and was conducting a very interesting conversation with two Councillors and with Andrei Filippovich. At a little distance from the two Councillors and Andrei Filippovich stood Anton Antonovich Setochkin and some of the other clerks, who were full of smiles, seeing that His Excellency was deigning to joke and laugh. The clerks crowding at the top of the staircase were also smiling and waiting for His Excellency to start laughing again. Just the pot-bellied doorman Fedoseyich alone was not smiling, as he stood fast by the door handles, at attention and waiting impatiently for a dose of his daily pleasure, which consisted in throwing one half of the doors wide open, all at once, with a single movement of his hand, and then, bending himself in half, respectfully letting His Excellency past him. But it was evidently Mr Golyadkin's unworthy and ignoble enemy who was glad and felt pleasure most of all. At this moment he had even forgotten about all the clerks, had even stopped winding his way and pattering among them, as was his vile custom, at this moment he had even forgotten to take advantage of the opportunity to suck up to someone or other. He had become all eyes and ears, had shrunk down strangely somehow, probably so as to listen more easily, without taking his eyes off His Excellency, and only from time to time did his arms, legs and head twitch with some scarcely noticeable spasms, which revealed all the inner, secret impulses of his soul.

'Just look at him, full of it,' thought our hero, 'looking like a favourite, the scoundrel! I'd like to know what it is precisely that makes him so successful in high-class society? No intelligence, no personality, no education, no feeling; the lucky rogue! My God! I mean, how quickly it is, when you think about it, that the man can go and "get in" with everyone! And the man will go, I swear on it, he'll go far, the rogue, he'll get there, the lucky rogue! I'd also like to find out what it is precisely he's whispering to them all? What confidences does he share with all these people, and what secrets are they talking about? My God! How can I, you know… and be with them a little bit as well… so to speak, it's like this, or perhaps ask him… so to speak, it's like this, and in future I won't; I'm at fault, so to speak, but a young man needs to work these days, Your Excellency; and I'm not at all embarrassed by my shady situation – that's how it is! And I won't be protesting in any way either, and I'll bear everything with patience and humility – there! So perhaps that's how I should act?… But anyway, you can't get to him, the rogue, you can't get through to him with any words; it's impossible to knock any sense into his wild head… But still, we'll have a try. If I happen to hit on a good time, then I can have a try…'

In his disquiet, in anguish and confusion, feeling it was impossible to remain like this, that the decisive moment was approaching, that he simply had to have things out with somebody, our hero began gradually moving towards the spot where his unworthy and mysterious friend was standing; but at this very moment His Excellency's long-awaited vehicle made a clatter by the porch. Fedoseyich tugged at the door and, bending himself in half three times, let His Excellency past him. All those waiting surged as one towards the exit and for a moment pushed Mr Golyadkin senior away from Mr Golyadkin junior. 'You won't escape!' said our hero, forcing his way through the crowd and not taking his eyes off the man he wanted. Finally the crowd thinned out. Our hero felt himself in the clear and dashed off in pursuit of his foe.

11

The breath caught in Mr Golyadkin's chest; as though on wings, he flew after his foe, who was rapidly moving away. He felt within himself a terrible energy. Yet despite this terrible energy, Mr Golyadkin could be confident that at that particular moment even a simple mosquito, if it could only have survived in St Petersburg at such a time, would have broken him very comfortably with its wing. He also felt that he had gone downhill and completely lost his strength, that he was being carried along by some quite special and external force, that he was not walking himself at all, that, on the contrary, his legs were buckling and refusing to work. However, it might all be arranged for the best. 'For the best – not for the best,' thought Mr Golyadkin, almost choking from the speed of his running, 'but that the business is lost, of that there can be not the slightest doubt now; that I'm utterly lost, that's already obvious, definite, signed and sealed.' Despite all this, it was as if our hero had risen from the dead, as if he had survived a battle, as if he had seized a victory when he came to catch hold of his foe's greatcoat as the latter was already setting one foot onto the droshky of the cabman he had just hired to take him somewhere. 'My dear sir! My dear sir!' he cried to the ignoble Mr Golyadkin junior, whom he had finally overtaken. 'My dear sir, I hope you…'

'No, please, don't you go hoping anything,' replied Mr Golyadkin's unfeeling foe evasively, standing with one foot on one of the droshky's footboards and endeavouring with all his might to get the other one onto the other side of the vehicle, vainly waving it in the air, trying to maintain his balance and at the same time trying as hard as he could to free his greatcoat from Mr Golyadkin senior, while the latter, for his part, clung on to it with all the means granted him by nature.

'Yakov Petrovich! Just ten minutes…'

'I'm sorry, I haven't the time, sir.'

'You must agree, Yakov Petrovich… please, Yakov Petrovich… for God's sake, Yakov Petrovich… it's like this – talk things over… on a bold footing… Just for a second, Yakov Petrovich!…'

'My dear, there isn't time,' replied Mr Golyadkin's falsely noble foe with discourteous familiarity, but in the guise of goodness of heart, 'another time, believe me, with all my soul and with a clear conscience; but now – well, truly, it's not possible.'

'Villain!' thought our hero.

'Yakov Petrovich!' he cried miserably, 'I've never been your enemy. It's wicked people who've described me unfairly… For my part, I'm prepared… Yakov Petrovich, would it suit you if you and I, Yakov Petrovich, just now popped into?… And there with a clear conscience, as you rightly said just now, and in straightforward, noble language… into this coffee house: then everything will explain itself – there, Yakov Petrovich! Then everything will explain itself for sure…'

'Into the coffee house? Very well, sir. I don't object, we'll pop into the coffee house on just one condition, my joy, with a single condition –

that there everything will explain itself. "It's like this, dear," so to speak,' said Mr Golyadkin junior, climbing down from the droshky and shamelessly patting our hero on the shoulder, 'you're such a great pal; for you, Yakov Petrovich, I'm prepared to go down a side street (as you were so good as to remark quite rightly in the old days, Yakov Petrovich). I mean, there's a scallywag, truly, he does whatever he wants with a man!' continued Mr Golyadkin's false friend with an easy little smile, spinning and twisting around him.

Far away from any main streets, the coffee house which the two Mr Golyadkins entered was at this moment completely empty. A rather fat German woman appeared at the counter just as soon as the ringing of the bell became audible. Mr Golyadkin and his unworthy foe went through into the second room, where a puffy little boy with closely cropped hair was busy with a bundle of firewood by the stove, struggling to restore the fire that was going out inside it. At Mr Golyadkin junior's demand, chocolate was served.

'That's a really tasty bit of skirt,' said Mr Golyadkin junior, winking roguishly at Mr Golyadkin senior.

Our hero blushed and held his tongue.

'Ah, yes, I'm sorry, I forgot. I know your taste. We're partial to slim little Germans, sir; I'm saying, Yakov Petrovich, you truthful soul, that you and I are partial to little Germans who are slim – albeit, incidentally, still not short of charm; we rent apartments from them, compromise their morality, in return for *bier* soup and *milch*[18] soup we dedicate our hearts to them and give them various written undertakings – that's what we do, you Faublas, you – you betrayer, you!'

Mr Golyadkin junior, in saying all this, was thus making an utterly worthless, albeit, however, a villainously cunning allusion to a certain person of the female sex, twisting all around Mr Golyadkin, smiling at him in the guise of civility, thus falsely showing him cordiality and joy at meeting with him. And remarking that Mr Golyadkin senior was by no means so stupid and by no means lacking to such a degree in education and fine manners as to believe him immediately, the ignoble man resolved to alter his tactics and conduct matters on an open footing. Straight away, having uttered his vile words, the fake Mr Golyadkin concluded by patting the respectable Mr Golyadkin on the shoulder with infuriating shamelessness and familiarity, and, not satisfied with this, he started playing around with him in a way completely improper in good society, namely he conceived the idea of repeating his earlier vile action, that is, despite the resistance and little cries of the indignant Mr Golyadkin senior, of pinching him on the cheek. Our hero flared up at the sight of such dissipation, but held his tongue... for the time being, anyway.

'That's the language of my enemies,' he finally replied, prudently restraining himself, in a quavering voice. At the same time our hero glanced round in disquiet at the door. The thing was that Mr Golyadkin junior was evidently in an excellent frame of mind and prepared to start on various little jokes, impermissible in a public place and, speaking in general, not tolerated by the laws of society and, principally, in company of exalted tone.

'Ah well, in that case, as you wish,' Mr Golyadkin junior retorted seriously to Mr Golyadkin senior's idea, putting his empty cup, which he had drained with unseemly greed, down on the table. 'Well, sir, there's no need for me to be with you for long, by the way... Well, sir, how are you getting on now, Yakov Petrovich?'

'There's only one thing I can say to you, Yakov Petrovich,' replied our hero with sangfroid and dignity, 'I have never been your enemy.'

'Hm.. Well, what about Petrushka, or whatever his name is? I think it's Petrushka, isn't it? Well, yes! Well, how's he? All right? As before?'

'And he too is as before, Yakov Petrovich,' replied the somewhat surprised Mr Golyadkin senior. 'I don't know, Yakov Petrovich... for my part... a noble, a candid part, Yakov Petrovich, you must agree, Yakov Petrovich...'

'Yes, sir. But you know it yourself, Yakov Petrovich,' replied Mr Golyadkin junior in a quiet and expressive voice, thus falsely representing himself as a sorrowful man, filled with repentance and worthy of pity, 'you know it yourself, our time's a hard one... I'll refer it to you, Yakov Petrovich; you're an intelligent man and you'll judge fairly,' Mr Golyadkin junior put in, basely flattering Mr Golyadkin senior. 'Life isn't a game, you know it yourself, Yakov Petrovich,' Mr Golyadkin junior concluded meaningfully, thus pretending to be an intelligent and learnt man capable of discussing elevated subjects.

'For my part, Yakov Petrovich,' replied our hero with animation, 'for my part I despise beating about the bush, and, speaking boldly and frankly, speaking in straightforward, noble language, and putting the whole business on a noble basis, I shall say to you, I can openly and nobly assert, Yakov Petrovich, that I am perfectly clean and that, you know it yourself, Yakov Petrovich, mutual delusion – anything can happen – society's judgement, the opinion of the servile herd… I'm speaking frankly, Yakov Petrovich, anything can happen. I'll say more, Yakov Petrovich, if you judge things like that, if you look at the business from a noble and elevated point of view, then I'll say boldly, I'll say without false shame, Yakov Petrovich, it will even be pleasant for me to discover that I was deluded, it will even be pleasant for me to confess to it. You know it yourself, you're an intelligent and, what's more, a noble man. Without shame, without false shame I'm prepared to confess to it…' concluded our hero with dignity and nobility.

'Destiny, fate! Yakov Petrovich… but let's leave all that,' said Mr Golyadkin junior with a sigh. 'Let's better use the brief moments of our meeting for a more useful and pleasant conversation, as should be the case between two colleagues… Truly, somehow I've not managed to say two words to you in all this time… I'm not the one to blame for it, Yakov Petrovich…'

'And neither am I,' our hero interrupted heatedly, 'and neither am I! My heart tells me, Yakov Petrovich, that I'm not the one to blame for all this. We'll blame it all on fate, Yakov Petrovich,' added Mr Golyadkin senior in a perfectly conciliatory tone. His voice was beginning little by little to weaken and tremble.

'Well, then? How's your health generally?' pronounced the errant one in a sweet voice.

'I've got a bit of a cough,' replied our hero even more sweetly.

'Take care. There are such epidemics all the time now, it's a simple matter to catch quinsy, and, I must admit, I'm already starting to wrap up in flannel.'

'Indeed, Yakov Petrovich, it's a simple matter to catch quinsy, sir… Yakov Petrovich!' pronounced our hero after a brief silence. 'Yakov Petrovich! I can see I was deluded… I think with tenderness of those happy minutes we were able to spend together under my poor, but,

I dare say, welcoming roof…'

'That's not what you wrote in your letter, though,' said the absolutely justified (but solely in this respect absolutely justified) Mr Golyadkin junior somewhat reproachfully.

'Yakov Petrovich! I was deluded… Now I see clearly that I was deluded in that wretched letter of mine. Yakov Petrovich, I'm ashamed to look at you, Yakov Petrovich, you won't believe it… Give me that letter so I can tear it up right in front of you, Yakov Petrovich, or if that really is quite impossible, I beg you to read it the other way round – completely the other way round, with a deliberately friendly intent – that is, giving the contrary sense to all my letter's words. I was deluded. Forgive me, Yakov Petrovich, I was completely… I was grievously deluded, Yakov Petrovich.'

'You're saying?' asked Mr Golyadkin senior's perfidious friend quite absent-mindedly and indifferently.

'I'm saying I was utterly deluded, Yakov Petrovich, and for my part, quite without false shame, I…'

'Ah, well, good! That's very good, that you were deluded,' replied Mr Golyadkin junior rudely.

'I even had the idea, Yakov Petrovich,' added our candid hero in a noble way, not noticing at all the terrible perfidy of his false friend, 'I even had the idea that, here, so to speak, there had been created two absolutely similar…'

'Ah! That's your idea!…'

Here Mr Golyadkin junior, known for his worthless nature, got up and seized his hat. Still not noticing the deceit, Mr Golyadkin senior got up too, smiling ingenuously and nobly at his false friend, trying in his innocence to be nice and reassuring to him and thus to strike up a new friendship with him…

'Farewell, Your Excellency!' Mr Golyadkin junior suddenly exclaimed. Our hero shuddered, remarking in his enemy's face something even Bacchic – and, solely in order just to get away, he put two fingers of his own hand into the hand the immoral one had stretched out to him; but here… here Mr Golyadkin junior's shamelessness exceeded all degrees. Seizing the two fingers of Mr Golyadkin senior's hand and having first shaken them, the unworthy one straight away, before Mr Golyadkin's very eyes, made up his mind to repeat his shameless joke of the morning. The measure of human patience was exhausted.

He was already putting away in his pocket the handkerchief with which he had wiped his fingers when Mr Golyadkin senior came to his senses and dashed after him into the neighbouring room, into which, as was his nasty habit, his irreconcilable enemy had immediately made haste to slip away. As if nothing were amiss, he was just standing by the counter eating pies and very calmly, like a man of virtue, paying compliments to the German pastry cook. 'Not in front of a lady,' thought our hero and also went up to the counter, beside himself with agitation.

'That bit of skirt really isn't bad, is she – what do you think?' Mr Golyadkin junior once again began his improper outbursts, probably reckoning on Mr Golyadkin's endless patience. And the fat German, for her part, since she evidently did not understand Russian, looked at her two customers with blank, glassy eyes and smiled cordially. Our hero flared up like fire at the words of Mr Golyadkin junior, who knew no shame, and, powerless to control himself, he finally threw himself at him with the evident intention of tearing him to pieces and thus finishing with him once and for all; but Mr Golyadkin junior, as was his vile custom, was already a long way off: he had taken flight and was already on the porch. It goes without saying that after the first momentary paralysis that naturally came upon Mr Golyadkin senior, he came to his senses and rushed as fast as his legs would carry him after the offender, who was already getting onto the droshky whose driver, waiting for him, had evidently agreed upon everything with him. But at this very moment the fat German, seeing the flight of the two customers, screamed and rang her bell for all she was worth. Our hero turned back and, all but on the wing and without demanding change, threw her down some money on account of both himself and the shameless one who had not paid – then, despite the fact that he had lingered, he nevertheless managed, albeit again only on the wing, to catch up with his foe. Clinging on to the side of the droshky with all the means granted him by nature, our hero sped along the street for some time, trying to clamber onto the vehicle, which Mr Golyadkin junior defended with all his might. The cab driver, meanwhile, with whip and reins and foot and words, was urging on his jaded nag, which, quite unexpectedly, taking the bit between its teeth, set off at a gallop, kicking out with its hind legs, as was its nasty habit, at every third stride. Finally our hero managed to perch on the droshky after all, facing his foe and with his back pressed against the driver, with his knees pressed against the knees of the shameless one and with his right hand locked by every means on to the very nasty fur collar of his dissipated and most bitter foe's greatcoat...

The enemies sped along and were silent for some time. Our hero could scarcely draw breath; the road was extremely bad, and he was jerking up and down at every stride in danger of breaking his neck. Moreover, his bitter foe would still not agree to admit himself beaten and was trying to push his adversary off into the mud. To crown all this unpleasantness, it was the most awful weather. Flakes of snow were falling thickly and trying for their part in every way to get somehow inside the real Mr Golyadkin's unbuttoned greatcoat. It was murky all around and not a thing could be seen. It was hard to make out where they were speeding to and along what streets... It seemed to Mr Golyadkin that something familiar was happening to him. For a moment he tried to remember whether he had had a premonition of anything the day before... in a dream, for example... Finally his anguish reached the utmost pitch of its ultimate agony. Throwing his weight onto his merciless adversary, he was on the point of beginning to cry out. But his cry died away on his lips... There was a minute when Mr Golyadkin forgot everything and decided that all this was quite all right, and that it was just happening in some inexplicable way somehow, and to make a protest on account of it would be superfluous and an utterly lost cause... But suddenly, and almost at that very moment when our hero was concluding all this, some incautious jolt changed the whole sense of the matter. Like a sack of flour, Mr Golyadkin toppled down from the droshky and rolled off somewhere, quite rightly acknowledging at the moment of his fall that he really had got excited very inappropriately. Finally jumping up, he saw that they had arrived somewhere; the droshky was standing in the middle of somebody's courtyard, and our hero noticed at first glance that this was the courtyard of that very building in which Olsufy Ivanovich lodged. At that same moment he noticed that his friend was already making his way onto the porch and probably to visit Olsufy Ivanovich. In his indescribable anguish he was about to rush off to overtake his foe, but, to his good fortune, he prudently had second thoughts in time. Not forgetting to settle up with the cab driver, Mr Golyadkin rushed into the street and started running for all he was worth, just following his nose. Flakes of snow were falling thickly as before; as before it was murky, wet and dark. Our hero did not walk, but flew, knocking over everyone in his way – men and women and children, and himself in his turn leaping aside from women, men and children. All around and in his wake fearful voices, screams and cries could be heard… But Mr Golyadkin seemed to be unconscious and did not mean to pay attention to anything… He came to his senses, however, when he was already by the Semyonovsky Bridge, yet even then only on account of managing to catch two women awkwardly, knocking them down along with some things they were selling in the street, and at the same time toppling over himself. 'It's all right,' thought Mr Golyadkin, 'this can all still quite possibly turn out for the best,' and straight away he put his hand in his pocket, wanting to get away with paying a silver rouble for the spilt gingerbread, apples, peas and all sorts. Suddenly a new light dawned on Mr Golyadkin; in his pocket he felt the letter handed to him in the morning by the scribe. Remembering, by the way, that not far off there was an inn he knew, he ran into the inn, without a moment's delay settled himself at a table illuminated by a tallow candle, and, paying no attention to anything, without listening to the waiter who had appeared to take his order, he broke the seal and began reading the following, which totally stunned him:

Noble man, who suffers on my behalf and is forever dear to my heart!

I am suffering, I am perishing – save me! A slanderer, a schemer and a man known for his worthless tendencies has entangled me in his toils and I am lost! I have fallen! But he is odious to me, whereas you!… We have been separated, my letters to you have been intercepted – and this has all been done by the immoral one, exploiting his sole better quality – his resemblance to you. In any event, one can be unattractive and yet captivate with intelligence, powerful emotion and pleasant manners... I am perishing! I am being married off by force – and scheming more than anyone here is my parent, my benefactor, State Councillor Olsufy Ivanovich, probably wishing to take over my place and my relations in good society... But I have made up my mind and I protest with all the means granted me by nature. Wait for me with your carriage today at exactly nine o'clock by the windows of Olsufy Ivanovich's apartment. We shall be giving a ball again, and the handsome lieutenant will be there. I shall come out and we shall fly away. What is more, there are other workplaces where it is still possible to be of service to the fatherland. In any event, remember, my friend, that innocence is strong just by virtue of its innocence. Farewell. Wait with the carriage by the entrance. I shall throw myself into the protection of your embrace at exactly two o'clock in the morning.

Yours to the grave,
Klara Olsufyevna

When he had finished reading the letter, our hero remained seemingly dumbstruck for several minutes. In terrible anguish, in terrible agitation, white as a sheet, with the letter in his hands, he walked around the room several times; to crown the calamities of his situation, our hero had failed to notice that he was at the present moment the object of exclusive attention for everybody in the room. Probably the disorder of his clothing, his uncontrollable agitation, his walking, or, to put it better, running, his gesticulation with both hands, perhaps the few enigmatic words, spoken to the wind in forgetfulness – all this was probably a very bad recommendation for Mr Golyadkin in the opinion of all the customers; and even the waiter himself was beginning to cast suspicious looks at him. Coming to, our hero noticed that he was standing in the middle of the room and was looking in an almost improper, impolite way at a little old man of most venerable appearance who, having eaten and said a prayer to God before the icon, had settled down again and, for his part, could not take his eyes off Mr Golyadkin either. Our hero gazed around vaguely and noticed that everyone, absolutely everyone was looking at him with the most ominous and suspicious air. Suddenly, a retired military man with a red collar loudly demanded *The Police Gazette*. Mr Golyadkin gave a start and blushed: somehow by chance he lowered his eyes to the ground and saw that he was in unseemly clothing such as he should not have worn even at home, let alone in a public place. His boots, trousers and entire left side were covered in mud, the stripe on his right trouser leg was torn off, while his tailcoat was even ripped in many places. In his inexhaustible anguish, our hero went up to the table at which he had been reading and saw that the inn servant was approaching him with some sort of strange and insolently persistent expression on his face. Flustered and completely deflated, our hero began examining the table at which he was now standing. On the table stood plates that had yet to be cleared away after somebody's meal, there was a soiled napkin, and the knife, fork and spoon that had just been in use were still lying around. 'Who can have been eating?' thought our hero. 'Surely not me? But anything's possible! Had a meal and didn't even notice; what on earth am I to do?' Raising his eyes, Mr Golyadkin again saw beside him the waiter, who was intending to say something to him.

'How much do I owe, old fellow?' asked our hero in a tremulous voice.

Loud laughter rang out all around Mr Golyadkin; the waiter himself gave a smirk. Mr Golyadkin realised that even here he had made a blunder and had done something terribly stupid. Realising all this, he became so confused that he was forced to delve into his pocket for his handkerchief, probably so as to be doing something and not just standing there; but to his indescribable amazement and that of all the people surrounding him, instead of a handkerchief he took out a phial with some sort of medicine, prescribed some four days before by Krestyan Ivanovich. 'Medicines at the same chemist's,' flashed through Mr Golyadkin's head… Suddenly he gave a start and almost screamed in horror. A new light was dawning… The ominous reflection of the dark, repulsive, reddish liquid shone into Mr Golyadkin's eyes… The bottle fell from his hands and instantly shattered. Our hero screamed and leapt back a couple of paces from the spilt liquid… all his limbs were trembling and sweat was breaking out on his temples and forehead. 'So my life is in danger!' Meanwhile, there had been movement and commotion in the room; everyone was surrounding Mr Golyadkin, everyone was talking to Mr Golyadkin, some were even grabbing hold of Mr Golyadkin. But our hero was dumb and immobile, seeing nothing, hearing nothing, feeling nothing... Finally, as if he had torn himself away, he rushed out of the inn, pushed aside each and every one who sought to restrain him, fell almost senseless onto the first cabman's droshky he came across and flew off to his apartment.

In the entrance lobby of his apartment he met Mikheyev, the Ministry watchman, with an official letter in his hands. 'I know, my friend, I know everything,' replied our worn-out hero in a weak, anguished voice, 'it's official...' In the letter there was indeed an order to Mr Golyadkin, signed by Andrei Filippovich, to hand over the files in his possession to Ivan Semyonovich. Taking the letter and giving the watchman ten kopeks, Mr Golyadkin entered his apartment and saw that Petrushka was making ready and collecting into a single pile all his bits and pieces, all his things, evidently meaning to abandon Mr Golyadkin and leave him for Karolina Ivanovna, who had enticed him over as her replacement for Yevstafy.

12

Petrushka came in, swaying a little, holding himself in a strangely offhanded way and with a look of servile triumph on his face. It was clear that he had conceived some plan, felt fully within his rights and looked like a completely detached person, that is, like someone else's servant, only not at all like Mr Golyadkin's former servant.

'Well, you see, my dear,' began our hero, panting, 'what time is it now, my dear?'

Petrushka set off in silence behind the partition, then returned and announced in quite an independent tone that it would very soon be half-past seven.

'Well, all right, my dear, all right. Well, you see, my dear... allow me to tell you, my dear, that everything seems to be over between us now.'

Petrushka was silent.

'Well, now that everything's already finished between us, you tell me now frankly, tell me as a friend, where have you been, old fellow?'

'Where've I been? Among good people, sir.'

'I know, my friend, I know. I was always pleased with you, my dear, and I'll give you a testimonial... Well, what are you doing there now?'

'What do you mean, sir! You're so good as to know for yourself, sir. It's clear, sir, a good man won't teach you bad ways.'

'I know, my dear, I know. Good people are rare nowadays, my friend; value them, my friend. Well, and how are they?'

'It's clear, sir, how, sir... Only I can't serve you, sir, any more now, sir; you're so good as to know it for yourself, sir.'

'I know, my dear, I know; I know your zeal and diligence; I've seen it all, my friend, I've taken note. I respect you, my friend. I respect a good and honest man, even if he is a flunkey.'

'Well, it's clear, sir! The likes of me, of course, you're so good as to know for yourself where he's best off. That's just the way it is, sir. What's it to me! It's clear, sir, you just can't manage without a good man, sir.'

'Well, all right, old fellow, all right; I sense it... Well, here's your money and here's your testimonial. Now let's kiss, old fellow, let's say goodbye... Well, now, my dear, I'll ask one service of you, a final service,' said Mr Golyadkin in a solemn tone. 'You see, my dear, all sorts of things happen. Grief, my friend, lurks even in gilded palaces, and you can't escape from it anywhere. You know, my friend, I think I've always been nice to you...'

Petrushka was silent.

'I think I've always been nice to you, my dear... Well, how much linen do we have now, my dear?'

'All's present and correct, sir. Six gingham shirts, sir; three pairs of leggings; four shirt fronts, sir; a flannel jersey; two items of underwear, sir. You know it for yourself, sir, that's all, sir. Nothing of yours, sir, I've not... I, sir, look after my master's property, sir. I, sir, you know, sir, you... it's clear, sir... and me guilty of anything – never, sir; you know that for yourself, sir...'

'I believe you, my friend, I believe you. I wasn't talking about that, my friend, not about that; you see, the thing is, my friend...'

'It's clear, sir; that we do know, sir. When I was still working for General Stolbnyakov, sir, they let me go, sir, they were going away themselves to Saratov... they had their family estate there...'

'No, my friend, it's not about that; I didn't mean anything... don't you go thinking anything, my dear friend...'

'It's clear, sir. What's the likes of me, sir, you're so good as to know it for yourself, sir, it doesn't take long to slander a man, sir. And people have been satisfied with me everywhere, sir. There've been ministers, generals, senators, counts, sir. I've been with the lot, sir, with Prince Svinchatkin, sir, with Pereborkin, the colonel, sir, with Nedobarov, the general, he went as well, went to his family estate, sir. It's clear, sir...'

'Yes, my friend, yes; very well, my friend, very well. And now I'm going away too, my friend... Everyone takes a different path, my dear, and it's unclear what road any one of us might come upon. Well, my friend, will you give me my things to get dressed now; yes, put my uniform jacket out as well... my other trousers, sheets, blankets, pillows...'

'Do you want me to tie it all into a bundle, sir?'

'Yes, my friend, yes; perhaps tie it into a bundle too... Who knows what might happen to us. Well, now, my dear, go and find a carriage...'

'A carriage, sir?...'

'Yes, my friend, a carriage, on the spacious side and for a period of time. But don't you go thinking anything, my friend...'

'And do you mean to go far, sir?'

'I don't know, my friend, I don't know that either. I think the mattress will need to be put in there as well. What do you yourself think, my friend? I'm counting on you, my dear...'

'Surely you'll not be so good as to be leaving now, sir?'

'Yes, my friend, yes! Such a circumstance has arisen... that's the way it is, my dear, that's the way it is.'

'That's clear, sir; it was the same with a lieutenant in our regiment, sir; a landowner's daughter, sir... carried off, sir...'

'Carried off?... How's that, my dear, you...'

'Yes, sir, carried off, sir, and they got married on another estate. Everything was prepared in advance, sir. They gave chase, sir; only then did the prince step in, sir, the late prince, sir – well, and the matter was settled, sir…'

'Got married, yes… and so how do you, my dear, how is it, then, that you know, my dear?'

'Well, it's clear, sir, nothing to it! News travels fast, sir. We know everything, sir… of course, who hasn't ever been at fault. Only I'll tell you now, sir, allow me to say it bluntly, sir, in a servant's way; if it's come to that now, then I'll tell you, sir: you do have an enemy – you have a rival, sir, a serious rival, sir, there…'

'I know, my friend, I know; you know it for yourself, my dear… Well, so I'm counting on you. How are we to do things now, my friend? What do you advise me?'

'Well, then, sir, if that's the way you're going now, sir, roughly speaking, sir, then what'll you need to buy, sir – well, sheets, pillows, another mattress, sir, a double one, sir, a good blanket, sir – from the neighbour here, sir, the woman downstairs, sir: she's a tradeswoman, sir; and there's a good fox-lined coat; you can have a look at it and buy it, you can go and have a look now, sir. You need to do it now, sir; it's a good coat, sir, made of satin, sir, lined with fox fur, sir…'

'Well, all right, my friend, all right; I agree, my friend, I'm counting on you, counting entirely; perhaps even the coat, my dear… Only quickly, quickly! For God's sake, quickly! I'll buy the coat too, only quickly, please! It'll soon be eight o'clock, quickly, for God's sake, my friend! Hurry, quickly, my friend!…'

Petrushka left unfinished the bundle of linen, pillows, sheets, a blanket and all sorts of rubbish he had begun to collect together and tie up, and rushed headlong out of the room. Mr Golyadkin meanwhile seized once more upon the letter – but was unable to read it. Taking his poor head in both hands, he leant against the wall in amazement. He was unable to think about anything, nor was he able to do anything; he did not even know himself what was happening to him. Finally, seeing that time was passing, but that neither Petrushka nor the coat had yet appeared, Mr Golyadkin made up his mind to set off himself. Opening the door into the entrance lobby, he heard noise, voices, arguing and debate… Several of the women living there were chattering, shouting, passing judgement, laying down the law about something – and Mr

Golyadkin knew precisely about what. Petrushka's voice could be heard; then someone's footsteps were heard. 'My God! They'll bring the whole world here!' groaned Mr Golyadkin, wringing his hands in despair and rushing back into his room. Running into his room, almost beside himself, he fell onto the couch with his face in a cushion. After lying thus for about a minute, he leapt up and, without waiting for Petrushka, put on his galoshes, hat and greatcoat, grabbed his wallet and ran headlong down the stairs. 'I don't need a thing, not a thing, my dear! I'll do it myself, I'll do it all myself. I don't need you for the time being, and meanwhile perhaps the matter will even be settled for the best,' Mr Golyadkin mumbled to Petrushka, meeting him on the staircase; then he ran out into the courtyard and straight out of the building; his heart was coming to a stop; he had not yet made up his mind... How was he to behave, what was he to do, how was he to act in the present and critical instance?...

'I mean, how am I to act, Lord God? And all this absolutely had to happen!' he finally exclaimed in despair, stumping along the street at random, just following his nose, 'all this absolutely had to happen! I mean, if it hadn't happened, specifically this, then everything would have been settled; once and for all, at a single stroke, at a single neat, energetic, firm stroke it would have been settled. I stake my finger that it would have been settled! I even know precisely the way it would have been settled. This is how it would have been done: I'd have said, you know, so to speak, it's like this, but, my dear sir, if you'll permit me to say it, it's neither here nor there for me; things aren't done like that, so to speak; my dear sir, so to speak, my good sir, things aren't done like that, and you won't succeed here with imposture; an impostor, my dear sir, is a man, you know, who is worthless and does the fatherland no service. Do you understand that? Do you understand that, so to speak, my dear sir?! That's how it would've, you know... But still, no, what do I mean... I mean, that's not it at all, not it at all... What am I lying for, like a complete idiot! Me, suicide that I am! That's not it at all, you suicide, you, so to speak... This, though, you depraved man, this is how it's being done now!... Well, where will I go now? Well, what will I do to myself, for example, now? Well, what am I good for now? Well, what are you good for now, to give an example, you Golyadkin, you, you unworthy fellow, you! Well, what now? I need to find a carriage; go and get a carriage for her, so to speak; we'll get our feet wet, so to speak, if there isn't a carriage... And so, who would have thought it? What a young miss, what a young lady! What a well-behaved girl, our much-vaunted one! You've excelled yourself, young lady, it can't be denied, excelled yourself!... And it all stems from an immoral upbringing; and now that I've had a good look and got to the bottom of it all, I can see that it stems from nothing other than immorality. Instead of, you know, from an early age... giving her the cane from time to time, they stuff her full of confectionery and all kinds of sweet things, and the little old man himself snivels over her: so to speak, you're my this and my that, you're a good girl, so to speak, I'll marry you off to a count!... And now she's turned out like this and shown us her cards; that's the way our game is! Instead of keeping her at home from an early age, they had to send her to boarding school, to madame the Frenchwoman, to some émigrée Falbala[19] or other; and she learns all kinds of good stuff with that émigrée Falbala – and so that's why everything turns out like this. Come and rejoice, so to speak! Be in a carriage at such and such an hour opposite the windows, so to speak, and sing a sentimental romance in Spanish; I await you and know that you love me, and we'll run away together and we'll live in a hut. But in the end it can't be done; while we're about it, my dear young lady, it can't be done like that, the laws forbid the carrying off of an honest and innocent young girl from her parental home like that without the consent of her parents! And, finally, to what purpose, why and what's the need? Well, if she went and married the person she ought to, the one predestined by fate, that would be an end to the matter. But I'm a working man; and I might lose my post because of this; I might end up in court, my dear young lady, because of this! That's how it is, if you didn't know! It's the German woman's work. It's from her, the witch, that it all stems, the sparks that set the forest alight all come from her. Because they've defamed a man, because they've invented women's gossip about him, a dramatised cock and bull story, on the advice of Andrei Filippovich, that's where it stems from. Otherwise why on earth should Petrushka get involved here? What's it to him? What need does the rogue have? No, I can't, young lady, I can't, not at all, I can't, not for anything... And on this occasion you just forgive me somehow, young lady. It's from you, young lady, that everything stems, it's not from the German that everything stems, not from the witch at all, but purely from you, because the witch is a good woman, because the witch isn't to blame for anything, whereas you, young lady, are to blame – that's how it is! You, young lady, are leading me into wrongful accusations… A man's disappearing here, a man's vanishing from himself here and can't hold himself in check – what wedding can there be here! And how will it all end? And how will it be arranged now? I'd pay dearly to find it all out!…'

Thus our hero reasoned in his despair. Suddenly coming to, he noticed he was standing somewhere on Liteinaya. The weather was awful: there was a thaw, snow was falling, it was raining – well, exactly like that unforgettable time when at the terrible midnight hour all Mr Golyadkin's misfortunes had begun. 'What voyage can there be here!' thought Mr Golyadkin, looking at the weather, 'there's death across the board here… My Lord God! Well, where am I to find a carriage here, for example? Over there on the corner there seems to be some black shape. Let's see, let's investigate… My Lord God!' continued our hero, turning his weak and unsteady footsteps in the direction where he had seen something resembling a carriage. 'No, this is what I'll do: I'll set off, fall at his feet, if possible, I'll humbly beg. It's like this, so to speak, I pass my fate into your hands, into the hands of my superiors; Your Excellency, so to speak, protect a man and be his benefactor; it's like this, so to speak, there's this and that, an illegal action; don't destroy me, I see you as a father, don't abandon… save my self-respect, honour, name and family… and save me from the villain, the depraved one… He's another man, Your Excellency, and I'm another man as well; he's separate and I'm myself as well: truly, myself, Your Excellency, truly, myself; that's how it is, so to speak. I can't resemble him, so to speak; change, have the kindness, order the change – and the annihilation of the godless, unauthorised substitution… to discourage others, Your Excellency. I see you as a father; superiors, of course, beneficent and solicitous superiors should encourage such impulses… There's even something chivalric about it. I see you, beneficent superiors, as fathers, so to speak, and entrust my fate and shan't contradict, I entrust myself and I myself relinquish my affairs… that's how it is, so to speak!'

'Well, then, my dear, are you a cabman?'

'Yes…'

'The carriage, old fellow, for the evening…'

'And will you be wanting to go a long distance?'

'For the evening, for the evening; wherever might be necessary, my dear, wherever might be necessary.'

'You won't be wanting to go out of town, will you?'

'Yes, my friend, maybe even out of town. I don't know for sure myself yet, my friend, I can't tell you for sure, my dear. The thing is, you see, my dear, maybe everything will even be settled for the best. It's so, my friend…'

'Yes, it is so, sir, of course; God grant, for everyone.'

'Yes, my friend, yes; thank you, my dear; well, what will you charge then, my dear?…'

'Will you be wanting to go now, sir?'

'Yes, now, that is, no, you'll wait in a particular place… you'll wait just a little, not for long, my dear…'

'Well, if you're hiring me for the whole time, sir, then I can't do it, sir, for less than six silver roubles in this weather…'

'Well, all right, my friend, all right; and I'll show my gratitude, my dear. Well, so you can take me with you now, my dear.'

'Get in; allow me, I'll adjust things a little here; now be so good as to get in. Where do you want to go?'

'To the Izmailovsky Bridge, my friend.'

The hired coachman clambered up onto the box and was about to set in motion towards the Izmailovsky Bridge his pair of emaciated nags, which he had difficulty tearing away from their trough of hay. But suddenly Mr Golyadkin pulled on the cord, stopped the coach and asked in an imploring voice to turn back, not towards the Izmailovsky Bridge, but into another street. The coachman turned into the other street, and ten minutes later Mr Golyadkin's newly acquired vehicle stopped in front of the building in which His Excellency lodged. Mr Golyadkin got out of the carriage, earnestly asked his coachman to wait, and, with his heart stopping, ran up the stairs to the first floor, he pulled on the bell cord, the door opened, and our hero found himself in His Excellency's hallway.

'Is His Excellency so good as to be at home?' asked Mr Golyadkin, addressing himself thus to the servant who had opened the door to him.

'And what do you want, sir?' asked the footman, looking Mr Golyadkin over from toe to head.

'Well, I'm, you know, my friend... Golyadkin, a civil servant, Titular Councillor Golyadkin. Say, it's like this, to explain things...'

'Wait; it's not possible, sir...'

'My friend, I can't wait: my business is important, it's a matter that won't brook delay...'

'Well, who are you from? Have you come with documents?...'

'No, my friend, I've come independently... Announce me, my friend – say, it's like this, to explain things. And I'll show you my gratitude, my dear...'

'It's not possible, sir. He gave orders to receive no one; he has guests, sir. Come in the morning at ten o'clock, sir.'

'Do announce me, my dear; I can't, it's not possible for me to wait... You'll answer for this, my dear...'

'Oh, go on, announce him; what's it to you: feeling sorry for your boots, or something?' said another footman, who was sprawling on a chest and had not said a word up until now.

'To hell with my boots! He gave orders no one was to be received, right? Their turn's in the mornings.'

'Oh, announce him. Is your tongue going to drop off, or something?'

'All right, I'll announce him: my tongue isn't going to drop off. He gave orders not to: I'm just saying – he gave orders not to. Go into that room, then.'

Mr Golyadkin went into the first room; a clock stood on a table. He looked: half-past eight. His heart started to ache in his chest. He already wanted to turn back; but at that very moment a lanky footman standing on the threshold of the next room loudly announced Mr Golyadkin's name. 'Now that's a voice, that is!' thought our hero in indescribable anguish... 'Well, if you'd said: you know... it's like this, so to speak, I've come most humbly and meekly to explain myself – you know... be so good as to receive me... But now there's my business ruined, there's my whole business blown to the winds; still... oh, well – never mind...'

There was no point in reasoning, however. The footman turned, said 'if you please' and led Mr Golyadkin into the study.

When our hero went in, he felt as if he had gone blind, for he could see positively nothing. Two or three figures did, however, flash before his eyes, 'Well, those are the guests,' flashed through Mr Golyadkin's head. Finally our hero began to distinguish clearly the star on His Excellency's black tailcoat, then, maintaining a gradual approach, he moved on to the black tailcoat too, and finally received the capacity for full contemplation…

'What, sir?' pronounced the familiar voice above Mr Golyadkin.

'Titular Councillor Golyadkin, Your Excellency.'

'Well?'

'Come to explain myself…'

'What's that?… What?…'

'Just that. It's like this, so to speak – come to explain myself, Your Excellency, sir…'

'And you… And who are you?…'

'M-M-Mr Golyadkin, Your Excellency, Titular Councillor.'

'Well, so what is it you want?'

'It's like this, so to speak – I regard him as a father, I am myself withdrawing from my work, and protect me from my enemy – that's how it is!'

'What's this?…'

'It's well known…'

'What's well known?'

Mr Golyadkin was silent; his chin was little by little beginning to twitch…

'Well?'

'Something chivalric, I thought, Your Excellency… That, so to speak, there was something chivalric about it, and I regard my superior as a father… it's like this, so to speak, protect me, I plai… plaintively en… entreat, and that such ten… tendencies sh… ould be en… en… encouraged…'

His Excellency turned away. For several moments our hero could not make anything out with his eyes. There was a tightness in his chest. He was short of breath. He did not know where he was standing… He felt ashamed somehow and sad. God knows what happened next... When he came to, our hero noticed that His Excellency was talking with his guests and was debating something with them seemingly sharply and seriously. Mr Golyadkin recognised one of the guests straight away. It was Andrei Filippovich; but the other he did not; however, the man was seemingly familiar as well – a tall, solid figure, advanced in years, endowed with very thick eyebrows and whiskers and an expressive, sharp gaze. There was a decoration around the stranger's neck, and in his mouth was a cigar. The stranger was smoking and, without taking the cigar from his mouth, nodding meaningfully, glancing from time to time at Mr Golyadkin. Mr Golyadkin began to feel awkward somehow; he turned his eyes away and at once saw another very strange guest. In the doorway, which our hero had taken for a mirror up until now, as had also been the case with him once before, *he* appeared – it's obvious who, Mr Golyadkin's very close acquaintance and friend. Up until now Mr Golyadkin junior really had been in another little room and had been writing something in a hurry; now it was evidently needed – and he appeared with papers under his arm, went up to His Excellency and very deftly, while waiting for exclusive attention to his person, managed to worm his way into the conversation and the counsel, taking up his position a little behind Andrei Filippovich's back and partly masking himself with the stranger smoking the cigar. Mr Golyadkin junior was evidently taking an extreme interest in the conversation, on which he was now eavesdropping in a noble way, nodding his head, pattering his feet, smiling, glancing at His Excellency at every moment, as though imploring with his gaze to be allowed to get a word in edgeways himself as well. 'Villain!' thought Mr Golyadkin, and involuntarily took a step forward. At this point the general turned around and himself went rather indecisively up to Mr Golyadkin.

'Well, all right, all right; off you go and God be with you. I'll have a little review of your business, and I'll have you seen off...' Here the general glanced at the stranger with the thick whiskers. He nodded his head as a sign of consent.

Mr Golyadkin sensed and understood clearly that he was being taken for something else and not at all as he should be. 'One way or another, I really must explain myself,' he thought, 'it's like this, so to speak, Your Excellency.' In his bewilderment he lowered his eyes to the ground at this point and, to his extreme astonishment, he saw a considerable white stain on His Excellency's boots. 'Surely they haven't split?' thought Mr Golyadkin. Soon, however, Mr Golyadkin discovered that His Excellency's boots had not split at all, but were only giving off a bright reflection – a phenomenon entirely explicable by the fact that the boots were lacquered and had a high shine. 'That's called a *highlight*,' thought our hero, 'and the term is retained in artists' studios in particular; whereas elsewhere such a reflection's called a *flash of light*.' Here Mr Golyadkin raised his eyes and saw that it was time to speak, because the matter might well take a turn for the worse… Our hero took a step forward.

'It's like this, so to speak, Your Excellency,' he said, 'you won't succeed in this day and age with imposture.'

The general made no reply, but rang firmly on the bell pull. Our hero took another step forward.

'He's a base and corrupt man, Your Excellency,' said our hero, beside himself, rooted to the ground by terror, but nevertheless boldly and resolutely indicating his unworthy twin, pattering at this moment around His Excellency, 'it's like this, so to speak, but I'm alluding to a certain person.'

Mr Golyadkin's words were followed by general movement. Andrei Filippovich and the unfamiliar figure began nodding their heads; His Excellency tugged impatiently with all his might at the bell pull, summoning the servants. Here Mr Golyadkin junior stepped forward in his turn.

'Your Excellency,' he said, 'I humbly request your permission to speak.' In Mr Golyadkin junior's voice there was something extremely resolute; everything about him showed that he felt himself completely within his rights.

'Permit me to ask you,' he began once more, forestalling His Excellency's reply with his zeal and turning on this occasion to Mr Golyadkin, 'permit me to ask you in whose presence are you explaining yourself thus? Before whom are you standing, whose study are you in?…' Mr Golyadkin junior was all abnormal agitation, all red and blazing with indignation and rage; tears even appeared in his eyes.

'The Bassavryukovs!' roared the footman, who had appeared in the doorway of the study, at the top of his voice. 'A good noble family originating in Little Russia,' thought Mr Golyadkin, and immediately felt that someone had laid a hand on his back in very friendly fashion; then another hand too was laid on his back; Mr Golyadkin's vile twin fussed around in front, showing the way, and our hero saw clearly that he was being directed, as it seemed, towards the large study doors. 'Exactly like at Olsufy Ivanovich's,' he thought, and found himself in the hallway. Glancing round, he saw beside him His Excellency's two footmen and one twin.

'The greatcoat, the greatcoat, the greatcoat, my friend's greatcoat! My best friend's greatcoat!' the corrupt man started twittering, tearing the greatcoat from the hands of a servant and tossing it for a vile and inauspicious joke right on Mr Golyadkin's head. Fighting his way out from under his greatcoat, Mr Golyadkin senior clearly heard the laughter of the two footmen. But, listening to nothing and paying no heed to anything extraneous, he was already walking out of the hallway and found himself on a lighted staircase. Mr Golyadkin junior was behind him.

'Farewell, Your Excellency!' he cried in Mr Golyadkin senior's wake.

'Villain!' said our hero, beside himself.

'So I'm a villain…'

'Profligate!'

'So I'm a profligate…' such was the reply to worthy Mr Golyadkin from his unworthy foe, and, with his characteristic vileness, he gazed from the height of the staircase directly and without batting an eyelid into Mr Golyadkin's eyes, as though asking him to continue. Our hero spat in indignation and ran out onto the porch; he was so crushed that he could not remember at all who put him in the carriage and how. Coming to, he saw that he was being carried along the Fontanka. 'To the Izmailovsky Bridge, then?' thought Mr Golyadkin… Here Mr Golyadkin wanted to think about something else, but it was not possible; and it was something so awful, it cannot even be explained. 'Well, never mind!' our hero concluded, and drove to the Izmailovsky Bridge.

13

…It seemed that the weather wanted to change for the better. Indeed, the damp snow that had been falling up until now in whole cloudfuls began little by little to grow sparser and sparser and finally stopped almost completely. The sky became visible, and little stars began to sparkle in it here and there. It was just wet, muddy, damp and stifling, especially for Mr Golyadkin, who was already scarcely able to catch his breath as it was. His now soaked and heavy greatcoat filled all his limbs with a sort of unpleasantly warm dampness, and its weight made his legs, already greatly weakened as they were, buckle. A sort of feverish trembling ran in sharp and caustic gooseflesh over his entire body; exhaustion squeezed out of him a cold, morbid sweat, so that Mr Golyadkin now forgot on this opportune occasion to repeat with his characteristic firmness and resolve his favourite phrase about it maybe, all the same, perhaps, somehow, probably, without fail, going and being settled for the best. 'Anyway, it's still all right for the moment,' added our strong and not dispirited hero, wiping from his face the drops of cold water that streamed in all directions from the brim of his round hat, which had become so drenched that the water would no longer stay on it. Having added that it was still all right, our hero tried to take a seat on quite a thick stump of wood that was lying about by a pile of firewood in Olsufy Ivanovich's courtyard. Of course, there was no longer any question of thinking about Spanish serenades and silk ladders; but it was necessary to think about a sheltered little corner, maybe not exactly warm, yet still cosy and secretive. He was much tempted, let it be said in passing, by that very little corner in the entrance lobby of Olsufy Ivanovich's apartment where once before, almost at the beginning of this truthful story, our hero had waited out his two hours between the cupboard and the old screens, among all sorts of domestic and unwanted rubbish, trash and junk. The thing was that now too Mr Golyadkin had already been standing and waiting for two whole hours in Olsufy Ivanovich's courtyard. But in respect of the sheltered and cosy little corner of before there were now certain inconveniences which there had not been previously. The first inconvenience was that the place had probably now been noted and certain preventive measures taken regarding it since the time of the incident at Olsufy Ivanovich's last ball; and secondly, it was necessary to wait for the agreed signal from Klara Olsufyevna, because there ought without fail to be an agreed signal of some sort. That was how it was always done and, 'so to speak, we're not the first and we won't be the last.' Just here Mr Golyadkin remembered, incidentally, in passing, some novel that he had read a long time ago now, where the heroine gave an agreed signal to Alfred in an absolutely similar situation by tying a pink ribbon to the window. But a pink ribbon now, at night, and in the St Petersburg climate, known for its dampness and unreliability, could not come into play and, in short, was quite impossible. 'No, this isn't the place for silk ladders,' thought our hero, 'and here, on my own and on the quiet, I'd better just... I'd better stand here, for example,' and he chose a spot in the courtyard, right opposite the windows, by a pile of stacked firewood. Of course, there were a lot of strangers going through the courtyard, postilions, coachmen; what is more, wheels clattered and horses snorted, etc.; but all the same, the place was convenient: whether anyone noticed or not, still now at least the advantage was the fact that the matter was taking place in a certain fashion in the shadows, and no one could see Mr Golyadkin; whereas he himself could see positively everything. The windows were brightly lit; there was some sort of ceremonial gathering at Olsufy Ivanovich's. Music, however, could not yet be heard. 'So it's not a ball, and they've just gathered for some other reason,' thought our hero, somewhat rooted to the spot. 'But then is it today?' flashed through his head. 'Could there be a mistake about the date? It's possible, anything's possible... And this is how anything's possible... It's just possible the letter was written yesterday, but didn't reach me, and it didn't reach me because Petrushka got mixed up in all this, scoundrel that he is! Or it was written tomorrow, that is, I... everything needed to be done tomorrow, waiting with the carriage, that is...' Here our hero went utterly cold and, in order to check, put his hand in his pocket for the letter. But to his surprise the letter was not to be found in his pocket. 'What's this?' whispered the half-dead Mr Golyadkin, 'where could I have left it? So have I lost it, then? That's all I needed!' he groaned in conclusion. 'Well, and if it falls into unfriendly hands now? (And perhaps it already has!) Good Lord! What will come of it? There'll be such a... Oh, you, my hateful fate!' Here Mr Golyadkin began trembling like a leaf at the thought that perhaps his improper twin, in throwing the greatcoat over his head, had had the specific objective of stealing the letter, of which he had somehow got wind from Mr Golyadkin's enemies. 'What's more, he's intercepting it,' thought our hero, 'as evidence... but who cares about evidence!...' After the initial fit and stupor of horror, the blood rushed to Mr Golyadkin's head. Groaning and gnashing his teeth, he took hold of his hot head, sank down onto his stump and started thinking of something... But the thoughts in his head somehow made no connection with anything. Faces of some sort appeared briefly, long-forgotten events of some sort came to mind, now indistinctly, now sharply, motifs of some sort from silly songs of some sort kept coming into his head... The anguish, the anguish was unnatural! 'My God! My God!' thought our hero when he had come to a little, suppressing the muffled sobbing in his breast, 'give me strength of spirit in the inexhaustible depths of my sorrows! That I'm lost, gone completely, there's no doubt of that at all, and it's all in the order of things, for it just cannot be any other way. Firstly, I've lost my job, lost it for sure, could not possibly not have lost it... Well, let's suppose it does somehow get sorted out. And suppose my little bit of money's enough to begin with; but some other little apartment, a bit of furniture of some sort's needed... And Petrushka, firstly, won't be with me. I can manage even without the scoundrel... so away from lodgers; well, that's good! Come in and leave whenever I like, and Petrushka won't be grumbling that you come home late – that's the way it is; that's why away from lodgers is good... Well, and suppose that's all good; only how is it I keep on talking about the wrong thing, talking about the wrong thing entirely?' Here a thought about the present situation again shed light on Mr Golyadkin's mind. He glanced around. 'Oh, my Lord God! Lord God! Just what is it I'm talking about now?' he thought, utterly confused and seizing hold of his hot head...

'Won't you be wanting to go soon, sir?' said a voice above Mr Golyadkin. Mr Golyadkin gave a start; but before him stood his cabman, also completely soaked to the skin and chilled to the bone, who in impatience, and having nothing to do, had taken it into his head to look in on Mr Golyadkin behind the firewood.

'I'm all right, my friend… I'll be along soon, my friend, very soon, so you wait…'

The cabman went away, grumbling to himself. 'What is it he's grumbling about?' thought Mr Golyadkin through his tears. 'I hired him for the evening after all – after all, I'm, you know… within my rights now… that's how it is! Hired him for the evening, and that's an end to it. Even if you have to stand like this, it makes no difference. It's all at my will. I'm free to go and free not to go. And the fact that I'm standing here behind the firewood, well, that's perfectly all right too… and you won't dare say a thing; the gentleman feels like standing behind the firewood, so to speak, so here he is standing behind the firewood… and he's not sullying anybody's honour – that's how it is! That's how it is, young lady, if you only want to know it. And in our day and age, young lady, so to speak, it's like this, nobody lives in a hut. That's what! And without good behaviour in our industrial day and age, young lady, you can't succeed, something of which you yourself now serve as a baneful example… You have to be a court official, so to speak, and live in a hut on the seashore. Firstly, young lady, there are no court officials on the seashore, and secondly, you and I can't even get him, that court official. For let's suppose, to give an example, I make an application, I present myself – so to speak, it's like this, become a court official, so to speak, you know… and protect me from my enemy… and you're told, young lady, so to speak, you know… there are lots of court officials and you're not at the émigrée Falbala's here, the place you learnt good behaviour, something of which you yourself serve as a baneful example. For good behaviour, young lady, means staying at home, respecting your father and not thinking about nice suitors before the time's right. For nice suitors, madam, will be found in good time – that's the way it is! Of course, various talents undeniably need to be had, such as playing a little on the fortepiano from time to time, speaking French, history, geography, divinity and arithmetic – that's the way it is! – but no more is needed. And in addition, cooking too; cooking should without fail enter into the sphere of knowledge of any well-behaved young girl! Otherwise what have you got here? Firstly, my beauty, my dear young lady, you won't be allowed to set off, but they'll set off in pursuit of you, and then you'll be over-trumped and into a nunnery. Then what, young lady? What will you require me to do then? Will you require me, young lady, after the fashion of certain silly novels, to go to a nearby hill and dissolve in tears while looking at the cold walls of your confinement, and finally to die, after the custom of certain bad German poets and novelists[20] – is that it, young lady? Well, firstly, allow me to tell you as a friend that things aren't done like that, and secondly, I'd punish both you and your parents with a really good thrashing for your having been given French books to read; for French books will teach you no good. There's poison there… noxious poison, young lady. Or do you think, allow me to ask you, or do you think that, so to speak, it's like this, we'll run away unpunished, and that's that… so to speak, a little hut for you on the seashore; and we'll start cooing and discussing various feelings, and we'll spend our whole life like that, in contentment and happiness; and then a nestling will appear, so we'll just, you know… it's like this, so to speak, our parent and State Councillor, Olsufy Ivanovich, there you are, so to speak, a nestling's appeared, so on this opportune occasion will you withdraw your curse and give the couple your blessing? No, young lady, and once again, things aren't done like that, and the first thing is that there'll be no cooing, don't be so good as to hope. A husband nowadays, young lady, is the master, and a good, well-brought-up wife should seek to please him in everything. But displays of affection, madam, aren't popular these days, in our industrial day and age; so to speak, the days of Jean-Jacques Rousseau are over. A husband, for example, comes home from work hungry nowadays – darling, so to speak, is there anything to have as a snack, some vodka to drink, some herring to eat? So, young lady, you should have both vodka and herring ready straight away. The husband will enjoy his bite to eat and won't even glance at you, but he'll say: off you go, so to speak, into the kitchen, my little kitten, and look after the dinner, and maybe, just maybe, he'll give you a kiss once a week, and even then with in-difference… That's how it is, the way we do it, young lady! And even then, so to speak, with indifference!… That's how it'll be, if that's the way we're talking, if that's what it's come to, if that's the way you have to start looking at the thing… And what have I got to do with it? Why, young lady, did you mix me up in your whims? "So to speak, you beneficent man, suffering on my behalf and dear to my heart in so many ways and so on." Well, firstly, young lady, I'm not suitable for you, you know it yourself, I'm no expert in compliments, I don't like mouthing all those various kinds of sweet-smelling female nonsense, I don't regard ladies' men with favour, and, I confess, I've not got a winning figure. You won't find false bragging and false modesty in us, but we'll confess to you now in all sincerity. So to speak, that's the way it is, we possess only a straightforward and open character and good sense; we don't get involved in intrigues. I'm not a schemer, so to speak, and I'm proud of it – that's the way it is!... I go among good men without a mask and, so as to tell you everything...'

Suddenly Mr Golyadkin gave a start. The utterly soaked ginger beard of his coachman again glanced in at him behind the firewood...

'In a minute, my friend; you know, my friend, straight away; just straight away, my friend,' replied Mr Golyadkin in a quavering and tortured voice.

The coachman scratched the back of his head, then stroked his beard, then took a step forward... stopped and glanced at Mr Golyadkin distrustfully.

'In a minute, my friend; you see, I... my friend... just a little, you see, my friend, only a second here... you see, my friend...'

'Won't you be going at all?' said the coachman finally, stepping up to Mr Golyadkin resolutely and decisively.

'No, my friend, in a minute. You see, my friend, I'm waiting...'

'Right, sir.'

'You see, my friend, I... what village are you from, my dear?'

'I'm a serf...'

'And are your masters good?...'

'Course...'

'Yes, my friend; you wait here, my friend. You see, my friend, have you been in St Petersburg long?'

'I've been driving for a year now...'

'And are you happy, my friend?'

'Course.'

'Yes, my friend, yes. Thank providence, my friend. You look out for a good man, my friend. Good men have become rare nowadays, my dear;

he'll bathe you, give you food and drink, my dear, a good man will…
But sometimes you see that even money doesn't bring happiness, my
friend… you see a sorry example; that's how it is, my dear…'

The cabman seemed to begin to feel sorry for Mr Golyadkin.

'Well, as you wish, I'll wait, sir. Will you be waiting long, sir?'

'No, my friend, no; I'm already, well, you know… I won't be waiting
now, my dear. What do you think, my friend? I'm counting on you.
I won't be waiting here now…'

'Won't you be going at all?'

'No, my friend; no, and I'll show you my gratitude, my dear… That's
how it is. How much do I owe you, my dear?'

'Well, just what you agreed to, sir, that's what you should give me.
I've been waiting a long time, sir; I'm sure you won't do a man down,
sir.'

'Well, here you are, my dear, here you are.' At this point Mr
Golyadkin gave the full six roubles in silver to the cabman and,
seriously resolving not to waste any more time – that is, to leave while
the going was good, all the more since the matter had already been
finally decided and the cabman released and, consequently, there was
no point in waiting any longer – he set off from the courtyard, went out
of the gates, turned to the left and, without a backward glance, panting
and rejoicing, he set off at the double. 'Perhaps it will all be settled for
the best,' he thought, 'and this way I've avoided calamity.' Suddenly Mr
Golyadkin's spirit really had become somehow unusually light. 'Ah, if
only it could be settled for the best!' thought our hero, without himself,
however, taking very much on trust. 'Now I can, you know…' he
thought. 'No, I'd do better like this, and on the other hand… Or would
it be better for me to do that?' Thus in doubt, and seeking a key and a
solution to his doubts, our hero ran as far as the Semyonovsky Bridge,
but having run as far as the Semyonovsky Bridge, he prudently and
definitively decided to return. 'It's better this way,' he thought. 'I'd do
better on the other hand, that is, like this. I'll be like this – I'll be an
outside observer and that'll be an end to it; so to speak, I'm an observer,
a figure on the outside – and that's all, and then whatever happens – I'm
not to blame. That's how it is! And that's the way it'll be now.'

Having decided to return, our hero really did return, all the more since, in accordance with his happy idea, he now considered himself a figure completely on the outside. 'This is better: you're not responsible for anything, and you'll see what happened next... that's how it is!' That is, the advantage was most definite, and that was an end to the matter. Having calmed himself, he again got himself into the peaceful shelter of his calming and protective pile of firewood and began to look attentively at the windows. This time he did not have to watch and wait for long. Suddenly, at all the windows at once, some strange sort of movement became evident, figures were glimpsed, curtains opened, whole groups of people crowded around Olsufy Ivanovich's windows, everybody was searching and looking out for something in the courtyard. Provided with his pile of firewood, our hero in his turn also began to follow the general movement with curiosity and to stretch his head out to left and right in concern, as much, at least, as he was allowed by the short shadow from the woodpile that was shielding him. Suddenly he was struck dumb, gave a start and all but sat down on the spot in horror. He had got the impression – in short he had guessed fully – that they were searching not for something and not for someone: they were searching simply for him, Mr Golyadkin. Everyone is looking in his direction, everyone is pointing in his direction. It was impossible to flee: they'd see... The dumbstruck Mr Golyadkin pressed as tightly as he could against the firewood and only here did he notice that the treacherous shadow was betraying him, that it was shielding not all of him. With the greatest pleasure would our hero have agreed to slip now into some mouse hole amidst the firewood, and to sit there quietly, if only it had been possible. But it was absolutely impossible. In his ultimate agony he finally began looking resolutely and directly at all the windows at once; that was better... And suddenly he completely burnt up in shame. He had been fully spotted, everybody had spotted him all at once, everybody was beckoning to him with their hands, everybody was nodding to him, everybody was calling him; then several transom windows clicked and opened; several voices began shouting something to him all at once... 'I'm amazed how it is these girls don't get thrashed while they're still children,' our hero muttered to himself, utterly confused. Suddenly *he* (it's obvious who) ran down from the porch wearing only his uniform jacket, hatless, puffing, fussing, pattering and jumping up and down, treacherously expressing his most awful joy at having finally seen Mr Golyadkin.

'Yakov Petrovich,' the man known for his worthless nature began to twitter, 'Yakov Petrovich, are you here? You'll catch cold. It's cold here, Yakov Petrovich. Do come inside.'

'Yakov Petrovich! No, sir, I'm all right, Yakov Petrovich,' muttered our hero in a submissive voice.

'No, sir, it's not possible, Yakov Petrovich: they're asking for you, asking most humbly, waiting for you. "Make us happy, so to speak, and bring Yakov Petrovich here." That's what, sir.'

'No, Yakov Petrovich; you see, I, I'd do better... I'd be better going home, Yakov Petrovich...' said our hero, burning on a low flame and freezing in shame and horror all at the same time.

'No-no-no-no!' the repulsive one twittered. 'No-no-no, not for anything! We're going!' he said decisively, and dragged Mr Golyadkin senior towards the porch. Mr Golyadkin senior did not want to go at all; but since everyone was looking and it would be silly to resist and dig his heels in, our hero went – although it could not be said that he went, because he himself had no idea at all what was happening to him. But then at the same time, that was all right!

Before our hero had had time to recover and come to his senses in any way, he found himself in the reception hall. He was pale, dishevelled, harrowed; he glanced with dull eyes around the whole crowd – horror! The reception hall, all the rooms – all, all was full to bursting; there were masses of people, an entire hothouse of ladies; all this clustered around Mr Golyadkin, all this sped towards Mr Golyadkin, all this carried Mr Golyadkin out aloft, and he remarked very clearly that he was being dragged off in a particular direction. 'But not to the doors,' flashed through Mr Golyadkin's head. Indeed, he was not being dragged away to the doors, but straight towards Olsufy Ivanovich's comfortable armchair. Beside the armchair on one side stood Klara Olsufyevna, pale, languid, sad, yet splendidly turned out. Mr Golyadkin was especially struck by the little white flowers in her black hair which created a superb effect. On the other side of the armchair Vladimir Semyonovich stood firm in a black tailcoat with his new decoration in his buttonhole. Mr Golyadkin was being led by the arms, and, as was stated above, straight towards Olsufy Ivanovich, on one side by Mr Golyadkin junior, who had assumed an extremely proper and loyal air – at which our hero was quite overjoyed – and on the other side he was directed by Andrei Filippovich with the most solemn expression on his face. 'What could this be?' thought Mr Golyadkin. And when he saw that he was being led towards Olsufy Ivanovich, it suddenly dawned upon him as if in a flash of lightning. A thought of the intercepted letter flickered in his head… In inexhaustible ultimate agony our hero stood before Olsufy Ivanovich's armchair. 'How should I behave now?' he thought to himself. 'It goes without saying, it should all be on a bold footing, that is, with a candour not lacking in nobility; it's like this, so to speak, and so on.' But the thing that our hero evidently feared did not happen. Olsufy Ivanovich seemed to receive Mr Golyadkin very well and, although he did not reach his hand out to him, at least, when looking at him, he shook his head, silver-haired and inspiring great respect, shook it with an air that was somehow solemn and sad, but at the same time well disposed. At least that was how it seemed to Mr Golyadkin. It even seemed to him that a tear shone in Olsufy Ivanovich's lacklustre gaze; he raised his eyes and saw that it was as if a little tear shone too on the eyelashes of Klara Olsufyevna, who was standing there as well; that in Vladimir Semyonovich's eyes too it was also as if there were something similar; that, finally, the inviolable and calm dignity of Andrei Filippovich was also fitting amid the general tearful sympathy; that, finally, the young man who had once borne a strong resemblance to an important Councillor was already sobbing bitterly, making the most of this particular minute… Or perhaps it all only seemed like this to Mr Golyadkin because he had himself become very tearful and could distinctly feel his hot tears flowing down his cold cheeks… In a voice filled with sobs, reconciled with men and fate and at this particular moment very fond not only of Olsufy Ivanovich, not only of all the guests taken together, but even of his pernicious twin too – who was evidently not at all pernicious now and not even Mr Golyadkin's twin, but a completely extraneous and in himself extremely amiable person – our hero tried to address Olsufy Ivanovich with a touching outpouring of his soul; but in the fullness of all that had accumulated within him he could not explain anything whatsoever, and, with a very eloquent gesture, merely pointed in silence to his heart... At last Andrei Filippovich, probably wishing to spare the sensitivity of the silver-haired elder, led Mr Golyadkin a little to one side and left him in what seemed a completely independent situation. Smiling, muttering something to himself, a little bewildered, but in any event almost completely reconciled with men and fate, our hero began making his way somewhere through the solid mass of guests. Everyone let him past, everyone looked at him with a sort of strange curiosity and a sort of inexplicable, mysterious sympathy. Our hero went through into another room – and everywhere there was the same attention; he indistinctly heard the whole crowd clustering in his wake, noting his every step, all surreptitiously discussing something very absorbing among themselves, shaking their heads, talking, passing judgement, laying down the law and whispering. Mr Golyadkin would very much have liked to find out what they were all passing judgement, laying down the law and whispering about like that. Looking round, our hero noticed Mr Golyadkin junior beside him. Feeling the need to seize his arm and lead him to one side, Mr Golyadkin asked the other Yakov Petrovich most earnestly to cooperate with him in all his future initiatives and not to abandon him in a critical situation. Mr Golyadkin junior nodded his head gravely and gave Mr Golyadkin senior's hand a firm squeeze. Our hero's heart began to palpitate from the excess of feeling in his breast. He was, incidentally, gasping for breath, he felt himself so constricted, so constricted; all those eyes directed towards him were oppressing and crushing him... Mr Golyadkin caught sight in passing of the Councillor, who wore a wig on his head. The Councillor was looking at him with a stern, searching gaze, not at all softened by the general sympathy... Our hero made up his mind to go to him directly so as to smile at him and immediately explain himself to him; but somehow he did not succeed in this. For a moment Mr Golyadkin almost lost consciousness completely, he lost both his awareness and his feelings... Coming to, he noted that he was spinning in a wide circle of guests who had gathered round him. Suddenly from another room there came a call for Mr Golyadkin; the call ran all at once through the entire crowd. All became agitated, all became noisy, everybody dashed towards the doors of the first reception hall; our hero was all but borne out aloft, and at this point the hard-hearted Councillor in the wig turned up right alongside Mr Golyadkin. Finally he took the latter by the arm and sat him down beside him, opposite Olsufy Ivanovich's seat, but at quite a significant distance from it. All who were in the rooms, all settled down in several rows around Mr Golyadkin and Olsufy Ivanovich. All fell quiet and became still, everyone observed a solemn silence, everyone kept looking at Olsufy Ivanovich, obviously expecting something not entirely ordinary. Mr Golyadkin noticed that the other Mr Golyadkin and Andrei Filippovich had taken their places beside Olsufy Ivanovich's armchair and also directly opposite the Councillor. The silence continued; something really was expected. 'Exactly like in a family when somebody's going away on a long journey; all that's needed is to stand up and say a prayer now,' thought our hero. Suddenly some extraordinary movement began, and it interrupted all Mr Golyadkin's reflections. Something long expected had happened. 'He's coming, he's coming!' ran through the crowd. 'Who's coming?' ran through Mr Golyadkin's head, and some strange sensation made him give a start. 'It's time!' said the Councillor with a careful look at Andrei Filippovich. Andrei Filippovich for his part glanced at Olsufy Ivanovich. Olsufy Ivanovich nodded his head gravely and solemnly. 'Up we get,' said the Councillor, helping Mr Golyadkin to his feet. Everyone got up. Then the Councillor took Mr Golyadkin senior by the arm, while Andrei Filippovich took Mr Golyadkin junior, and both solemnly brought the two absolutely similar men together in the midst of the crowd that had gathered around and focused upon them in expectation. Our hero looked about him in bewilderment, but he was immediately stopped and had Mr Golyadkin junior, who had stretched out his hand to him, pointed out to him. 'They want to reconcile us,' thought our hero and, moved, stretched out his hand to Mr Golyadkin junior; then – then he stretched his head out towards him. And the other Mr Golyadkin did the same... At this point it seemed to Mr Golyadkin senior that his treacherous friend was smiling, that he had given a quick and roguish wink to all the crowd surrounding them, that there was something ominous in the improper Mr Golyadkin junior's face, that he had even made a sort of grimace at the moment of his Judas' kiss. A ringing began in Mr Golyadkin's head, a darkness came into his eyes; it seemed to him that a mass, a whole string of absolutely similar Golyadkins was bursting noisily into every one of the room's doors; but it was too late... A resonant kiss of betrayal rang out and...

Here a completely unexpected event took place... The doors into the reception hall opened wide with a crash, and on the threshold there appeared a man whose look alone turned Mr Golyadkin to ice. His feet were rooted to the ground. A cry died away in his constricted breast. Still, Mr Golyadkin had known everything in advance and had long had a presentiment of something of the sort. The stranger approached Mr Golyadkin gravely and solemnly... Mr Golyadkin knew this figure very well. He had seen it, seen it very often, had seen it even today... The stranger was a tall, solid man in a black tailcoat with a significant decoration around his neck and endowed with thick, very black whiskers; only a cigar in the mouth was lacking for further resemblance... But still the stranger's gaze, as has already been stated, turned Mr Golyadkin to ice in horror. With a grave and solemn expression the terrible man came up to the sorry hero of our tale... Our hero stretched his hand out to him; the stranger took his hand and dragged him after him... With a lost, with a dead face our hero looked around...

'This, this is Krestyan Ivanovich Rutenspitz, Doctor of Medicine and Surgery, your acquaintance of long standing, Yakov Petrovich!' twittered an offensive voice right in Mr Golyadkin's ear. He looked round: it was Mr Golyadkin's twin, repulsive in the base qualities of his soul. An indecent, ominous joy shone in his face; he was rubbing his hands in delight, he was turning his head around in delight, he was pattering around each and every one in delight; he seemed ready to begin dancing right away in delight; finally he leapt forward, grabbed a candle from one of the servants and went on ahead, lighting the way for Mr Golyadkin and Krestyan Ivanovich. Mr Golyadkin distinctly heard all who were in the reception hall dash after him, everybody crowding and crushing one another and all together, with a single voice, beginning to repeat after Mr Golyadkin: ' it's all right; that you needn't be afraid, Yakov Petrovich after all, it's your old friend and

158

acquaintance, Krestyan Ivanovich Rutenspitz…' At last they came out onto the main, brightly lit staircase; on the staircase too there were heaps of people; the doors onto the porch opened wide with a crash, and Mr Golyadkin found himself on the porch together with Krestyan Ivanovich. By the entrance stood a carriage, harnessed with a team of four horses, which were snorting with impatience. The gloating Mr Golyadkin junior ran down the steps in three bounds and opened the carriage door himself. With an exhortative gesture, Krestyan Ivanovich asked Mr Golyadkin to get in. However, the exhortative gesture was quite unnecessary; there were enough people there to help him in… Freezing in horror, Mr Golyadkin looked back: the entire brightly lit staircase was covered with people; curious eyes were looking at him from everywhere; Olsufy Ivanovich himself presided in his comfortable armchair on the very top landing of the staircase and watched all that was being done attentively and with great sympathy. Everyone was waiting. A murmur of impatience ran through the crowd when Mr Golyadkin looked back.

'I hope that there's nothing here… nothing reprehensible… or that might excite everyone's severity… and attention with regard to my official relations?' said our hero in confusion. The sound of voices and noise rose up all around; everyone began shaking their heads in denial. Tears splashed from Mr Golyadkin's eyes.

'In that case, I'm prepared… I entrust myself fully… and deliver my fate into Krestyan Ivanovich's hands…'

No sooner had Mr Golyadkin pronounced that he delivered his fate fully into Krestyan Ivanovich's hands than a terrible, deafening, joyous cry burst out from all those surrounding him and rolled in the most ominous echo around the entire expectant crowd. At this point Krestyan Ivanovich on one side and Andrei Filippovich on the other took Mr Golyadkin by the arms and began putting him into the carriage; while the double, as was his vile little custom, helped him in from behind. The unfortunate Mr Golyadkin senior cast his final glance at everyone and at everything and, trembling like a kitten that has had cold water poured over it – if the comparison can be permitted – climbed into the carriage; Krestyan Ivanovich immediately got in behind him too. The carriage door slammed; a lash of the whip on the horses was heard, and with a jerk the horses got the vehicle moving… all dashed after Mr Golyadkin. The piercing, frenetic cries of all his enemies rolled after him as a sort of farewell. For a certain time some figures could still be glimpsed around the carriage that was carrying Mr Golyadkin away; but little by little they began to fall further and further behind and finally disappeared altogether. Longest of all remained Mr Golyadkin's indecent twin. With his hands in the side pockets of his green uniform trousers, he ran along with a contented air, bobbing up and down first on one, then on the other side of the vehicle; and at times, taking hold of the window frame and hanging from it, he poked his head through the window and sent Mr Golyadkin little kisses to wish him farewell; but he too began to get tired, appeared more and more rarely and finally disappeared completely. There was a dull ache in the heart in Mr Golyadkin's breast; hot spurts of blood beat into his head; it was stifling, and he wanted to unbutton himself and bare his breast, to sprinkle it with snow and pour cold water onto it. He fell at last into a half-conscious state… And when he came to, he saw that the horses were carrying him along some unfamiliar road. To right and left was the blackness of forests; it was remote and empty. Suddenly his heart stood still: two fiery eyes were looking at him in the darkness, and these two eyes shone with a sinister, diabolical joy. This was not Krestyan Ivanovich! Who was it? Or was it him? It was! It was Krestyan Ivanovich, only not the former one, it was another Krestyan Ivanovich! It was a dreadful Krestyan Ivanovich!…

'Krestyan Ivanovich, I… I seem to be all right, Krestyan Ivanovich,' our hero tried to begin, timid and trembling, wishing at least to some extent to mollify the dreadful Krestyan Ivanovich with his submissiveness and meekness.

'You haf official qvarters with firevood, vith *licht*[21] and vith serfants, of vhich you are unvurthy,' came Krestyan Ivanovich's reply, sternly and dreadfully, like sentence being passed.

Our hero cried out and took his head in his hands. Alas! He had already long had a presentiment of this!

NOTES

1. A Titular Councillor belonged to Class 9 (of 14) in the Table of Ranks originally created by Peter the Great in 1722. Other ranks mentioned in *The Double* are State Councillor (Class 5), Collegiate Councillor (Class 6), Collegiate Assessor (Class 8), Provincial Secretary (Class 12) and Collegiate Registrar (Class 14). The military ranks mentioned, General and Lieutenant, were the equivalents of, respectively, Classes 2 and 10.

2. Gostiny Dvor is the arcaded trading area on Nevsky Avenue.

3. Unceremonious (French).

4. Yeliseyev and Milyutin were the merchant founders of the premier grocery stores in St Petersburg.

5. See note 1.

6. Jean Baptiste Séraphin Joseph, Comte de Villèle (1773–1854), served as President of the Council under Louis XVIII in the 1820s.

7. *The Tale of the Adventure of the English Lord George and the Margravine Fredericka Louisa of Brandenburg with the Appended History of the Former Turkish Vizir Martsimiris and Queen Terezia of Sardinia* (1782) by M. Komarov (d. 1812).

8. Golyadkin's name is derived from the Russian word *golyadka*, meaning 'beggar'.

9. The Siamese twins Chang and Eng Bunker (1811–74) made a living by giving lectures and demonstrations worldwide.

10. Golyadkin quotes the closing line of the fable *The Casket* (1808) by Russia's foremost fabulist, Ivan Andreyevich Krylov (1769–1844).

11. From a book of anecdotes about Field Marshal Alexander Vasilyevich Suvorov (1729–1800), Russia's greatest commander of the eighteenth century, published in St Petersburg in 1827.

12. The huge canvas by Russia's leading Romantic painter, Karl Pavlovich Bryullov (1799–1852), *The Last Day of Pompeii*, was first exhibited in the St Petersburg Academy of Arts in 1834 to great acclaim from, among others, Alexander Pushkin and Nikolai Gogol, and long afterwards still remained one of the capital's chief artistic attractions.

13. A notoriously conservative newspaper with an unsophisticated readership.

14. One of the literary pseudonyms of Osip Ivanovich Senkovsky (1800–1858), editor of the popular journal *The Library for Reading* and a favourite of less sophisticated readers.

15. A genuine, well-known example of the sentimental verse commonly found in ladies' albums of the time.

16. Grigory Otrepyev became the figurehead for the opposition to the rule of Boris Godunov in 1604, when he claimed to be Dmitry, a son of Ivan the Terrible believed to have died in 1591. He was hailed as tsar after Godunov's death in 1605, but was deposed and killed in the following year.

17. The original Faublas was the cunning seducer in the novel by J.B. Louvet de Couvray (1760–97) *The Amorous Adventures of the Chevalier de Faublas* (1787–90).

18. Beer and milk, respectively (German).

19. The proprietor of the boarding school attended by the heroine of Alexander Pushkin's comic narrative poem *Count Nulin* (1828).

20. The allusion is to such situations as those found in Friedrich von Schiller's ballad *Ritter Toggenburg* (1797) and the Sentimental novel by Johann Martin Miller (1750–1814) *Siegwart* (1776).

21. Light (German).

BIOGRAPHICAL NOTE

Fyodor Mikhailovich Dostoevsky (1821–81) was born in Moscow. After the death of his mother in 1837, he was sent to the St Petersburg Engineering Academy, where he studied for five years and eventually graduated as an engineer. In 1844, however, Dostoevsky gave up engineering to write. His translation of Balzac's *Eugénie Grandet* came out in 1844, and his first novel, *Poor People*, was published in 1846. During this time Dostoevsky also became interested in Utopian Socialism – a political affiliation which would lead to his deportation, in 1850, to Siberia. He was imprisoned for four years in a penal settlement, and served for four more thereafter as as soldier in Semipalatinsk. The experience changed his life and writing: whilst in prison he became a member of the Russian Orthodox Church, and a monarchist, and upon his return to Moscow, he wrote about his experience as a prisoner in *Notes from the House of the Dead* (1862).

In 1862, Dostoevsky travelled around Europe for the first time, an experience which also marked his writing. He was a great admirer of the English novel, in particular the works of Charles Dickens, but he disliked Europe. London, above all, was Dostoevsky's 'Baal', the centre of world capitalism, and he used the Crystal Palace as a symbol of the corrupting influence of modernity in *Notes from the Underground* (1864). Upon his return to Russia, Dostoevsky wrote some of his best novels, including *Crime and Punishment* (1866), *The Idiot* (1868) and *The Brothers Karamazov* (1880), which he completed just before his death.

Having been largely ignored by English language readers in the nineteenth century, Dostoevsky is now considered to be the most popular and influential Russian author read in the twentieth and twenty-first centuries. The penetrating psychological nature of Dostoevsky's novels, his obsessive grappling with conscience, guilt and God, as well as the brilliance of his characterisation and plots, continue to inspire new generations of readers, writers and thinkers. Dostoevsky's novels are undisputed masterpieces.

Hugh Aplin studied Russian at the University of East Anglia and Voronezh State University, and worked at the Universities of Leeds and St Andrews before taking up his current post as Head of Russian at Westminster School, London. His previous translations include Anton Chekhov's *The Story of a Nobody* and *Three Years*, Nikolai Gogol's *The Squabble*, Fyodor Dostoevsky's *Poor People*, Leo Tolstoy's *Hadji Murat*, Ivan Turgenev's *Faust*, and Mikhail Bulgakov's *The Fatal Eggs*, all published by Hesperus Press.

SELECTED TITLES FROM HESPERUS PRESS

Author	Title	Foreword writer
Louisa May Alcott	Behind a Mask	Doris Lessing
Pedro Antonio de Alarcon	The Three-Cornered Hat	
Pietro Aretino	The School of Whoredom	Paul Bailey
Jane Austen	Love and Friendship	Fay Weldon
Honoré de Balzac	Colonel Chabert	A.N. Wilson
Charles Baudelaire	On Wine and Hashish	Margaret Drabble
Aphra Behn	The Lover's Watch	
Giovanni Boccaccio	Life of Dante	A.N. Wilson
Charlotte Brontë	The Green Dwarf	Libby Purves
Mikhail Bulgakov	The Fatal Eggs	Doris Lessing
Giacomo Casanova	The Duel	Tim Parks
Miguel de Cervantes	The Dialogue of the Dogs	Ben Okri
Anton Chekhov	The Story of a Nobody	Louis de Bernières
Anton Chekhov	Three Years	William Fiennes
Wilkie Collins	Who Killed Zebedee?	Martin Jarvis
Arthur Conan Doyle	The Tragedy of the Korosko	Tony Robinson
William Congreve	Incognita	Peter Ackroyd
Joseph Conrad	Heart of Darkness	A.N. Wilson
Joseph Conrad	The Return	Colm Tóibín
Gabriele D'Annunzio	The Book of the Virgins	Tim Parks
Dante Alighieri	New Life	Louis de Bernières
Daniel Defoe	The King of Pirates	Peter Ackroyd
Marquis de Sade	Incest	Janet Street-Porter
Charles Dickens	The Haunted House	Peter Ackroyd
Charles Dickens	A House to Let	
Fyodor Dostoevsky	Poor People	Charlotte Hobson
Joseph von Eichendorff	Life of a Good-for-nothing	
George Eliot	Amos Barton	Matthew Sweet

Henry Fielding	*Jonathan Wild the Great*	Peter Ackroyd
F. Scott Fitzgerald	*The Rich Boy*	John Updike
Gustave Flaubert	*Memoirs of a Madman*	Germaine Greer
E.M. Forster	*Arctic Summer*	Anita Desai
Ugo Foscolo	*Last Letters of Jacopo Ortis*	Valerio Massimo Manfredi
Giuseppe Garibaldi	*My Life*	Tim Parks
Elizabeth Gaskell	*Lois the Witch*	Jenny Uglow
Théophile Gautier	*The Jinx*	Gilbert Adair
André Gide	*Theseus*	
Nikolai Gogol	*The Squabble*	Patrick McCabe
Thomas Hardy	*Fellow-Townsmen*	Emma Tennant
L.P. Hartley	*Simonetta Perkins*	Margaret Drabble
Nathaniel Hawthorne	*Rappaccini's Daughter*	Simon Schama
E.T.A. Hoffmann	*Mademoiselle de Scudéri*	Gilbert Adair
Victor Hugo	*The Last Day of a Condemned Man*	Libby Purves
Joris-Karl Huysmans	*With the Flow*	Simon Callow
Henry James	*In the Cage*	Libby Purves
Franz Kafka	*Metamorphosis*	Martin Jarvis
John Keats	*Fugitive Poems*	Andrew Motion
Heinrich von Kleist	*The Marquise of O–*	Andrew Miller
D.H. Lawrence	*Daughters of the Vicar*	Anita Desai
D.H. Lawrence	*The Fox*	Doris Lessing
Leonardo da Vinci	*Prophecies*	Eraldo Affinati
Giacomo Leopardi	*Thoughts*	Edoardo Albinati
Nikolai Leskov	*Lady Macbeth of Mtsensk*	Gilbert Adair
Niccolò Machiavelli	*Life of Castruccio Castracani*	Richard Overy
Katherine Mansfield	*In a German Pension*	Linda Grant
Guy de Maupassant	*Butterball*	Germaine Greer
Lorenzino de' Medici	*Apology for a Murder*	Tim Parks
Herman Melville	*The Enchanted Isles*	Margaret Drabble

Sándor Petőfi	*John the Valiant*	George Szirtes
Francis Petrarch	*My Secret Book*	Germaine Greer
Luigi Pirandello	*Loveless Love*	
Edgar Allan Poe	*Eureka*	Sir Patrick Moore
Alexander Pope	*The Rape of the Lock and A Key to the Lock*	Peter Ackroyd
Alexander Pope	*Scriblerus*	Peter Ackroyd
Antoine François Prévost	*Manon Lescaut*	Germaine Greer
Marcel Proust	*Pleasures and Days*	A.N. Wilson
Alexander Pushkin	*Dubrovsky*	Patrick Neate
François Rabelais	*Gargantua*	Paul Bailey
François Rabelais	*Pantagruel*	Paul Bailey
Friedrich von Schiller	*The Ghost-seer*	Martin Jarvis
Percy Bysshe Shelley	*Zastrozzi*	Germaine Greer
Stendhal	*Memoirs of an Egotist*	Doris Lessing
Robert Louis Stevenson	*Dr Jekyll and Mr Hyde*	Helen Dunmore
Theodor Storm	*The Lake of the Bees*	Alan Sillitoe
Italo Svevo	*A Perfect Hoax*	Tim Parks
Jonathan Swift	*Directions to Servants*	Colm Tóibín
W.M. Thackeray	*Rebecca and Rowena*	Matthew Sweet
Leo Tolstoy	*Hadji Murat*	Colm Tóibín
Ivan Turgenev	*Faust*	Simon Callow
Mark Twain	*The Diary of Adam and Eve*	John Updike
Mark Twain	*Tom Sawyer, Detective*	
Giovanni Verga	*Life in the Country*	Paul Bailey
Jules Verne	*A Fantasy of Dr Ox*	Gilbert Adair
Edith Wharton	*The Touchstone*	Salley Vickers
Oscar Wilde	*The Portrait of Mr W.H.*	Peter Ackroyd
Virginia Woolf	*Carlyle's House and Other Sketches*	Doris Lessing
Virginia Woolf	*Monday or Tuesday*	Scarlett Thomas
Emile Zola	*For a Night of Love*	A.N. Wilson